Hellfire Origins

By Christopher J Sharman

Copyright © 2012 Christopher J Sharman

All rights reserved.

ISBN: 1514273624
ISBN-13: 978-1514273623

DEDICATION

This series of stories is dedicated to my partner Julie, for her support and encouragement given to me over my work for the last few years. Thank you for your patients and feedback, I love you very much.

CONTENTS

   Acknowledgments

1   First Command   Pg 1

2   Touched by Hell   Pg 15

3   Deadlock   Pg 55

4   Call to War   Pg 114

5   Planet of the Dead   Pg 186

ACKNOWLEDGMENTS

I would like to thank all of the people who have supported me in my work by purchasing one to all of my books. I would also like to thank my close friends and family who have given me both honest and constructive feedback. Then I would like to say thank you to the fans of my work who have not only purchased my books, but passed on to others the great review of how much they have enjoyed them.
Finally I must thank Isacc my son, who shows so much interest in my work and a want to become a writer himself. He makes me very proud and I love him very much.

HELLFIRE

FIRST COMMAND

VOLUME 1

BY CHRISTOPHER J SHARMAN

Christopher J Sharman

FIRST COMMAND

CONTENTS

Introduction	Pg 3
Just another day	Pg 4
Setting a trap	Pg 8
Facing hell fire	Pg 11
Losses and gains	Pg 13

INTRODUCTION

Personal log;

 I spent my whole life wanting to travel the stars. I guess that's why I applied for this job. All of my friends told me I was crazy, taking on a job commanding a cargo frigate during a time of war. But then working for a large company seemed a better option to me than joining the military.

I couldn't stand the thought of some jumped up captain barking orders at me every day. Besides when I applied for the captain's position, I didn't think I would actually get it. But when the conformation came, I found I had been given my first command.

It's not a large ship. But for a first command and with a crew of only six including myself, this ship is large enough. The haulage company say I'm the youngest captain on their books. But as I am only six months into this job, I guess I have a lot to learn. Log end…

Just another day

I approached the bridge door to start my shift for the day. I was on the late shift as usual, which suited me fine. I pushed the button to open the bulkhead door to the bridge, which hissed loudly as the hydraulics pulled the small door open. Stepping into the small room I could see the standard bridge layout in front of me. It had four chairs situated in front of the ship's various computer consoles, just under the ship's forward windows. The captain's chair was set up in the centre of the room with two control panels built into the arms of the chair. From here the whole ship could be controlled by just one person if needed, which was handy with such a small crew to hand. Then there was the holo ring communication device, which was built into the floor and ceiling of the room and set just in front of the captain's chair.

I looked out of the large forward windows and was still amazed by the sight of the stars and how clear they looked from out in the darkness of space. Over the last six months we had travelled much deeper into space and our current delivery was a first for me. As we were going to be supplying defence weapons and shield generator upgrades to a small colony situated in Caridian space. I knew this was a much more risky job to take, but then I also really wanted to explore the stars and the only other job on offer would take my ship back towards Earth. Besides other than that, the pay was a lot better with the added risk. I moved over to the captain's chair as my first officer stood up and turned around to look at me. He was a stocky man with blue eyes and short blond hair.

'Captain, you finally pulled yourself out of bed.' He stated as he smiled at me.

'You know I'm not a morning person, is there anything to report?'

But before he could reply, the communication's console lit up as it began to beep repeatedly.

We both looked at the console before Andrew said,

'Well, I was going to say nothing, but it looks like we are wanted.'

'We're not expecting any change of orders are we?'

'No, but maybe we should answer it.'

'I guess so.' I replied before moving over and stepping into the metallic holo ring that was situated just in front of the captain's chair. Andrew moved over to the communication's relay and activated the system.

'Channel open, Sir.'

The holo ring lit up around me at the same time as a projector began to show a holographic image of a man in his late thirties in a Caridian military uniform just in front of me. The man looked flustered as he said.

'Thank god; I am Captain Artos of the Caridian light cruiser, Storm. We have taken damage and are being pursued by a Plotation battleship. I need to speak with your Captain.'

I heard Andrew snigger at this as I replied,

'I am the Captain, how can we help?'

The man looked shocked before he bluntly stated out loud,

'No offence kid; but what ship exactly, are you in command of?'

'A class four Earth cargo frigate, why?'

The captain rubbed his hand across his face before he bluntly asked,

'Do you even have any weapon systems?'

'Yes, we have several level five pulse lasers equipped.'

'Great, look kid. I suggest you jump into warp space and keep out the way until we have passed through this sector.'

'That sounds great, but this ship doesn't have any jump engines.'

'No jump engines, that's all I need. Have you ever seen any combat?'

'We have had a few run-ins' with Raider over the last few months.'

The image flickered as I watched the captain steady himself and I could tell the ship was being fired upon as he replied,

'Well I guess that's better than nothing. But this isn't going to be anything like fighting off a few pirates kid, and your weapons won't even dent that battleship's shields. So we will need to find a way to knock them out first, if you're going help.'

Andrew turned to me as he quickly stated,

'Captain, there is a nearby asteroid field we could use for cover.'

I saw Artos's eyes light up at Andrew comment.

'That sounds like a plan. That Plotation battle cruiser may have speed and a hell of a lot of fire power, but it fly's like a rock. We will see you in there.' Artos replied as this gave me an idea.

'Hang on Captain.' I said before turning to my first officer and asking,

'Andrew, how long will we have before the Storm reaches the asteroid field?'

My first officer checked the console.

'About an hour. Why?'

I turned back to the image of Artos and then I said,

'Captain, don't worry about taking the shields out. Just make sure you keep some distance from that cruiser and we will do the rest.'

I could see the confusion on Artos's face as he curiously enquired,

'What the hell have you got planned kid?'

I could also see a look of bewilderment on my first officer's face as I replied,

'We still have some mining explosives in our cargo hold. If I can get them set up before you arrive, we will set a trap in the asteroid field.'

Artos grinned before he said,

'I like your thinking kid. We will see you there and follow your engine trail into the field, Storm out.'

He cut the communication link as the hologram image disappeared. Andrew was now looking at me like I was some sort of mad man before he said,

'Don't worry about the shields, ha. We have some explosives right.'

'It will work.' I replied.

Setting a trap

It was almost time for the Storm to arrive at the asteroid field. I had called all of my crew to the bridge for the coming battle, so we would be ready for the fight and I was now just waiting for my first officer to return. But just as our ship's shuttle returned after planting the explosives, I knew things were now set and we were probably in over our heads.

The plan seemed simple; we would wait until the Potation battleship was right in the middle of the blast zone before we would detonate all of the explosives together. In the hope that the mass explosion would damage the Plotation battleship enough to give us the upper hand in this battle. Then we would join forces with the Caridian ship as arranged over the com earlier, to overpower it quickly. We were now just waiting for the call to come in.

Richards my communication's officer quickly grabbed my attention as he stated.

'Sir, I have Captain Artos on a secure channel.'

'Put him through.' I replied before I moved back over to the holo ring. The metallic ring lit up as the image of the Caridian captain appeared in front of me.

'Ah kid. I hope you have everything ready, as we're losing our rear shields and I don't think this ship can take much more punishment.'

But before I could answer Andrew re-entered the bridge while saying out loud,

'Captain, that's the explosives set and armed. You should have control to detonate them from your chair's weapon control.'

I smiled at Andrew before I replied saying,

'Great work, now take up your station.'

I then turned back to the image of Artos as I replied,

'We're as ready as we can be, just follow our engine trail and we will do the rest.'

'Good luck out there kid, Storm out.'

The hologram image cut and I moved back over to my chair before I sat down. Moving my hand over the weapon's control, I activated the system just as Andrew said,

'Captain, the Storm is now passing through the blast zone.'

I now suddenly felt an overwhelming feeling of nerves at the imminent battle. The next minute seemed to last forever before Andrew then confirmed,

'Captain, the Storm is clear of the main blast zone and the Plotation war ship is now entering the trap right behind them.'

I held my finger over the detonation button for a moment, knowing I needed the ship to be right in the middle of the mine field to deal the maximum damage possible to the enemy vessel.

'What are you waiting for?' Andrew asked anxiously.

I check the scanner readout to find I had waited long enough before I quickly pushed the button and a blinding flash lit up the bridge, as all the explosives detonated together. I covered my eyes while the flash subsided before I heard Andrew shout out,

'Captain, we need to move now or the shock wave from that blast will cause our ship major damage.'

'Miller, get us out of here now.' I ordered.

'Yes Captain.'

The ship took off at speed, but after just a moment there was a loud bang that was quickly followed by a sharp jolt that caused the lights to flicker.

'Damage report?' I asked.

Miller replied while he steadied himself at his post,

'Shields down to sixty five percent, we have taken damage to the starboard cargo hold, and we have a hull breach on deck three, Captain.'

'And what about the Plotation battleship?'

'Their shields are down and they have taken heavy damage, with their power readings now registering as low.'

'Good, then what are we waiting for. Miller, spin us around and head straight for them, all weapons firing.' I ordered.

Facing hell fire

The ship turned around and I could now see the terrifying sight and size of the enemy vessel. We were closing in fast as Andrew called over to me,

'Captain, the Storm just lost power when the shock wave hit them. It looks like we are on our own.'

This wasn't good, but it was too late to regret my actions now. The Plotation battleship suddenly began to turn to face us as Andrew call out,

'Captain, they are powering up their main weapon systems again.'

I watched as our lasers hit the large battleship, tearing small holes in its outer hull. Then to my horror it began to fire its heavy energy cannons at us.

'Hold course, Miller.' I ordered as I watched their weapons fire rain in on us like hell's fire. Every shot hit the ship with an overwhelming blow, while our small frigate was slowly being torn apart.

'Captain, we have lost all power to our shields and the ship's hull is starting to break up.' Andrew shouted over to me with desperation in his voice.

I realised we only had one chance as the bridge began to burn. So gave the only order I felt would work.

'All hands abandon ship. Get to the shuttle and prep it to launch, while I rig things here.'

I heard the crew agree as they quickly moved to leave the bridge.

Andrew stopped at my side and put his hand on my shoulder before he left while saying,

'Come on you need to leave now.'

'I know, just get the shuttle ready and wait for me. I just need to lock the ship into this course so it will have maximum impact when it hits.'

Andrew patted my shoulder before he left saying,

'Don't take too long mate.'

'I don't intend to.' I replied while I continued to struggle with the ship's failing computer systems. Suddenly one of the front work stations exploded as I threw the ship's engines into full thrust, before the proximity alert went off. Just then the main lighting cut out leaving the room to be lit only by the flickering damaged computer consoles and fires that were now breaking out all over the bridge.

'Danger. Collision course set, impact in two minutes.'

I quickly locked the course in before I got up to leave the bridge, taking one last look out of the cracked front windows of my now doomed vessel. The whole ship seemed to be burning and the smoke was now beginning to choke me, as I quickly made my way to the frigate's shuttle through the burning corridors of my ship.

I was relieved to find Andrew standing at the shuttle door as I moved into the air lock corridor. I ran onto the shuttle as Andrew closed the door while he shouted out.

'Get us out of here, now.'

'Yes Commander.' Miller replied.

I sat down while the shuttle separated from the doomed frigate, just as my ship hit the Plotation battle cruiser head on. I moved over to the window at the rear of the shuttle while I watched my ship explode, tearing the Plotation cruiser in two, before both ships exploded in a blinding light. I heard the shuttle's alarm sound just before the shockwave hit the shuttle with an overwhelming blow. I was thrown to the floor along with my first officer as the lighting in the shuttle flickered on and off for a while. Then as the lighting returned to normal our shuttle went quiet.

Losses and gains

I pulled myself up off of the floor before checking my crew were all alright. Then I moved back over to the rear window.

Looking out into space I could now see nothing but the drifting wreckage of both vessels scattered finely amongst the stars, while the remains of the main Plotation's oversized hull still burnt while the last of its air escaped the destroyed vessel into space. My heart grew heavy at the loss of my ship. But I was still pleased to find that my crew had all managed to escape and with minimal injuries.

'What now, Captain?' Miller asked.

I turned and moved over to the front of our ship looking out of the forward windows at the damaged Caridian vessel.

'Open me up a channel to the Storm, asking if we can dock.'

'Yes Captain.'

Artos's voice could be heard over the com as the channel opened before he stated.

'Hay kid, that was one hell of a fireworks display out there. So I suppose you will need a lift?'

'That would be great.' I replied.

'No problem, I will have bay one ready for you. By the way, I never caught your name.'

'It's Chris.' I replied.

'Well Captain, I guess we owe you one. See you when you dock, Storm out.'

I continued to look out of the shuttle's forwards windows at the Caridian war ship. As I realised I had probably lost my job.

But then I knew this wasn't the end of my journeys through space and as I looked at my small crew. Well I could tell that I had some good friends to join me on our unset future journeys.

Hellfire

Touched by Hell
Volume 2   By Christopher. J. Sharman

Christopher J Sharman

TOUCHED BY HELL

CONTENTS

Introduction	Pg 17
Business as always	Pg 18
Boarding the unknown	Pg 22
Making contact	Pg 26
Parting of ways	Pg 29
The bridge	Pg 31
Time to leave	Pg 35
Rescue mission	Pg 41
The escape	Pg 50

INTRODUCTION

Aboard the small interplanetary shuttle Pay-check, the crew of the destroyed ship Payload are on their way back from Zedust colony, after making a delivery of expensive crystals for a customer that didn't want to pay the high customs taxes during the ongoing Plotation, Caridian war.

It has been a whole day since the shuttle left the colony with their pay for the job and even though the small crew get's on well with each other, the shuttle they are using is far from large enough to allow everyone to have their own space. But with war still playing out across the galaxy, work is coming in thick and fast for those willing to take a chance or two and this could mean a larger ship should be on the cards soon.

So everything seems to be going well, for now...

Business as always

I felt a hand on my shoulder gently shacking me as I heard the voice of my navigation's personnel Miller saying,

'Captain it is your shift, there is not much to report and I got to get some sleep. These long journeys are killing me.'

I opened my eyes and pull myself out of the make shift sleeping quarters as I replied,

'Ok, I'm up. Come on Andrew it's our shift, get up.'

I started to move over to the small door that led straight to the cabin of the shuttle before I turned and asked Miller,

'So everything is good, and we are still on course?'

'Yes Captain, but there is just one thing.'

'Well what is it Miller?'

'Nothing much, it's just that we seem to have picked up a ship on the edge of our scanners.'

'Who are they?' I asked.

'The ship is reading a Caridian signal and it seems to be moving slowly across the sector.'

'Do we have any communication from them yet?'

'No, I just guessed that they were patrolling the area, you know.'

'I suppose so, now get some sleep. Andrew come on, get up it's our watch.'

I moved through to the front of the shuttle and over to the pilot's seat before I put my hand on Phillips shoulder and stated,

'Come on you need to get some rest.'

'Thanks Chris. I just hope we can afford a better ship soon with real living quarters.'

I smiled at Tom Phillips as I replied,

'Just another couple of months now and we should be able to afford that star classed frigate. I know its second hand, but it's much bigger than this shuttle.'

'Yea, and then we can really make some credits.'

'Just keep that in mind, now go get some rest and that's an order.'

'Yes Captain, have a good shift.'

I sat down and gazed out at the stars before I checked over the ship's controls. Miller was right there was a Caridian military ship on the edge of our scanners. But it seemed to be moving very slowly away from us, so I just ignored it and continued to check the ship's other systems.

'Good morning Chris, how are you?' Andrew enquired as he took up the co pilot's seat.

'Good, but Phillips is right. We need a better ship.'

Andrew started to check over the systems as he rubbed his neck.

'Do you want a coffee?' I asked.

'Yea, but what's going on with this ship on the scanners?'

'It looks like it is just passing through.' I replied as I got up and moved over to the food dispenser on the wall. I punched in the order for the coffees and moved back over to the pilot's seat once I had got them. I then passed one of the drinks to my first officer.

'Thanks, but it looks more like it's drifting to me.' He replied.

I checked back over the scanner's readout and he seemed to be right.

So I pulled up the readout for the last hour before I checked it over.

'You are right it is drifting, I wonder if it has been attacked. Can you try to get them on an open channel, and see if they need any help?'

Andrew turned his chair to the communication's console as he opened up a channel before he relayed our message of assistance. He tried several times, but with no reply to our calls I said,

'Ok knock it on the head. Let's try a scan for life signs and if it shows up nothing, I will get onto the Caridian military to see what they have to say.'

'Scanning it now Chris.' Andrew replied

I turned to the readings we had already recorded on the ship to find that its fleet name was Nightfall and that it was an old destroyer class warship.

'Chris, I think you should know that there are no life readings aboard. Shall I open you up a channel to the military?'

I nodded in agreement as I continued to drink my coffee.

'Channel open, Captain.'

'This is the independent shuttle Pay-check. We have picked up a drifting Caridian warship called Nightfall on our scanners. It is reading no life signs, so would you like us to bring her in for you?'

There was a moments silence before we got a reply.

'Ha Chris is that you? Artos here, your message was relayed through to the closest warship. Anyway thanks for the offer. But that ship has been missing for five years now and its class was decommissioned two years ago. It's yours if you want it. I can give you some codes if you bring me a copy of the ship's last recorded logs, so what do you say?'

'Thanks, we will check it out then, and it's good to hear from you again Captain.'

'Likewise, just be careful kid. That ship was in uncharted space when it went missing. Now I have a war to fight, so Artos out.'

The com line cut and both Andrew and I looked at each other before he said,

'Well we need a bigger ship.'

'Yea, so let's alter course and get there before anyone else does.' I replied.

'Course altered and E.T.A in five hours.'

'Well, I will go and prep the boarding equipment, if you keep us on course.'

'Of course Chris, shall I let the rest of the crew know what's happening?'

'Not just yet, let's let them get some sleep first. Well for the next few hours at least.'

I got up and moved over to the middle of the shuttle's living area, where there was a large floor panel with a hidden release switch built under a small steel cover. I pulled the panel open and started to pull out several pieces of equipment, before I placed them on the floor next to me. Andrew got up from the controls as he said,

'I have locked the ship in on course. Do you fancy something to eat while we prep?'

'Yea why not, we have a few hours to kill.'

Boarding the unknown

Four and half hours later everything was ready and I had gathered the whole crew together for a briefing before we attempted to land on the drifting ship. All six of us were now in the cabin area of the shuttle while we fast approached the drifting ship. I look at my crew as I addressed them,

'Ok, as you know we are approaching a drifting Caridian warship. It has no life reading we can pick up on, and the military have said they have no need of it. So this means it is ours if we want it.'

'It all sounds too good to be true, so what's the catch?' Miller asked.

'Well that's it, the only thing is the ship has been missing for five years and from the information the military sent us. They say they lost contact with her in uncharted space. So we need to be careful.' I replied.

'Careful of what, you have already said that the ship has no life readings?' Phillips asked.

'Good question, but something must have happened to the crew and from the stories we have all heard about drifting ships. The ones with no life signs are the worst.' I replied.

'So we're going on old ghost ship stories, now are we?' Phillips sarcastically replied.

'Not exactly, but we do need to be careful. So until we know that the air is safe to breathe we will be using the face masks and I want everyone to be armed. Just in case this is a trap and something jumps out of the warp when we are all on board. Any questions anyone?'

The crew stayed quiet for a moment so I continued as I handed out the face masks and laser pistols saying,

'Ok then, keep these on and keep up your guard. We will keep in touch over the com and I will split us into three teams. Andrew and I will head for the bridge to take control of the ship. Hudson, Miller and Phillips you will need to head to the engine room to find out what state the ship is in before we try to move her. That leaves you Richards to keep watch on our shuttle. That means you will lock the door behind us once we leave and let us know if anything turns up on the shuttle's scanners that maybe of help to us. Any questions anyone?'

Again the crew stayed quiet and there seemed to be an air of excitement in the room.

'Ok then let's get to work and we should have a new ship by the end of the day. Miller, take the pilot's seat. Richards, take up the co pilot's seat and let's get this ship landed.'

I heard the crew agree as we switched places and I picked up my G8 Reaper gun and handmade energy sword. I saw Andrew look at me with a smile as he said,

'Don't you think that's a little over the top Captain?'

'Maybe, but if this is a trap, you know pirates like to use stabbing weapons and no one is going to argue with this gun, if they have any sense.'

'I'm glad I'm on your side mate.'

I smiled back at him before I turned to look out of the shuttle's forwards windows. Now we were approaching the drifting war ship. I could see that the ship must have been drifting for years now. Its outer hull was marked and scarred from being hit by space debris and asteroids. Still it looked in reasonable condition and we needed a bigger ship, even if it was on the old side.

'Well she looks like she could do with a good servicing.' Hudson stated with a warm grin on his face.

'Don't be too hasty yet, we have to make sure she is safe for space travel first.' I replied.'

'Oh don't worry Captain. I will have her ship shape in no time.'

'I bet you will, now what are we waiting for let's get landed.' I replied.

We came in close to the drifting ship as Miller flew our shuttle to the underside of its hull before he said,

'I have located the fighter bay and with any luck, we should be able to land in there without any trouble.'

He was right the doors to the bay were wide open and with the ship's shielding down, we could put down safely and close the doors by remote with the pass codes that captain Artos had sent us. I continued to watch from the shuttle's front windows as Miller began to land our ship. I also noticed that the shuttle bay seemed to be completely empty and in immaculate condition. Our ship gently bumped as Miller landed her before he said,

'That's it we're down and I am starting to close the doors behind us. Then it should take about five minutes to get a safe atmosphere in the fighter bay before we can leave the ship.'

'Great, now once that door opens I want everyone to be on full alert. I also need you to wear the face masks until we can confirm what happened to the crew and that the air is safe to breathe. Ok.'

Everyone agreed as I pulled on the breathing equipment and picked up my sword and gun. Andrew pulled on his face mask as he said,

'Now we have four hours of air in these things. So let's make sure we make this place as safe as we can, as fast as we can.'

The computer console beeped to indicate that the atmosphere outside of the ship was now at a safe level.

'Ok then, what are we waiting for? Let's get that door open and move out.' I ordered.

Miller released the shuttle's door and it hissed as the two atmospheres mixed. I could feel a cold blast of air come from the fighter bay and it was clear that the ship had not been heated for a long time.

'I moved boldly through the open doorway and stepped onto the strange ship as I ordered,

'Let's move out.'

My crew followed as I moved across the empty hanger bay towards an open doorway on the other side of the room.

I drew my gun as we approached the doorway and Andrew moved over to my side while he was looking at a portable scanner unit.

'Anything showing up yet?' I asked.

'It's strange Chris, I am getting no life signs at all from the corridors and rooms on this scanner, but.'

He paused as he stopped in his tracks. I also stopped and moved back over to him as he continued to say,

'Well, I seem to be getting movement from the rooms ahead of us and I have checked the scanner's systems over. It confirms that it is registering just six life reading and that is us.'

I looked at the screen to see that some of the rooms ahead of us were reading steady movement. But no life reading at all as I asked,

'Could the ship's walls be interfering with the scanner's read out?'

'No I don't think so, or the scanner would not be reading the movement from the rooms either.'

'Ok people, I think we should check out one of the rooms and find out what's moving in there. So ready your weapons and let's stay alert.'

'Agreed Captain. Now we should head this way.' Andrew replied as he pointed towards a doorway to the far right of the corridor we were standing in the entrance of. I moved into the corridor as my crew followed and we soon found ourselves at the closed door before I asked,

'Is this the first room reading movement?'

'Yes Captain, just one movement pattern. It seems to be circling the middle of the room.'

This all seemed strange and as I moved my hand over to the door release panel I said,

'Ok cover my back.'

Making contact

I pushed the open door button and the small doorway hissed while it slid open. The room was fully lit with little in there other than shelving racks lining all of the walls. I could see a figure standing facing the wall. It seemed to stop what it was doing as the door opened and I could see that it was wearing a dirty gray military overall. I pointed my gun at the man as I said out loud,

'Hello, do you need any help?'

The figure turned around to face me slowly and I could see that his lower jaw was missing. The man had a vacant look on his decayed looking face. But as he spotted me in the doorway his eyes seemed to glaze over and then without warning he grabbed for me while starting to moan. I didn't wait to find out what it wanted and fired off a single shot at its chest. The G8 Reaper's shot tore through his body, throwing the man like a ragdoll back against the wall where it slumped to the floor. My heart was pounding in my chest as I kept my gun trained in on it for a moment.

'Well I guess it is dead now Captain.' Miller said nervously.

'What the hell just happened?' I asked as Andrew moved passed me into the room, I lowered my gun while Andrew moved his scanner up in front of the dead man.

'I just need to get some closer reading and then we may kno…'

Suddenly Andrew fell back as the dead man suddenly moved forward towards him as it again started to moaned while reaching for my crewman. Andrew dropped his scanner as he grabbed for his laser pistol.

The man's top torso ripped off as it tried again to grab for him. There were then several laser shots as Andrew fired his gun at the things head until it slumped to the floor in a lifeless pile of blood and flesh.

'I think we should leave now.' Andrew stated while his hands shuck, before he began to pull himself up from the floor.

'Are you alright?' I asked.

'Yes, but it scared the hell out of me.'

I moved passed him and retrieved the scanner from the floor. I then moved back over to what was left of the dead man like thing and ran another scan of the body. Andrew moved back into the corridor as I heard him order,

'Weapons ready and cover our way ahead while we check over what is left of the body.'

He then came back into the room and moved over to my side, gun still pointing at the dead corpse as he asked,

'Well have we found anything out from the body?'

'More than I thought we would. The body is confirmed as humanoid, but in a state of advanced decay. The scanner readout from when the thing attacked me makes no sense. It had no heart beat or body heat, and the only thing the scanner could pick up on was a very low level of brain activity.'

'So what you're saying is the man was already dead. But he was still moving around because his brain was still active.'

'Yes, that's about it and once you shot it in the head, the brain stopped functioning and the body stopped.' I replied as Andrew looked at me with disbelief.

'You're saying we just had to shoot a Zombie.'

'It looks that way and we don't know how many more may still be aboard. But I am guessing that this is what may have happened to the crew.'

'So what do we do now?' Andrew asked.

I moved back out into the corridor passing the scanner to Andrew while I looked at my crew before I said,

'Ok then, it looks like the crew may still be here and moving around. So we can do two things. Leave now and let this ship be, or stick to the original plan which is Andrew and I will head to the bridge and you three can head to the engine room to find out if this ship is still salvageable. So what do you say?'

The crew looked at each other before Miller replied,

'I think we should check this ship out. There may only be a handful of those things here and this ship is a great opportunity for us all.'

'Yes Captain, I agree and this time we can be more ready for an encounter.' Andrew replied

'Ok then, let's move out. Andrew you're with me and the rest of you can make your way to engineering. Now be careful and don't let any of those things get close to you, until we know what we're dealing with, Ok.'

We all headed up the corridor towards what looked like an open area at its end. My crew all had their laser pistols drawn except Andrew who was still using the scanner to see if there was anything moving ahead. We soon came quickly to the end of the corridor and emerged into a small open space, where I could see two large closed doorway with a control panel between them.

'These should be the main lift shafts for the ship Captain.' Andrew said.

'Good let's get moving and be ready for anything that may come out from those doors.'

I moved in front of one of the lift doorways as I pressed the call button. I then stepped back and pointed my gun at the closed door while we waited for the lift car to arrive. Andrew pushed the small scanner into his pocket and drew his pistol as he stood next to me, while the rest of my crew covered the door to the other lift. I could see the look on his face as he looked at his small laser pistol even before he asked,

'I don't suppose you want to swap guns for the day, Captain?'

'I smiled at him as I replied,

'And you said this was a little over the top.'

Andrew laughed as the lift in front of us stopped and the doors began to slid open.

Parting of ways

Empty; we both sighed with relief as I asked,

'Do you gents want to take this one?'

'No thanks Captain, we will get the next one.' Phillips replied.

'Ok then we will see you later.'

'Good luck Captain, and we will get in touch when we get down to the engine room.' Miller replied.

'Just be careful and we will see you once the ship is secured.'

Both Andrew and I moved into the lift car as he pushed the button for deck one. The doors closed and I could feel the lift as it quickly ascended up through the ship's main hull.

'What do you think we will find on the bridge?' Andrew asked.

'Nothing I hope, then this will be a very easy mission.'

'That would be great.'

The lift car came to a stop and the doors slid open to reveal an empty long and poorly lit corridor. The first thing I noticed was a skeleton of a man that had been completely stripped of any flesh leaving it clean. The corridor on the other hand was smeared with dried blood and bits of fabric from clothing. I stepped out of the lift with my gun aimed forwards ready for anything that may come.

The corridor ahead had several doorways leading off from it and I could see that some were open while others were blocked off with debris, like make shift barriers.

'I'm starting to get the feeling we should have left this ship alone.' I said quietly to Andrew.

We both moved off towards the bridge as I noticed Andrew looking behind us. I stopped and turned to see what he was looking at as I asked,

'What wrong?'

'Nothing, I just get the feeling that we should check the corridor out behind the main lift shaft.'

'It's just the crews living area isn't it?'

'Yes, but I'm just getting a bad feeling about it Captain.'

'I now have a bad feeling about the whole thing. But we should find out what happened first.'

'Agreed, and then maybe we can get this placed warmed through.' Andrew stated while sort of laughing as we started moving again. We both pointed our guns at the bridge's heavy bulkhead doors as we approached. I knew the doors should open automatically as we stood in front of them, but we both had to stop when nothing happened.

'Well what do we do now?' Andrew asked. I looked around the door frame until I saw a control panel. I then moved over to the controls and started to type in several security overrides that Artos had sent us. Again nothing happened.

'Do you have any other bright ideas Chris?'

'Just one, now stand back just a few steps.'

We both moved back as I pointed my G8 Reaper at the door control.

Then I fired it just once; the shot exploded as it hit the panel smashing it right into the wall. There were several sparks before the hole where the control panel used to be started to smoke. I then moved over to the hole and put my hand in as I grabbed hold of just one wire. I then rubbed the wire against each connection and bare wires in turn until the door hissed and pulled opened slowly.

The bridge

We both moved onto the bridge to find what looked like three dead bodies slumped over some of the ship's control systems. Nothing moved so we lowered our guns before we moved across the room and over to one of the ship's main computer systems.

'Andrew, can you start accessing the ship's main systems? While I look into what happened and find some heating, it is freezing in here.'

'I'm on it Chris.'

Andrew started to work at the ship's computer systems while I started to pull up the ship's logs and reports on what had happened to this vessel.

'Chris, It should start to warm up in here and I now have the ship's main systems online.'

'Great now bring this ship to a full stop and let's see what Hudson and his team are up too.'

'Yes Captain.'

I found the ship's last month's worth of recorded log's as I felt the temperature in the room start to rise. I started to look over the last captain's report as I watched with disbelief at what was happening. The log stated that the whole crew had been infected by some sort of virus, and that the three members of the bridge crew, were the only crewmen left that had not been infected up to this point. But they were locked on the bridge and needed to escape the ship before they died of starvation or were bitten and infected by the virus.

'Bitten?' I said out loudly.

'What did you say Chris?'

I continued to read back through the logs as I replied,

'Yes, it looks like this virus was picked up from a small abandoned alien asteroid base that still held an atmosphere. It looks like they found a small alien creature that didn't read any life signs. Then they captured it to bring aboard for tests. The earliest log on this, states that the creature bit one of the medics before the ship's captain ordered it to be destroyed.'

'What happed to the medic?' Andrew asked.

'Well the report says that the man fell ill as the virus spread throughout his nervous system, before it then spread to his brain. Then he died.'

'So what was that thing we found in that store room?'

'One of the crew, the dead man got up ten minutes later and started to attack the crew. The report says that he was shot twenty times before one of the ship's guards shot him in the head. But by that time the dead man had bitten twelve other crew members.'

'And I guess it spread from there right.' Andrew replied.

'You got it in one. It looks like the cold has slowed the decay of the bodies and kept the virus in a slowed state of activity.'

I looked at Andrew as he looked back at me with a look of horror on his face.

'But if we turned the heating back on in the ship, wouldn't that make the virus more active again?'

Suddenly there was a groan come from one of the dead bodies.

'Shut it down now.'

I turned to where the moan had come from to see that the dead body was pulling its self off of the console it was lay over. I quickly looked around to find the other bodies were also getting up slowly. I quickly went for my gun as the zombie in front of me started to head in my direction while its blackened eyes stayed fixed on me. I remembered what the report said and fired off a single shot at its head. This stopped it in its tracks as its body fell to the floor.

The loud bang from my G8 gun seemed to excite the other zombies causing them to run for me. I again took another shot at the second zombie hitting it in the chest. The force from my gun shot tore the decaying man in two, as it throw him back across the room. I turned to find the third zombie almost on top of me just as I heard a laser shot and it fell to the floor at my feet.

I stood looking at Andrew while he still had his gun pointed at me while he said,

'A little too close for you, right Captain?'

But before I could reply, I noticed the upper torso of a body pulling its self over to Andrew's feet. I quickly pulled up my gun firing off another shot, blowing the thing into pieces, where it lay on the ground still groaning.

'Now we're even, right?'

'Yes but we should warn the others.' Andrew replied.

'Do it and tell them to head straight back to our ship. I will let Richards know we're on our way back.'

I could feel the warmth in the room as I pulled my com link from my belt and I knew the place would now take at least half an hour to cool back down again. I opened up a channel as I said,

'Richards, we're aborting the mission. This ship is too dangerous for us to salvage. Also you may want to monitor the hanger bay until we get back, and don't open the shuttle door until you have voice contact from one of our crew, understood.'

'Yes Captain, but what's going on out there?'

'Trust me you don't want to know, just don't let anything in. Ok!'

'Yes Captain.'

I cut the com line and replaced my com link back on my belt. Then I turned to Andrew as he stated.

'Chris, they have already run into trouble and they are held up in engineering. Everyone is ok but they say it may take them some time to get back to the shuttle.'

'Ok, tell them we will wait, unless they need any help and I will set up a warning message to tell anything to keep away from this ship.'

I could hear Andrew relaying my message while I set up the warning beckon. I could also still hear groaning coming from the other side of the bridge. I activated the message and then moved over to where the groaning was coming from. I had my gun drawn ready as I moved around the ship's control consoles. Only to find that the noise was coming from the dismembered head that was still trying to bit at me as it lay on the metal grilled floor. Its eyes were wild and its jaw snapped as it saw me. I stepped back as I said out loud,

'We should never have come here, now let get back to the shuttle.'

Andrew looked at the severed head with horror before he simply replied,

'Agreed, let's go.'

Time to leave

We both turned to leave the bridge and headed back into the corridor that would lead us back to the main lift shaft. We were heading back the way we had come, just as a zombie emerged from one of the open doorways. Andrew took a shot at the decaying man slowing it down while he fired again at its head. This finished the thing off but as we started to move again more of the dead started too emerged from the open doorways in front of us, we stopped and I turned to find that we were now surrounded. We both looked at each other with a desperate look on our faces before I said,

'In there, we can fight them off better if they are only coming at us from one direction.'

I knew if I fired my gun now it would set the things off running at us. So I drew my sword and headed blindly into the darkened side room. Andrew followed quickly after me, hitting the close door button once we were in the room and as the door slid closed after him the lights raised.

I was now facing a woman sitting on a bed with a large open wound to her stomach. I nearly gagged as I watched the woman sitting there eating her own inners. She looked up with a look of hunger on her blooded face before she dragged herself to her feet. I didn't wait to see what she was going to do so I used my twin bladed sword to cut her head from her shoulders. Her body then fell to the floor as her head rolled off to the left still snapping with its blood covered jaws. I moved over quickly plunging my sword into the head, causing the thing go still and silent.

Suddenly there were several loud bags on the door and both Andrew and I looked at the door before looking back at each other.

'Well what do we do now?' Andrew asked with a hopeless look on his face.

I looked around the room as the banging continued before it hit me.

'The bed, come on help me pull it in front of the door.'

We both lifted the heavy bed over the dead zombie's body before we moved it in front of the door.

'I don't think that will stop them.' Andrew replied.

'It's not supposed to, just get ready to shoot.'

'That's ok for you to say with that G8, but I have this tiny laser gun and no sword.'

'Well next time bring a bigger gun.' I replied as Andrew looked at me with a desperate look on his face.

'Ok, give me your pistol and you can use this.'

I moved over to Andrew and passed him my gun. His eyes lit up with a spark of power as he quickly gave me his pistol like a child that was worried I would change my mind. I looked at the small pistol as I said,

'I'm worried I'm going to break this thing.'

Suddenly the door slid open as the zombies tried to push their way in.

'Didn't you lock the door?' I shouted at Andrew as I shot the first zombie in the head.

'I thought you did.'

'Just shut up and shoot.'

I shot another zombie in the head while they started to scramble over the bed that was in their way. Suddenly Andrew let the G8 Reaper gun fire on automatic. The heavy gun shots cleared the doorway quickly leaving nothing but a blooded pile of mangled decaying bodies. I could still hear movement as I activated the power unit on my sword. The twin blades crackled with energy as another round of zombies came around the door frame.

Andrew fired another short burst of ammo until the gun clicked empty.

'I'm out of ammo Chris.'

'Here catch this.' I threw him another couple of ammo clips while I continued to say,

'And put that gun back on single shot or we will run out of ammo before we get off this deck.'

I took another zombie out as the first of the dead crawled over the bed and into the room. I could see Andrew franticly trying to reload his gun and I knew we needed to stop them from getting into the room if we were to survive. I fired again taking out the zombie that was now in the room before I moved into the doorway to take out the rest of the zombies with my sword. This was brutal and bloody as my sword cut the decaying bodies heads in two, but it had to be done. The pile of bodies started to build and I felt like I was going to gag at the sight and smell of what was now in front of me. But I knew I had to finish this or we would not be going anywhere. I cut the last zombie's head off as I heard the G8 gun's ammo clips click into place.

'Ok move out of the way.'

I stepped back from the door before I turned back to Andrew. I didn't have to say anything as Andrew said,

'Ok then, I guess that we should get moving.'

'Yea, and let's make it quick.'

I climbed over the pile of dead zombies and made my way back into the corridor. I turned back to see Andrew pulling himself out of the room as he steadied himself from falling with his free hand.

'That is disgusting and my hand is now covered in zombie slime.'

I watched as he wiped the mess across the wall before I said,

'Come on we need to get back to the ship and I don't want to run into another round of those things.'

We both started to move quickly towards the lift shaft as a zombie grabbed for Andrew from one of the barricaded doors. Andrew quickly shot the thing with the G8 at point blank range, blowing its rotten body apart and back into the room it came from.

We reached the lift shaft and I pushed the button to call for the lift, while Andrew fired off several more rounds back up the corridor,

'Chris, I hope that lift gets here soon as I am running low on rounds again.'

I noticed zombies coming around both sides of the lift shaft from the back of the ship and it was now clear that we were more than outnumbered before I replied,

'Andrew, watch your back, we have more incoming.'

I shot several more shots knocking down three more of the un-dead, but they were still closing in on us fast.

'Andrew, concentrate on the closest for now to buy us some time.'

'What the hell do you think I have been doing?'

Suddenly the lift doors slid open while Andrew fired off another few rounds.

'Get in the lift now.' I shouted while I cut one of the zombies down from in front of me.

'Come on Captain, I only have one shot left.'

I pulled back into the lift car as I plunged my sword into another decaying crewman while it lunged at me. Andrew hit the close door button while I pulled back, but as the doors started to close several zombies put their blooded hands into the doorway trying to force them open again. Andrew quickly pulled up the G8 gun, firing off the last shell at the narrow opening between the doors. The blast was nearly deafening in the small space, but it did clear the doorway allowing it to close. I quickly hit the button for the hanger deck and to my relief the lift started to move while the ringing in my ears subsided.

We both sighed with relief as we looked at each other.

'That was too close and I am now out of ammo.'

I quickly pulled another two ammo clips from my pocket as I handed them to Andrew and said,

'Take these. That's the last I have, so make them count. And Thanks, I think I owe you one.'

Andrew reloaded his gun as the lift came to a stop and I drew my sword again ready for another round. The doors opened to reveal the same empty corridor we were first in and I could see the opening to the hanger bay from out of the lift car doors. We both moved out of the lift as my com link went off making us both jump. I pulled the com link from my belt and answered it saying,

'Go ahead, Chris here.'

Miller's voice sounded desperate as he replied,

'Captain, we need help. We're all held up in the main engine room and several of those things are blocking our escape.'

'How many of them are there?'

'Only about seven and they don't seem to know how to use the ladder we climbed up to escape them.'

'Why don't you just shoot them and get out?'

'We can't risk hitting any of the equipment in here. Hudson says that one missed shot could fracture the main reactor and blow us all to kingdom come.'

I looked at Andrew as I cut the open com line. I could see the concern in his eyes and I knew he could see the worry in mine. I looked down at the laser pistol's power read out before I said,

'Well I have at least nineteen shots worth of power left in this thing and if you just reloaded, you should have twenty-two rounds in the G8.'

We both looked back down the corridor towards the hanger bay before I said,

'You don't have to come. It's my fault we are all in this mess.'

Andrew looked at me like I had just said something stupid before he replied,

'We all made the decision to come here.'

'Captain are you still there...Captain?'

Miller's voice sounded even more desperate as I reopened the com line saying,

'Stay calm I'm on my way, now what deck are you on?'

'Thank god; I thought you had gone there for a minute. We're all held up on deck twelve.'

'Ok, we will be there as soon as we can.'

'Trust us we're not going anywhere right now Captain. But I must tell you the computers on this deck are reading a lot of movement from outside of this room.'

'Thanks for the warning, now stay safe.'

Rescue mission

I again cut the com line and replaced the link back on my belt as Andrew pushed the button for deck twelve. The doors slid closed again and we looked at each other.

'Well Captain, who wants to live forever anyway?'

We both smiled at each other as the lift came to a stop, but as the doors slid open both of us raised our guns in readiness for whatever lay ahead. The first thing I saw was a zombie walking away from us up the corridor. I stepped out of the lift slowly with my sword drawn and pistol raised. I quickly looked around to find a zombie walking slowly towards me. It reached out for me so I quickly slashed my sword at the things neck cutting its head from its shoulders, and causing the thing to drop to the floor like a sack of spanners. This also caught the attention of the other dead man as I spotted it stopping before it turned around, and then it made a run for me. I quickly raised my gun but before I could shoot, I heard a single round fire from the G8. The shot passed just inches from my side and within moments it had taken the zombies head off. I looked back briefly as Andrew stepped out of the lift saying,

'I think we should get moving before more of them come.'

I nodded in agreement as we both moved quickly around the lift shaft. So we could head towards the main engine room. The first thing I saw as we moved around the main lift shaft was a short but wide open corridor.

It had several archways leading off to other areas of the ship's engineering section and a large door at the end packed with zombies, all heavily banging on the steel and glass bulkhead door.

Both of us stopped in our tracks as we looked on at the mass of zombies blocking our way ahead.

'Please tell me there is another way into that room.'

Andrew checked his scanner before he answered,

'I'm afraid not Captain, but at least they haven't spotted us yet.'

'Ok then, let's do this right. We don't have a lot of ammo so I need you to fire off about five rounds into the group, then get my back and I will fight off what's left with my sword.'

Andrew looked at me like I was crazy as he said,

'There has to be around twenty five of those things there. Do you really think you can take that on?'

'Well let's find out shall we.'

'Ok mate, but it's your funeral.'

I watched as Andrew raised the G8 before he fired off five rounds at the mass of zombies. I again turned the power to my sword on as I watched the shots hit the decaying mass of bodies, knocking most of them down to the floor. I knew this was it as the first of the dead started to run for me. It looked like the shots had taken down around a dozen of the targets and with half gone the rest were mine.

I started to move forwards raising my pistol. I took several shots at the fastest closing zombies taking out another four while I continued to move towards the rest of the un-dead, as they drew much closer to me. Shooting two more in the head before they were close enough for me to use my sword. I quickly slashed out hitting three of the closest zombies with the twin power charged blades. The sword removed one of the zombie's head's instantly, while the others were thrown back towards the wall with a 50'000 volt energy shock. I stood my ground as I slashed at another zombie as it came into range, again cutting its head in two. I quickly shot two more of the zombies as they approached knocking them to the floor with close range head shots. Before I glanced around to see the two zombies I had first knocked down starting to get up while several mangled zombies dragged themselves along the floor in our direction from the bulkhead door.

I moved in as I plunged my sword into one of the zombie's heads just as the other one grabbed for my leg.

'Captain, look out behind you.' I heard Andrew shout as I shot the zombie in the head as it pulled at my clothing. I turned quickly to find another zombie coming from out of the corridor behind me.

So I switched the power on my sword off, just for a second as I placed my boot on the zombie's head my sword was plunged into, before ripping it free from the dead creature. The zombie moved in quickly as I reactivated the power on my sword before again cutting its head off. I turned back towards the bulkhead door to find six mangled zombies still slowly pulling themselves in my direction.

I moved forwards as again I cut the heads from the mangled remains of zombie bodies until the corridor fell back into the undertone hum of the engineering deck. Again I looked around to see if there was any movement. But all I could see was the decayed blood and remains of the now dead zombie mass.

'Come on we need to get off this ship and I don't have much ammo left.'

Andrew moved along to my side with a look of astonishment on his face before he asked,

'Where the hell did you learn to fight like that?'

'I used to sword fight as a kid, why the hell do you think I made this thing?'

I raised the sword in front of him for a moment as he replied,

'What war zone did you grow up in?'

I just smiled in reply as we quickly reached the battered bulkhead to find the small window in the door had been smashed by the force of our earlier gun shots.

'Well I guess this is main engineering.' Andrew stated.

I moved over to the small broken window in the door to see what was on the other side. But before I could see anything a rotten and blooded hand grabbed at me from the other side of the broken window. I pulled back quickly as I heard Miller's voice shouting at me from the sealed room.

'Is that you Captain? We're stuck in here with several of these things, Captain?'

As he spoke the zombie's hand disappeared back into the room. I pulled my com link from my belt as I turned to Andrew and said,

'Ok keep this corridor clear for our escape and I will take it from here.'

'You can count on me, just be careful in there.'

I smiled as I replied

'Trust me.'

Then I opened up the channel to Miller so we could speak clearly.

'Ok Miller, we're outside and I'm going to get you all out of there. But I need you to do something for me first.'

'What is it Captain?'

'I need you to check that no one has been bitten, ok.'

I could hear the zombies over the com while Miller checked with the other crewmen to see if everyone was alright. The pause seemed to last forever before his voice came back over the com.

'We are all fine, no injuries at all.'

'That's great, now I'm going to open this door but I need you to buy me some time by distracting those things.'

'And how the hell do you think we can do that?' His voice had again returned to a state of panic at facing the zombies.

'It's ok; I don't want you to do anything dangerous. But you can make as much noise as possible. I'm hoping it will keep them focused on you guys while I pick them off one by one. Have you got me?'

'Ok Captain, we will do our best.'

'Great now make some noise and don't stop, ok.'

I cut the com link and pulled my sword up as I reached for the door control. I could now hear my crewmen shouting and banging on what was around them and I knew it was time to take the only chance they all had of getting out of there in one piece. I reached out to the door control panel and typed in the code to open the door.

The magnetic locks banged loudly as they released and the door hissed and groaned as it was pulled slowly open. I knew Andrew had my back as I moved into the opening doorway to be met by the first of the zombies.

I quickly thrust my power sword into the opening doorway at the zombie's head where it crunched into the dead man skull. I could now clearly see into the room as I pulled my sword back out of the dead zombie head. The noise from the opening doorway had now attracted the attention of several more of the un-dead which were now heading quickly for me.

I moved forwards taking down another zombie with my sword as I heard the G8 gun fire behind me. I hoped that Andrew was ok as I took down another zombie, cutting its head from its shoulders. The dead zombie fell to the floor as I pulled back while the next two zombies walked over the dead ones lying in their way. I could now see four zombies clearly coming for me as I again heard two more shots come from the G8 but closer now. I slashed again at the two closest zombies knocking them to the floor with the shock from my power sword.

I stepped back again as I glanced behind me to find Andrew slowly falling back towards the main engine room. I looked back into the room to find the last two zombies were almost on me. I stabbed the closest one in the head while I quickly pulled up my laser pistol, again shooting the other zombie in the head.

'Come on, let's get out of here while we have the chance.' I shouted over to my crewmen.

The room now looked clear other than the two zombies that were pulling themselves up off the floor. So I moved over quickly swinging my sword at them beheading one with the first blow while my sword blades knocked the other back to the floor again.

'Captain, I could do with a little help out here, I have about a dozen incoming and fast.'

I quickly plunged my sword blades into the zombie's head killing it out right before I turned and headed back towards the bulkhead door as I again shouted out,

'Come on let's move out.'

'Captain, I could really do with some back up now.' Andrew shouted out in desperation. I quickly move back into the corridor to find Andrew almost shooting zombies at point blank range.

I could now see about forty zombies heading for us as I moved back to Andrew's side.

I slashed out at two of the closest zombies killing one and knocking the other to the floor as I asked,

'Where the hell did all these come from?'

I pulled up my pistol shooting three more zombies in the head as Andrew replied,

'It looks like they came from the other side of the lift shaft.'

I heard my crew behind me as Hudson said,

'Maybe we should go back into the room Captain?'

'Just start shooting at them, unless you know of another way out of engineering?'

Miller stood at my side as he started to shoot and there were now four of us taking zombies down as Andrew's gun clicked empty.

'I'm out Chris, what you got?'

'Here take this, it's got about eight shots left and make them count.'

I looked around quickly to see that Phillips was missing,

'Where is Phillips?'

Miller replied as he briefly looked back while still shooting at the oncoming zombies,

'He was just behind us, he should be there.'

There seemed to be more zombies coming from the corridor in front of us as I said,

'Hold the line I won't be long. Andrew, cover Miller and Hudson's back while I check engineering.

'With what Captain, I have three shoots left?'

'Just do it I won't be long.'

I moved quickly back into the engine room to find Phillips struggling to hold off a zombie while it held him against the wall. I moved over quickly using my sword to behead the decaying man.

Its head rolled to the floor as its body was thrown to the ground by Phillips.

'Thanks Captain, I thought I was a goanna.'

'Well, let's get back to the others before they get over run.'

We both moved back to the main bulkhead door as Phillips asked,

'Captain, what did you mean when you asked if anyone had been bitten?'

I stopped and turn to him to see he was holding the back of his neck.

'Why?'

'Well that thing got me from behind before I knew it was there. I managed to hold it off, but I can feel blood running down the back of my neck and it hurts like hell. So what did you mean?'

Andrew moved into the doorway as he desperately stated,

'Captain, we need your help and I only have one shot left.'

'Here take my gun, and give me yours, I haven't used it yet.' Phillips replied as he held out his pistol while his hand shuck. Andrew looked at us both so I took the gun and passed it to Andrew. Then he passed me his gun as I said,

'Ok just start to push forwards towards the lift I will be there soon.'

'Captain?'

'Just do it, ok.'

Andrew left as I heard him relay my orders. So I turned back to Phillips before I said,

'Let me take a look at that.'

He turned around and moved his hand away from his neck as he winced with pain. There was a tear across the back of his neck and I could see a human tooth lodged in the wound.

'Sorry; it looks like it got you.'

Phillips turned back to face me with a look of fear on his face as he said,

'So does this mean I am going to become one of those things?'

I didn't know how to tell him as I replied,

'Yes, I am so sorry and I really don't know what to do about it.'

'How long have I got and don't lie to me?' His voice wobbled as he spoke and I knew I had to leave.

'About ten minutes, sorry.'

Phillips looked back around the room before he held his hand out for the pistol.

'Give me the gun.'

'I can't let you shoot yourself.' I replied.

'I'm not going to shoot myself. I'm going to shoot the main reactor core once I shut down the shielding. Now get out of here and I will give you all as long as I can.'

'There has to be another way.'

Phillips looked at me with an expression of defeat on his face as he replied,

'You know as well as I do that we cannot let this ship find its way back to a populated world. Now go before you run out of time.'

I handed him the pistol as I said,

'I owe you one.'

'Just get out Chris and make sure this ship takes no more lives.'

'I will Tom.'

I didn't want to leave him in there, but knew he was right. So I quickly moved out of the room and back into the corridor closing the bulkhead door behind me sealing Phillips in. My crew had only moved ten meters up the corridor while they continued to shoot at the zombies. So I quickened my pace to catch up with them as I stated,

'We don't have the time for a long shootout. Hudson give me your gun and quickly.'

Hudson passed me his pistol as I asked,

'Is there any other way off this deck other than that lift shaft?'

Hudson turned to me as he watched me pull open the laser pistol while I started to swap the energy power emitter around, before he answered.

'Well the ship should have service tubes between decks but it will take about three minutes to get between each deck and they are all very narrow, if you know what I mean.'

'And how many decks are there down to the hanger deck?'

Hudson continued to watch me as I fed the power safety back into the guns own power pack as he replied.

'Are you really going to...?'

'Yes it's a bomb; now how many decks?'

'Six Captain, why?'

'Ok then pull back everyone and that's an order.'

I picked up one of the G8 guns empty shell's as I pulled the trigger and shoved the shell into the space where you would put your finger, jamming the trigger into its firing position. I could hear the power building up as the gun started to get hot, so I throw it at the oncoming zombies. The gun quickly hit the floor as it disappeared into the mass of zombies before it exploded.

The blast knocked all of the zombies to the floor and I knew we had wasted enough time already. I quickly raised my sword and activated its power blades as I ordered,

'Let's get back to the lift and don't let anything touch you.'

The escape

I moved quickly towards the crawling remains of the un-dead as I cut the heads off anything that was in my way. I quickly moved around to the other side of the lift to find several more zombies heading in our direction.

'Andrew, call the lift. Miller, cover the others while I hold off anything that gets to close.'

I slashed out at the closest zombie removing its head with my sword blades as Miller and Andrew continued to fire.

'That's it Captain my gun is drained.' Miller stated.

I cut down another zombie as the lift doors opened and I heard Andrew shout out,

'Get in the lift, come on.'

I pulled back into the lift car as Hudson hit the button for the hanger deck. The doors started to close as one of the zombies put its rotten arm through the narrowing space between the doors as it grabbed for my crew. I quickly thrust my sword through the small space stabbing the zombie in the head. Then I removed the blades with a crunch letting the zombie fall backwards, while allowing the doors to close fully.

The lift started to descend as I readied myself for what maybe on the next deck while I asked,

'Where the hell did all of those things come from?'

'This ship's cargo hold is located in front of the main engineering section, it's a huge open space for equipment and food.' Hudson replied.

'I wish I had known that before, the captain's logs stated that once the infection had spread throughout most of the crew they were all placed in the ship's storage area until a cure could be found.'

The lift drew to a stop and the doors slid open as I moved quickly back into the first corridor we had entered this hell hole of a ship on.

'Come on we need to leave now. Miller, let Richards know we will be with him shortly and that he needs to have the ship ready to leave as soon as we are aboard.'

'Where's phi...'

Hudson was cut short as the whole ship jolted sharply with a huge bang. Suddenly the ship started to shudder violently as it began to groan.

'Get out of the lift now.' I shouted while the ship's cold computer voice tannoy system kicked in saying,

'Reactor containment failure, all crew to evacuate the ship. This is not a drill.'

'Move it now, everyone back to the shuttle.'

My crew moved quickly out of the lift car as all the doors in the corridor we were in slid open.

'Why the hell are the doors opening?' Andrew asked.

'It is standard ship protocol. The computer is making it as easy as it can for the crew to leave the ship, it's old military programming.' Hudson replied.

'Come on we have to leave now.' I stated as I spotted a zombie coming out from one of the open doors.

'If anyone has any ammo left start shooting anything in our way.'

I could hear a sound of thunder rumbling throughout the ship's hull behind me and I knew it wasn't good. Andrew shot down a zombie in front of us as my crew moved quickly towards the hanger bay.

I followed with my sword ready while the ship continued to tear its self apart with the explosion in engineering.

We were nearly at the hanger bay as the explosion burst out from the lift shaft behind us.

I glanced back to see several zombies running after us, and they were being quickly caught up by a massive wall of flames from the explosion.

We all made it to the hanger bay where our shuttle was waiting with its engines running. I hit the close door button to the bay before I turn to make the last dash to my shuttle. I glanced back to see the zombies had all now been engulfed in the flames and that the wall of fire was just behind me. I hit the door control button to lock off the hanger as the last of my crew ran past me. The hanger door banged closed as the magnetic locks activated just as the force of the explosion hit the metal door with a loud thud.

The whole ship jolted again violently with another massive bang as several areas of the hanger roof and floor blow up around us all. The force of the blast thrown my whole crew to the floor and I found myself also thrown several feet through the air before I hit the floor with a painful thud. I looked up from the floor to see my crew pulling themselves up from the burning deck as the ship continued to tear its self apart. The hanger roof was now falling in on us as I scrambled to my feet and again headed for my shuttle. I heard Andrew calling for me as I realised that he was trying to free Hudson from some fallen wreckage. The whole ship now looked to be burning around us and I knew we only had minutes before the ship was nothing but a burning wreck. I rushed over to my first officer while he was trying to free Hudson from some twisted metal. Andrew looked up at me through the broken glass of his face mask as he said,

'I can't free him, it's too heavy.'

'Come on, I promised Phillips I wasn't going to let this ship get anyone else, now lift.'

We both lifted the twisted piece of metal that was pinning Hudson to the deck. We could hardly move it, but we did manage to lift the twisted metal plating just a few inches.

'Hudson, can you pull yourself out?' I asked through gritted teeth.

'I will be out of here if it is the last thing I do, Captain.'

I watched as Hudson dragged himself out from under the wreckage while both Andrew and I struggled to hold the heavy plating. Suddenly the ship jolted sharply again as the deck exploded in several areas around us.

The jolt caused us both to drop the plating as something hard hit me across the back of my left arm and shoulder. I again found myself lying on the deck just feet from where I was standing before. I looked up through the cracked glass of my mask and to my relief Hudson was free from the wreckage, but now lying on the deck. I started to pull myself back up from the floor as a huge amount of pain shot down my arm and shoulder. I felt a hand grab hold of my side as I looked up to see Andrew pulling me up from the floor. I groaned with the pain as I got to my feet before I said,

'Help Hudson back to the shuttle, I'm ok.'

Andrew looked at me in disbelief before he moved quickly over to Hudson. I started to head back for the shuttle as I struggled to avoid the burning areas of the deck that were all around me. My shuttle lifted up from the deck and started to move over to Andrew and Hudson in front of me. I watched as it picked them up while I continued in its direction. Again the ship groaned as the deck under my feet started to tear apart. I stepped to one side as I watched the tear run quickly across the deck towards the hangar space doors. I began to run for my life towards the shuttle as the ship violently began to break up around me.

'Captain, come on.' Miller shouted as he held out his hand as far as he could reach. I jumped over a burning hole in the deck just as the room we were in started to lose atmosphere from the hanger bay doors. I just caught hold of Miller's hand and he pulled me into the shuttle. Andrew hit the door control closing the shuttle off from the exploding ship as he shouted,

'Raise the shields and get us out of here, now.'

I pulled myself up into a seated position on the floor as the shuttle worked its way out of the collapsing hanger bay doors. I looked around to see we had everyone but Phillips while the shuttle shot back into space. I pulled my cracked face mask off just as there was a blinding flash come from the rear shuttle window, which was followed by a sharp jolt as the shuttle was hit by the exploding ship's shock wave.

'Well we cut that one close.' Andrew sort of laughed.

Richards looked back from the pilot's seat before he asked,

'Is everyone ok back there?'

'I think we need to get Hudson and the Captain checked over by a medic, so put out a call to the Caridian military asking if they have any ships nearby. Then set course for the closest colony while I check everyone over.'

Andrew moved over to a wall panel and pulled out a medical kit as he looked at both me and Hudson.

I smiled through the pain I was in as I said,

'Check Hudson first, and Thanks again.'

I tried to relax against the wall as I moved myself into a more comfortable position while Andrew started to check over Hudson. I couldn't help but think we had made a really big mistake today and that the loss of Phillips was my fault. But then I also knew that these men trusted me more now than ever, and that we would have many more difficult decisions to make together in the years to come.

HELLFIRE

DEADLOCK

VOLUME 3   By Christopher J Sharman

DEADLOCK

Contents

Introduction Final days of the war	Pg 57
Earth date 12.08.2302 AD	Pg 62
Hope arrives	Pg 65
A debt owed	Pg 72
Death arrives	Pg 76
Deadlock	Pg 82
Calm before the storm	Pg 86
Confrontation and loose ends	Pg 89
Ending the deadlock	Pg 97
One ending and new beginnings	Pg 109

INTRODUCTION

The final days of the Darkness war

Captain's log Earth date 22.03.354 BC. This war against the Darkness is coming to an end and I fear as the final battle approaches we may still fall at the last hurdle. The crew of the Hellfire are all tired of fighting, but then we all know we are fighting to save our own future and this war must end with the final defeat of this Darkness race. Even if none of us have ever even seen the enemy creatures we are fighting against, due to the fact that they stay hidden in the shadows and their ships. The Darkness have gathered all their ships, allies and weapons together for this final conflict and this battle will take place just outside of the Kaliens own solar system. Our fleet is in place, but I know the risk to their home world and this has made me realise that the time has come to send Starlight and her family to our own time for safety. I know this means I will have to say goodbye to my sweet Starlight and that I may not see her again. But then I know it has to be this way, Log end.

'Captain to the bridge.'

I moved over to the wall tannoy system and answered the call saying,

'I'm on my way.'

With this I left my quarters as I grabbed my long command coat from my bed, putting it on before I moved out into the corridor.

I quickly reached the ship's bridge and moved into the busy room where I was met by my first officer.

He moved over to me handing me a tactical computer pad as he stated,

'Captain, the fleet is in place and the Darkness forces will be here in under an hour. The Kalien Dreadnoughts have the experimental gateway ready and are waiting on your orders.'

'Good, then let's hope this works or there will be nothing left to fight with. Now my friend, what about Starlight's family and have they arrived yet?'

'Their ship will be here in under five minutes Captain.'

'Does she know what I have planned?'

'No but Chris, are you sure about this. I mean you know what will happen.'

'I don't have a choice, besides I would not change any of the time we have had together over the years, even if it means I will not see her again.'

I could see Andrew knew how much this was going to hurt me but then he knew I was right. But before he could reply Richards stated,

'Captain, Starlight's family's ship has just touched down in hanger bay one.'

'Thank you Richards, let Starlight know they are here and tell her I will meet her in bay one in five minutes.'

I turned to leave the bridge just as Andrew grabbed my arm. I turned back to see the worried look on his face as he said,

'Chris, as your friend I need you to think about this. Can't it wait until after the battle, then you could look at this without the stress of this war?'

'It's too risky and you know it has to be this way.'

Andrew let hold of my arm just as Miller informed me,

'Captain, the Darkness fleet will be within firing range in thirty five minutes and our fleet is requesting our next move.'

'Tell them to hold for now. If this plan is going to work then we need to wait right until the last minute before we act. Andrew, you have the bridge and I will be back soon.'

I turned and left the bridge as I heard my first officer take control of the ship. I had waited long enough and while I headed toward the ship's main lift shaft I found Starlight waiting for the lift.

I walked up to her as she turned around to see me and a smile beamed on her soft pale blue face before her wings fluttered lightly and she said,

'Chris, what are you doing here? I thought you would be on the bridge.'

I moved over to her and gave her a huge hug before I kissed her on the forehead and replied,

'If you are going to spend some time with your family, then I wanted to say goodbye.'

Starlight stepped into the lift once the doors had opened and I followed hitting the button for the ship's hanger level. The door slid closed and I stared at her for a moment trying hard to burn her image into my mind.

'What's wrong my love and why the sad face?'

I smiled at her as I replied softly,

'Starlight you know this ship is not from this time and that once this war is over we will be going back.'

'Yes, but why does that make you feel sad?'

'Well your family are here because I am sending them ahead with you.'

'But I thought we were just going somewhere safe.'

'You are, there is no Darkness war in my time and your home world is safe. It's just too risky for you to be here right now.'

The lift car stopped and we both stepped out into the corridor before we continued to make our way to the hanger bay.

'I will see you again, after this battle right?'

She held my hand as she stopped in the middle of the corridor. But before I could answer Hudson interrupted saying,

'Ah Captain, Starlight, the ship will be ready for the time jump in just five minutes. I just need to input the emitter codes and adjust the power levels so it will work. Then once this war is over we can get you two back together, when our ships meet back up with each other.'

'Great work Hudson and set the date and time to this date.'

I handed him a small computer pad before he left as he thanked me. Starlight smiled at me again before she said,

'Chris, I will be looking forwards to seeing you again. Stay safe.'

I held Starlight's hands as I looked at her while wondering how to say my next words,

'Starlight, when you are in my time there will be a day you will meet me again, but I will not know you.'

'What do you mean? We have known each other for nearly my whole life.'

'Look it is your future so I can only say this. You will meet me but before I have the Hellfire. I will need your help and you must promise me you will not tell me any of what is in my future.'

'But why?'

'Look it may change what time we have already had together. You will know it is me and your dad will not accept the young me as well as, well me.'

'You are not making any sense. What do you mean?'

'Do you remember when we met, just as this war was starting?'

'Yes of course, but what does that have to do with this?'

'Well I had met you before and that is how I knew you. You will understand what I am saying when it happens.'

'But I met you when I was five, so of course you knew me.'

'I haven't lived that day yet. Look it is kind of weird but it will all make sense one day.'

'So will I see you again like we are now?'

'I don't know, but it is possible.'

'Chris I don't like this, it feels wrong. What are you not telling me?'

'Look I have so much I want to tell you but can't. Just remember there will be a choice to make and it will be your decision. It must be your choice and your choice alone. I know you will make the right decision.

Now we must get you to safety.'

We moved through to the hanger bay and I could see Starlight's mum waiting for her just outside of their small transport ship. We both moved over to her as her mum greeted us both with a friendly embrace, just as the tannoy announced,

'Captain, the Darkness fleet has stepped up its speed and will be within firing range in just a few minutes.'

Starlight looked up at me with a desperate look as she said,

'I will miss you so much.'

'Me too, now go and be safe. I will see you again soon. Go while I finish this war once and for all.'

The ship jolted as the red alert sounded and I knew I needed to be back on the bridge. I kissed Starlight passionately once more before she left with her mother, and as the Kalien ship closed its doors before it began its take off. I quickly headed back to the bridge, just as the ship jolted again while the tannoy stated,

'Captain to the bridge, we have a problem.'

I stepped onto the bridge to find the battle had started as I asked,

'Is Starlight's ship clear?'

'Yes Captain and they have made the time jump.'

'Great then what are we waiting for. Let's begin the attack and give them Hell. All of it.'

Earth date 12.08.2302AD

The Kalien cargo ship Enlightenment is journeying to a small Kalien colony within the Caridian boarders, with a shipment of shield generators and technical equipment meant for a low tech settlement. So they can better its defenses during the ongoing war. The ship's captain, called Talstead and his daughter Starlight are on the small bridge chatting about their next visit home, when the ship's sensors alert them both to an explosion two sectors away. Starlight springs lightly across to the array of crystal like controls, running her hands over them until a holographic image is displayed in front of her of the star system where the explosion has just occurred.

'Father you should come and see this.'

'Leave it alone, it is probably just a skirmish between the Plotations and the Caridians again. We are near their borders.' He replied with a sound of un-interest in his voice.

'No Father, this is from much deeper within Caridian space, and it looks like a small ship has survived.'

'You know our race has opted not to take sides in this war and after the war with the Darkness, we are too few to start fighting again. They will make their way to a colony, we should let the younger racers find their own way in the universe.'

'I know Father, but they are sending out a call for help and we could be there in just a few minutes.'

'Starlight, I said No. We cannot be seen to be taking sides with the military. Let it be my child.'

His words were firm but Starlight couldn't just leave it until she knew the survivors were ok. She lightly sprung across to the other side of the bridge as she replied,

'At least let me listen to the call for help, so I will know we are not leaving them for dead.'

Talstead shuck his head before he looked at her and then replied,

'You are just like your mother. You can listen to the message, but that is all.'

Starlight fluttered her delicate looking wings with excitement as she moved two crystals. Suddenly the distorted voice of a man could be heard throughout the room and she listen with intent.

'I repeat, this is the independent shuttle Pay-check, too any friendly nearby ship. We have escaped an exploding vessel and we have injured. Can anyone offer assistance?'

'Father did you hear that?'

'Yes, and if they are not military who are they?'

Talstead had concern in his voice, but he could see his daughter would not leave this alone, as she said.

'Let me find out.'

'No, I will do that my child.' Talstead moved gracefully over to the ship's main controls as he began to move crystals and wave his hand over various lights. He looked for a moment with a puzzled look about his face.

'Well what is it?' Starlight asked with excitement.

'The shuttle checks out to be an Earth built ship. It has no weapons and a small crew.'

'So we should help them right?'

'Maybe, but I think we should find out what has happened first.'

Starlight smiled as again her wings fluttered while her father moved over to the communication's console.

'This is the Kalien transport, Enlightenment. What is your status and what injured do you have?'

A different voice could now be heard with a strong accent throughout the room as the voice answered.

'Hi; my name is Andrew, our shuttle took a bit of a knock when the ship blew up. But that's not really the problem. Our engineer and captain are both injured and need medical assistance. We have little aboard we can do for them, so can you help us?'

'There is a colony just half a sector away from your location. They should have the resources you require.'

'That colony will take us three days to get to, now that the ship's engines are damaged. What do you want me to do, let them bleed to death?'

Talstead cut the communication as he looked at his daughter.

'So we are going to help them, right?' she asked.

'You will never forgive me if we don't.'

Talstead reopened the communication channel before he replied,

'We will be with you in just a few minutes. Please hold your position.'

'Thank you we are very grateful, Pay-check out.'

Talstead turned to his daughter before he said,

'You had better prepare the healing rooms, I will tell Callter to ready our shuttle bay for the guests.

Hope arrives

'Captain just hold on, we have help on the way.'

I watch as Andrew moves back over to me before he kneeled at my side still looking worried. I could feel my clothing sticking to my shoulder and arm but remain still as it hurt too much to move, then I asked,

'How's Hudson doing?'

'He passed out with the pain, the scanner is reading that he is stable for now, but it looks like he has broken his leg in two places. Now how are you?'

Andrew waved the small scanner in front of me as his concerned look deepened.

'I have had better days. Now what's all this about help?'

I tried not to show the pain I was in as I sat there, but I could see Andrew knew my injuries were too bad to leave as he replied,

'A Kalien ship has answered our call for help and should be here soon. So can I get you anything?'

'How about a coffee and... I don't think I have ever met a Kalien before.'

'Not many people have, they keep themselves to themselves and avoid any kind of conflict. So we should be safe with them.'

Suddenly there was a blinding series of lightning flashers come from outside the shuttle's front windows as Richards said,

'We have a jump gate opening five hundred meters off our port side.'

'Go check it out, you have command right now my friend.'

Andrew got up and ran over to the shuttle's cockpit as he ordered,

'Give me a report on that gateway.'

'Sir, we have a medium sized transport ship emerging from the gateway. But it...'

Miller paused as the ship appeared and Andrew asked,

'But what, come on what is it?'

'Just the gateway Sir, its readings are different from the normal jump gate signals.'

The lightning faded as the ship pulled in front of our shuttle and its gateway closed behind it. Then Richards interrupted as he said,

'We're getting a call coming through. Shall I put it on?'

'Yes of course.' Andrew replied before Miller fed the message through.

'Captain Talstead here, we have readied our shuttle bay and you are free to dock. I have our ship's healer waiting in the bay for your injured.'

'Thank you we will start docking procedure now.' Andrew replied.

'No need, just fly in close and we will do the rest. I will meet with you once you have landed, Talstead out.'

The com cut and Miller looked at Andrew with a slight look of fear on his face.

'Well Miller, bring us in close. Let's not keep our hosts waiting.'

The shuttle bumped lightly onto the deck of the alien ship. Then I watched Andrew move over to the door. He released the lock and our shuttle door hissed as it opened. He then kneeled down at my side before he asked,

'Chris, do you think you can get up?'

'Just give me a hand mate and please be careful.'

Andrew grabbed hold of my arm and pulled me to my feet. The pain was unbearable as I moaned while I steadied myself and stood upright.

'Funny but it didn't seem to hurt this much when it first happened.'

I sort of laughed through the pain as I headed out of the shuttle door while Andrew followed close behind me.

'Chris, you really need to get some medical help.' Andrew stated with an uneasy tone in his voice.

We walked across the open space as we approached two blue skinned winged aliens. This was the first time I had seen a Kalien and was taken by how beautiful a race they were. I couldn't seem to take my eyes off of the young woman that now stood several feet in front of me. Her pale blue skin seemed to shine under the ship's lighting and I could see she had an amazingly hot figure under her light brown fitted robes. She looked right at me like she recognised me while her fairy like wings fluttered before she said,

'Chris?'

Then she turned to the male Kalien as I held my hand out before I realised it was covered in blood. I pulled my hand back as Andrew quickly cut in saying,

'Captain Talstead, I am First Officer Cygnarowski and this is Captain Sharman. We are hoping you can help us.'

The Kalien man stood there as he replied calmly,

'I thought you had said your Captain was badly injured, yet he stands in front of us?'

'Hi, I am here you know. Look, call me Chris and if you have a medical bay, then please may we use it. Then we will be on our way.'

I struggled to speak and stay standing as my vision blurred slightly. I staggered a little so Andrew grabbed hold of my arm to stop me from falling. The jolt sent a huge amount of pain down my back and arm causing me to groaned out loud. Suddenly I found the young Kalien woman now at my side before she said,

'Father, his wounds are extensive, we need to move him now.'

'Hudson, make sure they see to Hudson as well.' I said out loud.

Andrew steadied me before helping me follow the Kalien man, while the young woman pressed my shoulder as she said softly,

'This will help with the pain.'

Then the pain subsided while my vision blurred before the room seemed to go black.

I could hear voices as I opened my eyes to find I was now in a brightly lit room. I was comfortable while I lay on my side so I began to try to focus on the room I was in. The voices in the room became clear enough to make out what they were saying. So I stayed still as I listened carefully.

'Starlight, I can see the similarities but it is impossible. Humans don't live that long, besides he looks so young.'

'But Father, you have seen the holo-records of us for yourself. He is identical, even his voice matchers the old war records from our archives. Beside's I should know him and his crew and I can see you see it too.'

'Starlight, you know we fled that war on our savior's orders and we vowed never to speak of it outside of our race. The war against the Darkness was many millenniums ago now and although it has only been a few hundred years for us, we must stay silent about it until the Darkness is prophesied to return.'

'Yes Father but.'

'You must say nothing my child.'

I needed to move, as my arm was starting to go sleep. But as I moved pain shot through my body and I let out a groan, so I started to pull myself up into a seated position.'

'Our guest is starting to come around. You may need to ease the pain from his injuries again.'

I sat up on a silk like bed before I looked around the beautifully elegant and brightly lit room. I watched as this beautiful pale blue skinned fairy like creature crossed the room. I couldn't help but smile at her as she gazed with a look of concern in her big green eyes. She moved over to my side before she gently placed her hand on my shoulder while the Kalien man left through the open doorway.

I tried not to show the pain I was in but jolted as I was touched.

'Sorry, but I need to remove the bindings to check your wounds.'

'It's ok. So tell me, how bad I was hit.'

The fairy like creature undressed the wound as she replied,

'I had to fuse your shoulder blade back together and three ribs also needed fusing. I have stopped any internal bleeding. But you still have some open surface wounds and a lot of bruising to go with the tissue damage. That will heal in time, now I need you just to rest hear for a few days.'

I felt the pain ease in my shoulder before the young fairy like girl redressed the wound.

'I need to check on my crew and ship.'

'They are fine and I will let them know you are here and awake.'

I smiled at her as I pulled myself off of the bed and stood up. I hurt all over but could stand as Starlight moved in front of me.

'You need to stay here while you heal.'

I could see she didn't want me to leave the room so I said,

'Ok, but do you mind if I look out of the window?'

She smiled and stepped to one side before I moved over to a floor to ceiling window. Starlight watched me with interest as I stopped in front of the window and looked out into space. She then moved over to my side before she asked,

'What are you looking at?'

'The stars, they are the reason I ended up here.'

I could see Starlight through the reflection of the window smiling at me before she then asked,

'Knowing what you do now, would you still have come to the stars?'

'Yes of course.'

She placed her hand on my shoulder as it started to glow and my pain eased.

'What are you doing?'

'I am born of the healing cast, I have the gift to heal the sick and injured. My father says it was passed to me by my mother.'

I turned to face her as she moved her hand away from my wounds. We looked into each other's eyes and I could see she was looking at me like she already knew me and like she had known me for many years. I was going to ask her just as Andrew entered the room carrying some clothing.

'Captain you're up. That's great to see but, if I am interrupting something. I can come back later.'

'It's good to see you my friend, what have you got there?'

'A clean set of clothing for you. I am sure you don't want to walk around half naked do you?'

I smiled as I looked back at Starlight while she finished redressing my wounds. I was going to ask her if I could look around but she could see what I was going to say as she stated,

'Ok you can leave, just make sure you ask for me before the pain becomes too much for you again.'

'I will and thank you; it sounds like I owe you my life.'

She smiled as her wings fluttered lightly and then she turned away. I smiled back at her and then moved over to Andrew as he handed me my clothing.

'So how are you, or is that a stupid question?'

'I feel like I have been hit by a star freighter.'

I pull on the suit like jacket as gently as I could while I tried not to show I was still in pain. Andrew looked at me as he then said,

'You know, when I saw you get hit by that bulkhead door I thought we had lost you. It only missed me by a few inches. Then I saw you start to move and figured I should help.'

I eased my hand into my trouser pocket to make my arm feel more comfortable before I replied,

'It's funny but I didn't feel anything after I hit the deck until I tried to get up and then I just guessed that I was ok. Anyway how is Hudson doing?'

He is in the next room. Do you want to go and see him?'

'Why not, and you can lead the way as you seem to know your way around this place.'

Andrew headed for the arched doorway and I followed him into the corridor while I was considering how lucky I was to still be alive. I looked back at the Kalien girl to find she was still staring at me before she turned away from me while her wings again fluttered lightly.

'Thanks again and....Sorry I didn't get your name?' I said out loud knowing her answer from listening to their conversation.

'Starlight.' She replied.

'That's a beautiful name.' I said as her wings fluttered lightly while she broke into a full smile before we then left the room.

A debt owed

I walked aboard the Pay-check and moved back over to the shuttle's pilot seat before I sat down. Then I activated the control systems and started to go over the control readouts.

'Ha Chris, Starlight said I would find you here. What are you up to?'

'Just checking the ship over, it's great here but I don't want us to out stay our welcome and we don't have a lot to offer them as thanks for everything they have done for us.'

'What about Starlight?' Andrew asked.

I got up out of the pilot's seat and moved over to the food dispenser before I punched in the order for a coffee. Andrew moved over to my side as he again asked,

'I know you two have become close. So what are you going to do?'

I picked up the coffee as I jolted with pain.

'Are you ok?'

'Yea, I just forget that it hurts to pick things up with this arm still.'

'Should I get Starlight for you?'

I could see the concern in his eyes as I passed the coffee to my good arm before I replied,

'No, I'm ok. But you do have a point. I don't want to leave her here and we can't stay, but then I don't know if she will come with us. After all we have only known each other for about a week now.'

'It won't work you know. You're both different races. I mean what do you see in her?'

I looked at Andrew like this was a stupid question before I replied,

'She is stunning, gentle and we just seem to get on so well.'

'You've slept with her haven't you?'

I didn't answer as I turned back to the ship's controls.

'That means you have and we have only been aboard for six days.'

'I know, look I will sort things out. It's not like I planned this, it just sort of happened.'

'If you haven't forgotten mate, we're onboard her father's ship and she is a fairy.'

'She is a Kalien and I don't think that matters, besides you have to admit she has an amazing body and her eyes, I could look into them forever.'

'Chris, I have seen that look before and it only causes trouble.'

'I know but then she just seems to know me.'

'Chris.'

'And she...'

'Chris!'

'She's, standing behind me isn't she?'

Andrew nodded in agreement as I turn feeling a little embarrassed. Starlight stood in the doorway of the shuttle as we looked into each other's eyes for a moment.

'Hi' I said as she smiled at me.

'Well at least I know you really care for me. So when are we going to tell my father that I'm leaving with you?'

I looked back at Andrew and then back at Starlight while they both stayed focused on me. Andrew looked nervous and Starlight had a glimmer of excitement in her eyes.

'Well I guess whenever you are ready. I think we should speak to him alone after my crew has offered some sort of payment for the assistance your father and his crew have given us.'

Starlight moved aboard the shuttle before she replied,

'My father will not take payment for the help we offered you. But he will be expecting the conversation about my going with you. As he has already asked me if I am involved with you.'

'What did you say?' I asked nervously.

'Let's just say, he told me I should distance myself from you. He thinks you are trouble.'

'I can see this will go well then.' I replied as the shuttles scanners kicked in with an alert warning sound.

I quickly moved over to the controls with Andrew as we both looked over the different readouts.

'Jump gate opening and it's a big one.' Andrew stated.

'I recognised that jump frequency code; it's a pirate code.' I replied

I quickly opened up the ship's communication relay as I stated,

'Captain Talstead, if you have shields raise them now.'

His voice came over the com as he replied,

'What for, we have no fight with anyone?'

'Just raise your shields. It's a pirate jump gate frequency and most pirates don't leave survivors.'

'How can you be sure?'

'Talstead, just raise your shields and we can discuss this later, Pay-Check out.'

I cut the communication as I span the chair I was on around.

Starlight looked at me worried while I pulled myself over to the floor panel in the centre of the shuttle's floor.

'What are you doing?' Starlight asked.

I pulled the panel open and pulled out my sword and gun as I jolted with pain. I lay the weapons on the floor before I grabbed for two ammo clips and two of the ship's pistols.

'Look we need to show a sign of strength or these pirates will just attack us and kill everyone. Now we owe you and your crew that at least. Andrew, take these.'

I passed him the two pistols before I loaded the G8 Reaper and fitted the holster to my belt and leg. I pulled myself up from the floor with an involuntary moan of pain as Andrew stated,

'Chris, you are in no fit state to start fighting.'

'Hopefully we won't have too, now let's get to the bridge. Starlight, lead the way and let's hope you dad has put the shields up.'

She looked concerned as she left the shuttle, but lead the way quickly as we followed.

Death arrives

We were just feet from the bridge's arched doorway as the ship shuddered with two sharp jolts.

'Well I guess the shields are up.' Andrew said out loud.

'Yea they will be the warning shots, now come on.'

We moved quickly onto the small but elegantly decorated bridge before we moved over to Talstead who turn to face us with a look of fear on his face.

'You were right, they are pirates and they have demanded we lower our shields to be boarded.' Talstead stated.

'What have you said to them?' I asked slightly breathlessly.

'Nothing yet, that's why they shot at us.'

I looked blankly across the mass of crystal controls and displays before I asked,

'What weapons does this ship have?'

Starlight's father just looked down as he replied,

'None, we have not been in any kind of conflict since we left the last.... Well for a long time now.'

'Great so what are we up against?' I asked.

Starlight quickly moved over to the controls as she moved crystals and waved her hand over several displays.

Then a hologram came up of the pirate vessel.

I looked over the hologram as a shiver ran down my spine and my heart sank.

'It's a Falsec hive ship.' Andrew replied with defeat in his voice.

I could see from the readout that it was heavily armed and much bigger than the Kalien vessel we were on.

'Ok, anyone got any ideas?' I asked.

Captain Talstead looked across the display before he replied,

'If we cannot fight them why don't we just give them what they want?'

'That would not be wise. The Falsec race takes what they like and slaughter anyone or anything that is in their way. Then they destroy what is left to cover their tracks.' Andrew replied.

The ship jolted again as the pirate vessel fired once more at the Kalien ship while I looked over the hologram readout again.

'Ok, we need to buy ourselves some time. Captain Talstead, do we have your permission to use whatever is aboard to better our chances?' I asked

'Yes, but I don't see what good it will do.'

'Andrew, get Hudson down to engineering, then get Miller and Richards down to the cargo hold. Let's see if we can't put something together to make that ship think twice about attacking us.'

'Yes Captain.'

'Starlight, ready the ship's jump engines, you said this ship crossed two sectors in just a few minutes last night. Maybe we can out run them.'

Starlight almost blushed as she moved over to another set of crystals before she said,

Do you want me to open the gateway now Chris?'

'Yes, maybe they will not expect us to make a run for it.'

I watched as Starlight began to operate the controls as she moved crystals and waved her hands over lights before the ship began to move.

I monitored the hive ship's readout as suddenly the ship jolted sharply and one of the consoles blew up in front of Starlight.

I moved quickly over to her side, checking if she was ok while she shut down the engines before she said,

'It's no good Chris, they have our ship in a holding field and the control system just blew out trying to get free from it.'

'It was a long shot. Are you ok?'

'Yes, I think so.'

Starlight smiled at me as the ship jolted sharply again. Her smile faded quickly back to worry before she then asked,

'So what do we do now?'

'Plan B.' I replied.'

'So what is Plan B?'

'I don't know yet, but it will work when I figure it out.' I replied as again the ship jolted sharply.

'I guess some things will never change.' Starlight muttered to herself.

Captain Talstead moved over to us both as he spoke,

'Look, I don't know what you think we can achieve from this. But maybe we can reason with them.'

'You're right, that ship could have destroyed us by now, so we know they want or need the ship or something aboard. I have an idea, but I need you both to do exactly as I ask no matter what.'

Talstead looked at me with unease as he asked,

'How do I know we can trust you with our life's?'

'How many crewmembers do you have?' I asked.

'Thirty five why?'

'And I have four, that's a lot of people life's at stake and I'm not ready to let my crew or yours die just yet, ok?

Now open me up a visual communication link before we don't have any shielding left to work with.'

'I guess we have no choice in the matter then.'

Talstead moved over to one of the control systems before he activated the holo link and an image of the Insect like creature was projected in front of me. I stood up straight trying not to let the pain in my shoulder and arm show as I addressed the oversized bug like alien.

'I am Captain C. J. Sharman of the ship Pay-check. You are firing on a civilian vessel, which is classed as an act of war within the Caridian Empire. Now stand down and leave before the war ships we have called in, arrive to sort out this dispute.'

The creature laughed out loud before it replied,

'Captain, your communications are blocked and our sensors read no military ships that can come to your aid for at least ninety cronons, or three of your earth hours. Now lower your shields and your deaths will be swift.'

'Well if we are going to die. What do you want from this ship?' I asked trying to figure out what to do next.

'The ship's drive units and power core. You can give it to us or we will take it by force. Either way you will die quickly.'

This gave me an idea as I smiled at the Hologram image,

'Look, this is where we have a problem. You want the ship's engines and power core and we don't want you to have them. So let's make this easy, you shoot at this ship once more and I will blow the whole ship to nothing but atoms. Probably taking some of your own ship with it, or you can let us go on our way and we all leave here no harm done. So what do you say?'

'You would not do such a thing; killing your own is not Kalien practice. You make me out to be a fool Captain.'

I hoped that Starlight would do as I now asked or this bluff would not work as I replied to the pirate captain,

'As you may have noticed I am not Kalien and I can see this will go nowhere, so I will just start to overload the ship's systems now.

Starlight, power up the ship's main reactor to go critical and then shut down our shield systems at the last moment to cause maximum damage to their vessel when we blow. If we're going to die, I want to take as many of them with us as we possibly can.'

I could see the look of horror in her eyes at what I had just asked her to do, but she uneasily replied anyway,

'Yes Chris, I will jus...'

'Wait. Maybe we can sort something out.' The Falsec captain shouted. I turned to Starlight and gave her a wink as I ordered,

'Hold on that order for now. So what do you suggest, Captain?'

'I don't know, this has not come up before. But I can see you mean business.'

'I tell you what, I will give you one Earth hour to come up with an offer or leave, and if nothing is sorted by then. Well then I will blow up the ship. Cut the communication.'

The Hologram faded out quickly and I sighed with relief before I looked at Talstead and Starlight. They both looked at me like I was crazy before Talstead asked,

'How do you know they will not still attack us now you have closed down the communication?'

'I don't, but I'm guessing that they would have shot at us by now if they knew I had no intention of blowing this ship up.'

'You risked everything on the slim chance that they would believe you?'

'Well they want the ship and if we blow it up they get nothing but damage to their own unshielded vessel. So I have created a sort of deadlock situation, where the Falsec pirates get nothing if they let us go or they get nothing if they attack us. I figured that at least now we have an hour to sort something out.' I replied.

Starlight moved over to my side as she put her hand on my back. I jolted with pain slightly as she moved her hand down to mine, holding it gently before she spoke.

'You need another healing session.'

'No time, we need to find out everything we can about that ship and the Falsec race. We need anything that maybe of use to us.'

'Like what?' Talstead replied as he looked at Starlight with discontent while she held my hand.

'Weaknesses, laws or rules they obey, anything that may give us something to work with while we try to make some sort of weapon systems for this ship and boost its shielding systems. Now Starlight, can you open up an internal channel to my crew.

'Yes Chris, I will get straight on to it.'

She moved away from me and as she faced the controls I had to let the pain show. I moved over to a seat and eased myself into it as I sighed with relief. Talstead moved over to me before he said in a low voice,

'I do not agree with your ways and I don't want you near my daughter. You are not who she thinks you are. If we get out of this you will leave before she becomes too attached to you.'

'Look, I didn't nearly get killed trying to save my crew from a hoard of undead Caridians, for a bunch of jumped up pirates to go and kill them all a few days later. And as for your daughter, she is old enough to make her own decisions.'

We both looked into each other's eyes as Starlight called over to me.

'You have an open channel Chris.'

Deadlock

Things were all too clear now as Starlight shut down the ship's intercom to my crew. I knew there was no way we could even put up a mild fight against that hive ship, and weapons were out of the question as we could do nothing more than put a few antimatter torpedoes together from the ship's sensor probes and power converter control unit. But I did have a hunch that the hive ship was not as capable of destroying us as it looked. I stared at the stars outside of the ship as Starlight moved over to my side saying,

'So what do we do now?'

I looked into her beautiful eyes as I smiled trying to hide my concern, before I replied,

'Well Hudson is boosting the shield generators to give us some more protection, Andrew and Miller are building three torpedoes out of what they can find so we can fight back and Richards is looking into the Falsec race records in the Pay-Check's data banks. So I guess we have to wait while I try to figure out a plan.'

I was still sitting in the chair as Starlight moved to my side.

'I cannot see a way out of this Chris. So what chance do we really have against a ship that big?'

I was just about to answer as the intercom opened up with the voice of Richards my communication's personal.

'Captain, I may have found something.'

He sounded both excited and nervous at the same time as I replied,

'Well what have you got for me?'

There was a moment's pause before Richards continued saying,

'Well I found a report from one of the haulage ship's from the company we used to work for. It states that they were held by a Falsec pirate ship and didn't have a way out.'

'So what did they do?' I asked impatiently.

'The captain challenged the pirate leader to a hand to hand fight to the death for his ship and crew.'

'Go on, did it work?'

'Yes the ship's captain said if he lost the pirates could have the ship but spare his crew, and if he won they would have to leave them unharmed.'

'So he won right and the Falsec pirates let them be!' I replied.

'No, he was torn to pieces. But the pirates kept their word and let the rest of the crew go in the frigate's shuttle, unharmed.'

This was much better than I had hoped. All that I now had to do was fight off one Falsec pirate and not the whole hive ship.

'Thanks Richards, get on to Hudson and get him to create a gateway through our shields just big enough to let a small shuttle through, and tell him we don't have much time. Then see if you can find anything else out that may get us out of here.'

'Yes Captain.'

'So all we need is someone to fight the pirate captain, right?' Starlight asked.

'Yes, that's about it.'

'So what do we do now?'

'Just wait I suppose, we can't do much more right now.' I replied

Starlight held her hand out to me as she said,

'Come with me Chris, I need to look at your injuries and I have something for you.'

She smiled as I took her hand before I pulled myself out of the seat I was sat in. Talstead stood in our path as we both moved towards the bridge's exit.

'Starlight, I forbid you to leave this room with this, Human.'

He stood firm and glared at her with disapproval. I looked at Starlight as she looked up at her father and sharply replied,

'Father, this is not your choice, I am four hundred and thirty six years old, now step aside.'

Talstead didn't move as he replied desperately,

'I beg of you my child, this man cannot be who you want him to be. Besides he is nothing compared to the Captain of the Hellfire you loved, even if he looks the same.'

'Father, he loves me and I will leave with him when this is over. So you can be my father and back me, or lose me as a daughter when I leave here. It is your choice.'

She firmly glared at him until he stepped aside before we both moved out of the room. I moved to her side before I asked,

'Well that was one way of telling him, but how old did you say you are, and the captain of what?'

'Kaliens can live for up to nine hundred years.'

I looked at her surprised before I asked,

'Is there anything else you aren't telling me?'

Starlight smiled at me as we both stopped in the corridor and gazed into each other's eyes.

'More than you can ever know right now. Is that a problem?'

'No, like surprises.'

'Good then come with me. I want you to have something.' She replied as she fluttered her wings and moved her lips up to mine before gently kissing me. Then she took my hand again and started off up the corridor as her feet left the floor. I had to run to keep up and this was hard to do with my injuries so I said,

'Slow down, remember.'

She stopped and turned to look at me with concern.

'Sorry, I'm just happy I found you. Now let's get those wounds healed. I want to be with you.'

We both moved up the corridor as I smiled to myself while wondering what she wasn't telling me.'

Calm before the storm

I sat on Starlight's bed as she sat behind me. Her hands glowed with golden light while she healed my injuries. The light was warm and soothing and after a few minutes she stopped and moved her hands away from my shoulder and arm. I turned to face her as she sat behind me and I could see she now looked exhausted.

'What's wrong?'

'Nothing, it just takes a lot out of me to heal wounds that quickly.'

Starlight looked up at me as she smiled sweetly before she then said,

'Look in the mirror and you will see what I mean.'

I moved over to the huge elegant golden edged mirror on the other side of the room and turn my shoulder and arm that had been injured to face the mirror. I was surprised to find my wounds had gone. I didn't even have any scarring. So I turn to Starlight to find she was now sitting on the bed smiling at me. I moved over to her and put my hand through her black straight hair. Moving in close I kissed her before she pulled me onto the bed, then she rolled me over so she was sitting on my lap.

'I thought you were tired?' I asked as she just beamed at me happily.

'Just be quiet, I want to be with you.' She replied as she moved in for another passionate kiss, while we both started to undress each other quickly.

We both lay on the bed naked, Starlight's head on my chest while we held hands.

'I wish we could stay like this forever.' She said softly.

'Well when this is all over we will have all the time we need.'

Suddenly the ship's intercom kicked in as the voice of my first officer could be heard.

'Captain, the hour is almost up, Have you come up with a plan yet.'

I stroked Starlight's hair as I asked,

'How do I reply to him?'

Starlight held me close as she said out loud,

'Computer, activate voice link.'

The intercom beeped once as she then said,

'You can speak to him now.'

'Has Richards found anything else out yet?'

'No Captain, so it looks like someone will have to fight the pirate captain, if we want to get out of this mess.'

'Ok, I will meet you on the bridge in a few minutes. I have a plan, and we are getting out of this.'

'I can't wait to find out what you have cooked up mate.'

'You will find out soon enough, just get our crew together. Chris out.'

'Computer close voice link. So what do you have planned?' Starlight asked as she sat up.

'You will find out soon, now maybe we should get dressed and head for the bridge.'

I picked my clothes up off of the floor and started to get dressed. I watched Starlight as she put on her clothes and we both smiled at each other lovingly before I picked up my G8 Reaper gun. Starlight moved over to me picking up my sword.

She stopped for a moment while she stared at the weapon before she handed it to me saying,

'It has been a long time since I have seen a sword like this.'

'It's a one of a kind, you must be mistaken.' I replied as I took the sword from her and fitted it to my belt. Her wings fluttered a little as she smiled at me with a warm glow about her.

'How do you know it is a one off?'

'I built it to my own design. It is the only one in the universe.' I replied. Again she smiled and then she said,

'I knew you were going to say that. Now we should head to the bridge my love.'

We both kissed passionately before we left her room and headed for the bridge.

We both arrived on the bridge to find my crew and captain Talstead waiting. All eyes were on us both as we moved over to them before Andrew asked,

'So what's the plan?'

'Ok Hudson, did you get that gateway through our shield set up and ready to use?'

'Yes Captain, I have set up a shield generator to project an energy corridor out to the main ship's shields. Once the two shields meet it will open a hole just big enough to get our shuttle through. But the hole will lead right out in front of the Falsec hive ship.'

'Great work that is just what I wanted. What about the torpedoes?'

'We have three ready and they can be launched from the same shuttle bay.' Miller replied.

'Ok then Talstead you had better open me a visual communication line up to that hive ship so I can get this sorted.'

Confrontation and loose ends

I moved to the centre of the bridge as the holographic image of the Falsec pirate captain appeared.

'Captain, sorry I didn't get your name.' I said casually.

'My name is of no importance to you, just that you will die before I let you leave.'

'I see you have not changed your mind then, so what do you propose Captain?'

'I have monitored the system and found no ships coming to your aid and you have no weapon systems that can hurt this vessel, so lower your shields and I will make your deaths swift.'

'Ok let's look at it like this. I'm guessing that you are in need of this ship's power core because your ship's own reactors are damaged. So I don't think you can really hold this ship and attack us effectively without using up what power you have left. Am I right?'

The Falsec pirate looked shocked at what I had just said before he replied,

'What has led you to this wild guess? I should just destroy you now.'

'Well I don't think you can you see. Your shields are down and holding this ship will be taking up a lot of your power. Also when I threatened to blow this ship up, anyone with half a brain would have just raised their shields and attacked us anyway. So I think you can only really destroy us if you let hold of this vessel, and then we may just escape before you can take down our shielding right?'

The Falsec pirate just stared at me for a moment before he said,

'You are not as stupid as you look Human. But you cannot escape and we will have your vessel.'

'Now while you have been figuring out how to take this ship, we have been busy as well. We have increased our shield strength and built several ant-matter torpedoes. Not enough to destroy your ship. But we have located your bridge and one good shot should slow you down enough for us to escape. So here we are still stuck in this deadlock. You want this ship and I don't want to give it to you.'

'So what do you propose, Human?'

'Let's sort this out with a duel, captain to captain. Blade weapons only, what do you say?'

'And if I agree to this fight what are the terms you suggest, Human?'

'You win; you get the ship but let everyone on board live. I win you leave this ship and never attack it again.'

'Why should I agree to this?'

'Are you afraid to fight me?' I replied knowing his answer as he laughed out loud before he replied,

'Puny human you will be crushed by my blades. Once you are dead, I will let your crew live but the ship will be mine. No tricks.'

'No tricks, my first officer will follow my order if I lose.'

'Lower your shields and I will come to my new ship and provide your death.'

'Hang on just a minute. I don't trust you that much either, we will open a small hole in our shielding to let one shuttle come aboard. If you try sending more I will have them destroyed. Have you got me?'

'I look forwards to fighting you. Your head will make a great trophy to the story of your end. I will prepare my shuttle and you will see me and my first crewmate in half of one of your Earth hours.'

'I will be looking forwards to it, Enlightenment out.'

Talstead cut the communication and the oversized insect like creature's image faded out. I sighed as I turned to face my crew to see they were all looking at me with bewilderment.

I looked at Andrew and then said,

'Ok then, we now have thirty minutes to increase the shield strength and locate that holding field emitter. Andrew, work with Miller on locating the emitter so we can knock it out. Hudson, work with the Enlightenment's crew to increase the shield integrity even more and Richards, prep the shuttle bay for the fight.'

Andrew still looked at me like I was crazy as he said,

'Captain, as your friend I have to tell you I will not let you fight that thing with your injuries.'

I smiled at him as I replied,

'I'm not injured anymore, besides if you lot sort out the shields and locate that emitter, I won't have to fight, as we can make a run for it.'

Andrew moved over to my side as he asked,

'Can I look at your shoulder?'

'Yes.' I replied as I took off my jacket and move my t shirt. Andrew pulled the small scanner out of his pocket and ran a scan before he replied,

'I don't think I have seen anything like this before, you have no tissue damage or any trace of broken bones. How?'

Starlight moved over to us both as she replied,

'I did it. I gave him some of my life's energy to regenerate his own cellular structure.'

'But that must have taken an immense amount of energy.' Andrew replied.

'About twenty five years of my life span.'

'What, I would not have le....'

'Shush my love. I knew you would be fighting and you need to be well. Now come with me I have one more thing for you.'

She took my hand and started to lead me off of the bridge as Andrew's jaw dropped open before he asked,

'So what do you want us to do?'

I turned back as I said,

'You have your orders. Now let's see if we can avoid the fight.'

'Yes Captain.'

Both Starlight and I moved into the corridor as she asked me,

'Do you think they well get that stuff done?'

'Yes, but not before I have to fight that thing and if I stall them any longer, they will know I have been bluffing all along.'

Starlight turned to face me with a look of sadness in her eyes.

'Do you think you can win?'

'I don't know, but I don't see we have any other options.'

'I don't want you to fight.' Starlight replied as she ran her hand down the side of my face. I looked into her beautiful green eyes wishing things could be different. But knowing time was short as I replied,

'Look I have something I need to do. I will meet you in your room in ten minutes, ok.'

With this I kissed her on the forehead and move quickly up the corridor. I turned back to smile at her only to find a deepening look of sadness fall across her face.

'I won't be long.' I said as I headed for my ship.

I stepped aboard the Pay-Check and moved quickly over to the communication's console activating the record message system before I spoke,

'If you find you have received this message then I didn't make it. I just need to send my love to my Mum, Dad and the rest of the family. I had planned on coming home soon and I have met a girl. I think you will like her, so do me a favour. If she visits you make her feel welcome. Now I have to go, so love to everyone. Goodbye and I will see you on the other side.'

I hit the shut down button and made a copy of the recording. I took the data stick out of the console and turned my chair around to find Andrew standing in front of me. I could see the uneasy look on his face while we looked at each other for a moment.

'So I guess you don't think you can beat this creature then mate?'

'I don't know my friend, but there is a couple of things you can do for me.'

'Anything just let me know.'

I handed him the data stick as I replied,

'Make sure my family get this message if I don't make it, and take care of Starlight for me. If I do die here today, I would like to know she is going to be ok. Aright my friend?'

Andrew took the data stick as he smiled at me and said,

'I don't know if I could do what you are going to do today mate.'

'I'm sure you would if you thought you could save your friends. I saw you in that hanger bay trying to save Hudson. Now take my gun and if the Falsec pirate tries to go back on his word, nail him for me.'

Andrew took my G8 Reaper gun as I moved across to the shuttles door before he said,

'Go see Starlight, she seems upset and I will see you back here in about twenty minutes. Good luck mate.'

'Thanks.' I replied as I headed off out of our ship and back towards Starlight's room.

I arrived at Starlight's door and it opened as I stood in front of it. I moved into the room and over to the window on the far side of her bed. I looked out of the window at the stars, I could see the oversized Falsec hive ship and it was clear that the pirate ship could destroy this small vessel with ease. But then all I had to do was beat this one creature.

It sounded easy but I knew it wasn't. I felt a hand run down my back softly as Starlight's reflection came into the view of the window.

'How are you?' I asked.

'Fine, but I am worried about you.'

I turned to her and ran my hand down her arm to where her hand was. I held it gently before I spoke,

'You said that part of your gift was to heal and the other was a perception of the future. Look into my eyes and tell me if I'm not going to make it today.'

Starlight looked up at me. She smiled as a tear ran down her face before she replied,

'I cannot say for sure, the future is not set.'

'So why the tears? I can tell you are not telling me everything.'

'I know now why you will hold pain in your eyes, and I know there is a choice to be made.'

Starlight pulled away from me and moved away from the window. Her wings were lowered and her head down. I moved over to her and put my hands on her shoulders before I softly said,

'What choices?'

'I have said too much, hold me just for now, I need to feel your warmth once more.'

'You are talking like this is the last time we will be together.'

She turned to me and I held her in close. We just stood there for a few minutes holding the embrace. Starlight let go as we both stepped back from each other, I smiled at her and she smiled back as I said,

'Now we don't have long and you said you wanted to show me something.'

Starlight's wings rose again and she hopped lightly over to a wall panel. She ran her hand over a crystal display and a wall panel slid open. She pulled a heavy black folded garment out and moved back over to me before she said,

'I made this for someone I knew. I know it will fit you and I know it is your style.'

She handed the folded garment to me with both a smile and an undertone of sadness in her eyes. I unfolded the material to find it was a long black military styled command coat. The paneling and detail was amazing as I said,

'I can't take this. It must have taken you months to make.'

'Try it on and I will not take no for an answer.'

I pulled the coat on to find it fitted me like a glove. Starlight grabbed hold of my hand and pulled me over to her mirror, where she stood me in front of it. While looking at my reflection I spotted Starlight beaming at me. I turned around and pulled her into me as I kissed her passionately. She stepped back smiling before she said,

'It suits you just like I reme... Well that doesn't matter right now, and you must wear it for the battle, I feel it will bring you luck.'

I gazed into her eyes as I replied,

'Thank you I will.'

Starlight stared at me for a moment before she said,

'Now don't take any chances in this fight.'

'It's funny but when I was fighting off those things on the Nightfall before it was destroyed, I wasn't concerned for myself, just my crew. Now I'm facing this pirate I find I'm worried that I may not make it and I don't want this, well us to end.'

Starlight moved in and held my hand as she replied,

'We will always have each other no matter what happens here today. But what do you mean creatures?'

'It doesn't matter, not now anyway.'

I could see she looked concerned as she replied,

'No, tell me. All things hold importance it is just that sometimes we do not see it.'

'Well we found a drifting ship with no life sign and needed a new vessel. I suppose it all looked too good to be true, but when we boarded we found the crew. Well what was the crew?'

'What do you mean?' Starlight asked with greater interest.

'The scanner read them as dead no life signs, heartbeat or warmth, just a low level brain activity. Just like zombies.'

A look of horror quickly passed across Starlight's face as she grabbed my hand while she said with urgency,

'We have to inform my father and now.'

She pulled my arm as we headed for the door to her room while I asked,

'What is the rush?'

She stopped and turned to me before she said,

'Many millennia ago there was a war with a powerful Darkness. It nearly wiped out my race and many others. It was beaten but prophesied to return, what you have just described is a weapon that Darkness once used. We have to inform my people.'

She turned again and pulled me out of the room before we headed to the bridge.

Ending the deadlock

We both reached the bridge to find Talstead looking over the status of the Falsec hive ship. Starlight ran over to her father as she blurted out,

'Father there is something you need to know.'

'Starlight, I can see we are in grave danger, this hive ship still has more than enough power to destroy this ship and there is no way we can make a run for it even if this man can knock out the energy field that is holding us. I feel we may have to trust these pirates at their word.'

'No Father, this is much bigger than that. The Darkness has made its first move.'

'You must be mistaken my child. Now explain what you have discovered.'

The ship's communication system sounded before Starlight could speak and her father put his hand up in front of her asking her to wait while he moved over to the controls and said,

'Captain, it is the hive ship, I will put it on for you.'

He waved his hand over some of the controls before the image of the Falsec pirate captain appeared in front of me. The strange insect like creature spoke angrily and without hesitation.

'I have had enough of this waiting around. Open up the gateway through your shielding so I can take your worthless life and my prize. Or I will attack this vessel and our deal is off, Human.'

I calmly smiled back at the image which seemed to just anger him more before I replied,

'Captain, good to see you. I was just going to give you a call.'

'Stop stalling and open up the gateway, now.'

'Open up the gateway Starlight. Now I will meet you in the hanger bay so we can get this dispute sorted out.'

'You will mee...'

'And cut the communication; it's bad enough I have to look at him without having to listen to his ego as well.'

The holographic image faded out while the Falsec captain ranted to himself. I turned to Starlight and her father as I said,

'Starlight, let your dad know what you have told me and I will go down to the hanger bay for this duel. Wish me luck.'

I turned away as I saw the desperate look in Starlight's eyes. Then I moved back towards the corridor as I felt Starlight grab my shoulder. I turned around as she pulled me in for a passionate kiss before she said,

'Be careful my love and I will be there shortly.'

'Just tell your dad what he needs to know and I will try to make sure the crew survive so you can inform your people. Now I have to go.'

I kissed her head gently and left the bridge before I quickly headed off towards the hanger bay, where the fight would take place.

I walked into the hanger bay to be met by some of my crew standing and waiting. I moved over to Andrew as I asked,

'Did we find out if we can knockout the holding field?'

Andrew put his head down before he replied,

'Sorry Chris, it looks like we could weaken the field but not take it down completely.'

'Well let's get this fight over and done with. Now how long do I have before the Falsec shuttle lands?'

Miller pointed to the open hanger door as a strange spiked cone like ship drew closer. Its brown hull looked dirty and scratched from boarding other ships forcefully. I watched as the ship touched down with a thud before a heavy panel on its side split into three pieces and opened up into a doorway. I turned to face Hudson and Miller as I quickly said,

'Look I need you two to find some way of knocking that holding field out. Now look over the information again and you don't have long. Andrew, I've got a bad feeling this pirate is going to go back on his word. If he tries anything at all shoot him down and then take out the others, don't let them leave.'

'Yes Sir, but what about you?'

'I'm going to try my best to stay alive, but if I don't make it take care of the crew and Starlight. She is very important to me.'

I turned back to see two eight foot tall insect like creatures climb out of the open doorway. They both moved quickly into the open space on their four thin spike like legs. One of the creatures stepped back as it drew an alien looking large blaster from its back before it pointed it at us. I noticed Andrew pull up the G8 Reaper in defense as the other creature that I recognised as the captain scuttled forwards. I raised my hand to Andrew as I also stepped forwards before saying,

'Ok let's lower the guns. I believe the deal was your Captain and I, are going to sort this out in a bladed weapon fight. Or are we just making this up as we go?'

The Falsec captain signaled for his crewman to lower his gun before he replied,

'Human, your crew have made preparations to leave this ship on your death?'

'Yes they will leave if I lose and your crew will let hold of this ship if I win?'

The creature laughed out loud as he replied,

'You look small and feeble Human, you will not win and my crew have their orders if you do.'

'And what orders are they?' I asked as I stepped closer to him.

The Falsec captain seemed offended at my comment, but replied with discontent.

'My first crew mate is here to ensure the rules are followed. If you win, which is unlikely, he will return my body to my ship and we will leave.'

Suddenly his crewman raised his gun again but towards the hanger door this time. I quickly rose my hand as I turn back to find Starlight and her father entering the room.

'Wait, they are not here to fight.'

The Falsec captain again told his shipmate to lower his weapon as he watched Starlight run over to my side. Starlight grabbed my hand as she pulled me in and whispered into my ear,

'My love you have to win this. Please be careful, it is very important that we get the information about the Darkness to my people.'

She then kissed me gently on the lips before she continued to say,

'Besides, I don't want to lose you my love.'

I kissed her forehead as I held her in and replied,

'I have no intention of dying here. Now stay back and whatever happens. Stay with Andrew, he will look after you. Ok?'

She looked up at me as she replied,

'Ok, just remember I love you.'

She stepped back as the Falsec captain cut in saying,

'You Human like creatures disgust me. Now are we going to fight or do I have to come over there and strike you down while you flirt with the fairy?'

I smiled at Starlight as I said to her,

'I love you too, now get back.'

I then turned to the Falsec captain as I drew my twin bladed sword before I stated,

'Well let's get this show on the road.'

I started to slowly move towards the Insect like creature as I gave a wrist flick with the sword in readiness for the fight. I looked up at the creature while trying not to show my fear at its size and menacing look.

The pirate captain pulled two long serrated blade swords from its back as it also started to scuttle towards me.

'This will be like taking sweet cane from larva.' It boasted.

We were now standing just a few feet apart with our weapons raised as I replied saying,

'I thought you would be bigger.'

This angered the captain as he swung out with one of his swords while he bragged,

'You will pay for your insults, Human.'

I moved quickly out of the way as I replied,

'You will have to do better than that.'

Again the Falsec captain swung out at me, but with the other sword this time. I moved back to miss the first blade as I defended the second blade that was coming at my head. Our blades clashed with a huge amount of force and I found I had to steady myself from the blow. The captain drew back his swords to attack again as I slashed out at one of his four spiked legs. The captain pulled his leg back just as my sword blades clipped below its knee like joint. A dark yellow blood sprayed from the wound as the creature attacked with a powerful two sword strike. I pulled my sword up to defend as our blades locked.

'You will suffer greatly for that lucky hit, Human.'

We looked into each other's eyes as the Falsec captain pushed down on me with his overpowering strength. Its mandibles chattered as its sword blades drew ever closer to my head and then he said,

'Now you will die a slow and painful death.'

'Not if I can help it.' I replied through gritted teeth as I hit the power button on my sword. The 50'000 volt blades cracked loudly as the jolt from my sword throw the Falsec pirate's sword blades back, knocking him to the floor. I quickly stepped back while I regained my fighting stance.

Before the Falsec captain screamed for a moment as it rolled over quickly from its back while it struggled to take back a fighting stance of its own. I could see the pirate captain was trying not to put weight on its injured leg as it pulled its blades back up to continue the fight.

'Have you had enough yet, or do I have to kill you first?'

I gave another flick of my sword which unnerved the captain as I again stepped forwards. The captain put one of his swords back behind his back as he then tore some of his armour from his shoulder protection while he replied.

'Clever; but your cheap tricks will not save you.'

I watched as he put the armour piece around one of the sword handles. I quickly realised he was insulating the sword from his clawed hand and quickly moved back in for the attack. I slashed out at the creature's neck as the Falsec captain deafened with his sword while sparks flew out when our blades met. We both pulled our swords back before we struck at each other again. This time the blades of my sword locked in the teeth of the Falsec sword. The pirate captain reared up on to his back legs which throw me off balance before he kicked me with one of his front legs. The blow to my chest, throw me across the room about ten feet where I hit the deck with a thud. I deactivated the power on my sword as I rolled to a painful stop. I looked up to find the pirate captain quickly moving in my direction. He thrust his sword right at me as I rolled to the side, the blade stuck into the ship's steel deck where it became wedge between two floor panels. I quickly took advantage of this slashing out with my sword, cutting one of the Falsec's front legs off at the knee. The creature screamed out with pain as it grabbed me with its free hand while steadying its self with its sword.

I found I had now been lifted several feet off of the floor as the captain pulled me up to his face before he said,

'I have underestimated you Human, now I will finish this and quickly.'

'Are you still taking?' I replied as the captain screamed in my face before throwing me back across the room. I again hit the deck just feet from where Starlight was standing, with another painful thud. I quickly looked up to see the creature tying one of his swords to his bleeding stumped leg. I started to get up as Starlight rushed over to my side.

'Are you alright?' I could see the worry in her eyes and hear the concern in her voice as I pulled myself into a crouched position while I held my chest with my free hand. I looked at her as I replied,

'Get back my love, you need to stay back.'

She looked up behind me with horror as I heard a metal clicking moving across the floor.

I realised the Falsec captain must have been coming in for the attack.

'Chris.' Starlight shouted out as I turn while raising my sword to defend.

The Falsec captain was just feet from me and closing fast as it swung its blade down hard towards my head. I defended the heavy blow as I pulled up my other hand to hold back the blade.

'You cannot hold your death off for much longer Human, and I will enjoy tearing the wings from your fairy companion for interfering. I may even let you live long enough to see her die.'

The Falsec blade was slowly pushing down on me as I replied through gritted teeth,

'Get back Starlight, and you leave her alone. Beside what the hell do you think you are going to do while our swords are locked?'

'This you foolish Human.'

The Falsec pirate quickly raised its stumped leg with the sword attached. I could see what was going to happen but before I had chance to react, it thrust the sword blade at my body. The serrated blade hit my chest hard as it crunched through the left side of my rib cage before tearing out of the back of my body. The pain was instant and as the Falsec captain drew back the sword from above my head. I activated the power unit on my own sword before putting all my efforts into slashing upwards at where the blade was attached to the Falsec's stumped leg. This cut the blade free as the power from my sword throw the captain back while also cutting its abdomen open. Again the captain hit the floor where this time it lay still.

I fell back to the floor onto my side where I lay with the sword still impaled through my body. I could see the pirate captain twitching on the floor several feet from where I lay as I struggled to breath. I could feel the blood draining from my body as I heard Starlight screaming my name. I felt her warm hand touch my face as I looked up to see she was now in front of me crying. I moved my blood covered hand over to her as I began to feel cold.

'Don't move Chris, I can help.' She said gently to me.

'I don't think even you can fix this.' I replied while starting to choke on my own blood.

'Starlight!' I heard Andrew call out as she spoke to me.

'I said there was a choice but I didn't say...'

Her words were cut short as the Falsec's sword blade ripped through her chest spraying me with her blood before it disappeared again and she fell to the floor. The Falsce captain now stood over us both covered in its own blood as he laughed out loud before saying,

'The ship is now mine Human and you will both die together.'

I used what little strength I had left to pull myself into a crouched position while still holding my sword as the pain caused me to yell out loud as I moved. The Falsec captain looked down at me confidently as it stated,

'Why don't you just die?'

It moved its free blood covered clawed hand over to me as it took hold of the sword that was impaled through my body, twisting it as it laughed before saying,

'Hurt does it, watch your fairy die. Then I will kill you.'

I moaned with the insurmountable pain while the creature drew as close as he could get. I looked down at Starlight as she looked up at me helplessly before I struggled to say,

'Funny but it's not over yet.'

I hit the power button on my sword as the pirate captain realised what I was going to do. Then I thrust my sword blades into the creature's body, while the blade in my chest crunched my ribs as I moved. The power from my sword quickly hit us both blowing us apart from each other. Thought all the pain I still felt the sword blade rip from my chest before I hit the deck.

I watched Andrew rush over to Starlight as he tried to move her from the place she was laying. I could hear them saying the Falsec captain was down and I could also hear Starlight asking to be moved over to me as my vision started to burr for a moment.

Andrew kept his gun trained in on the Falsec's first shipmate as he watched it move over to its captain. Talstead quickly moved over to his daughter frantic with worry as he said to Andrew.

'Leave her alone, you people have done enough.'

Starlight grabbed hold of her father's hand as she tried hard to speak.

'Father, you know what I must do. Take me to Chris quickly.'

Her voice was strained and weak as her father replied,

'But I cannot lose you now my child.'

Tears ran down his face while Andrew ran a scan of her body.

'I am sorry but she is dying. If it is her last wish they should both be together before they die.'

Talstead looked at both Andrew and Starlight as he nodded and replied,

'Ok my child, I will help.'

'Thank you.' Starlight said as she started to choke on her own blood.

I was getting cold as I tried to make sense of what was around me. I could hear movement and voices getting closer, I groaned through the pain as I dragged my torn body over and pushed against the pain to pull myself to my knees. I could barely lift my head let alone stand as I felt a small hand on my chest. It seemed to ease the pain a little as I turned my head to the side to see Starlight next to me. She was being held up by her father as her hand glowed while she held it against my open chest wound. I could feel my breathing getting easier as the area around my wounds started to glow with bright yellow energy.

'What are you doing?' I asked Starlight. She smiled through her own pain as she replied.

'Shush my love and don't move. This is my decision.'

I moved my hand to her face and gently ran my fingers across her cheek. Starlight looked up at me with tears running down her face as I realised that my whole body was now glowing with energy. She smiled at me as I asked,

'Why Starlight?'

She choked as she replied weakly,

'Because I must, I have known this would come from the first day I met you. I just didn't think it would happen this way.'

'Heal yourself please.' I pleaded to her.

'I cannot self heal, it does not work that way. Now everyone should stand back.'

'Captain?' I heard Andrew call out.

'Do as she is asking please.' I replied as Starlight moved her hand over to my arm so she could hold herself up.

'Please my love, hold on to me and don't let go. And I am sorry but this will hurt a lot.'

I moved closer to her as I put my arms around her and pulled her in close. Suddenly there was a blast of pain run throughout my body as we both seemed to be consumed by a golden yellow light.

'Ahrrrrr.'

I cried out as there was a final blast of energy hit my body. Before Starlight just slumped lifelessly in my arms. I lay her down on my lap as I placed my hand on her chest. My whole body was still glowing with energy as I felt her weak heart beat. I turned to find Andrew looking at me gob smacked as I said,

'Andrew, take hold of Starlight, she is still alive.'

Andrew moved over to my side and took Starlight in his arms as he continued to stare at me. I pulled myself up off of the floor while I could feel energy burning throughout my veins. Quickly I picked my sword up as I headed for the two Falsec pirates. I could feel energy running through my body as my mind turned to getting these creatures off this ship so I could try to save Starlight. I could feel my anger building as I drew close to the two Falsec pirates. The battered captain had just pulled himself up off of the floor. He stumbled before he drew his two swords and looked across at me.

'What are you?'

'I don't know, but I am going to give you one last chance to leave this ship or die.'

I activated my power sword as I continued to walk forward while the energy from my body mixed with the energy from my sword blades causing energy ribbon to run across my whole body.

The battered captain started to move back as he shouted out.

'Kill him, kill him now.'

The first mate pulled his gun up to shoot as I jumped forwards several feet, slashing out at his head. The Falsec gun fired as my sword cut the creatures head from its body. The blast shot passed me hitting the wall while the now dead Falsec pirate dropped to the floor. I continued to move towards the captain as he backed off towards his shuttle keeping me in sight.

'You have no intention of letting this ship go, do you?'

'No, even if you kill me my crew have been ordered to cut you all down and take this vessel.'

The pirate captain was almost at his ship just as Miller ran into the hanger bay shouting,

'I have located the hive ship's main power converter... Captain!'

With the interruption the battered and bleeding pirate captain scuttled aboard his shuttle and closed the door behind him. I turned to Miller as I ordered,

'Miller, get those torpedoes ready to fire. Talstead, get to the bridge and ready a jump gate so we can get out of here.'

The Falsec shuttle lifted off the deck and turned to leave as it moved back through the atmospheric shielding into space. I rushed back over to Starlight and Andrew to find she was trying to tell Andrew something. He looked up at me with a hopeless look on his face as I took her from him and cradled her in my arms. I placed my hand on her wound as she looked at me and tried to smile.

'How do I use this energy to heal you?' I asked desperately.

'You cannot, but I am glad of one thing.'

'What?'

'I got to spend my last days with you again... and...'

She coughed weakly as she tried to catch her breath.

'What, what is it?'

'I got to see your wings. Thank you... and I am sorry.'

I could feel the tears running down my face as I picked her up off the floor and held her close in my arms. I turned to Andrew as I said,

'Get to the bridge, tell them we have to get Starlight back to her own kind, too someone who can help her.'

'Yes Captain.'

As Andrew replied the torpedoes fired out into space and within moments there was an explosion. I could feel the ship move as I said,

'Go, we don't have much time. Her mum can help her.'

'What are you going to do? Andrew asked.

The ship jolted sharply as I steadied myself and replied,

'I am going to take her to her room where I can make her more comfortable. Now go.'

Andrew ran out of the hanger bay as I headed towards Starlight's room.

One ending and a new beginning

I lay Starlight on her bed; she was now growing cold and her pulse was even weaker than ever. I found some fabric and wrapped it around her open wounds to stem the bleeding, as several flashers of light came from her window. I could see the ship was soon travelling through some sort of energy corridor from her window before I heard Andrew's voice come over the ship's communication relay.

'Captain, we should be at the Kalien home world in just a few minutes. How is Starlight?'

'Computer, open voice relay.' The system bleeped so I continued.

'She is very weak, just please get her help.'

'We will be there very soon, just hold on, bridge out.'

I ran my fingers across her face gently as I said,

'Just hold on my love, you will be home soon.'

I could see the blue energy corridor dissipate as the ship entered normal space again. And now it was clear what Starlight had said to me as I looked at my reflection in her window. My body was still glowing with energy and this energy was spraying out from my back like wings. I felt Starlight grasp my hand weakly as she tried to speak.

'Chris, I feel so cold, please hold me so I can feel your warmth.' Her voice was quiet and breathless as I moved onto the bed before gently cradling her in my arms.

'Is there anything I can do to help you?'

'Just hold me close and let me look at you one last time.'

'Don't say that my love.'

Starlight looked up at me and smiled. I smiled back at her as I felt a tear run down my face. Starlight moved her hand up to my face to stroke my cheek as she said,

'You are beautiful with your wings. Thank you for everything.'

Her eyes widened as her hand fell away from me and she sighed out her final breath. Her whole body relaxed and I pulled her in as close as I could while my heart hurt like it was being torn open and tears flooded down my face.

I just sat on her bed holding her as the light energy that surrounded me began to dissipate. I found that I had not turned the lights on in her room and once the healing light from my body was gone. I found I was sitting in the darkness still holding on to her lifeless body alone.

The ship's intercom interrupted the silence with the worried voice of my first office as he said,

'Captain, we are here and there is a shuttle on its way up to the ship to help Starlight.'

I wiped the tears from my face and took a deep breath before I spoke,

'Computer, open voice relay.'

I paused as I didn't really know what to say and found it hard to find any words that didn't seem impossible to form.

'Captain, are you there?'

'Yes but...' I didn't want to say it as Andrew replied.

'But what?'

'She has gone. It is too late.' Again I started to cry quietly to myself as Andrew quickly replied,

'Stay there I am on my way.'

The communication channel cut and I sat in silence trying to gather my thoughts.

Personal log; It has been four days since the pirate incident and we are about to leave the Enlightenment to return to Caridian Prime. We are all packed and my shuttle is ready to depart. But still I am finding it hard to concentrate on what we need to do next. Starlight's father stayed back on their home world and I was surprised to find we were accepted there so readily by her family after all that had happened. Still there seemed to be a lot that wasn't said there and Andrew and my crew are still not sure what to say to me. I have decided to take one last look at Starlight's room, just to say goodbye before we leave, even though Andrew thinks it is a bad idea. Still I don't think I can hurt much more than I do right now and maybe I will find some peace before we leave. Then there is the mention of this Darkness, which seemed to get the Kaliens all riled up. I don't know what to make of it myself, but I do know that it maybe something we will come across again in the future, Log end.

I turned my chair around to find Andrew standing behind me as he said,

'Well if you are going to do this, then we had better get a move on.'

I smiled at Andrew as I got up out of my chair and picked up the coat that Starlight had given to me. I put it on and moved over to the shuttle's door as I said,

'You don't have to come you know. I can do this on my own.'

'Well what are friends for, now let's move before this ship reaches Caridian Prime.'

We both left the shuttle and moved out of the hanger bay as Andrew said,

'You should get that thing fixed. No one is going to believe you were wearing it when those holes were made.'

I stood in front of the door to Starlight's room as I waved my hand over the release panel. The door quietly slid open to reveal a very empty room with not much more than her bed and the fixed wall storage units. My boots echoed as I walked across the metal floor and I found my thoughts turning to unanswered questions. I stopped by the window and looked out at the stars as I asked,

'Andrew, Starlight was trying to tell you something during the fight, after she had been injured. What did she say?'

'It didn't really make any sense mate.'

I turned to him and moved over to the bed where I sat down before I looked back up at his face.

'But what did she say?'

Andrew looked a little uneasy as he answered,

'She just said the word hellfire.'

'What?'

'She said hellfire twice, and that you would know what it meant one day soon.'

I looked down at the floor even more confused than ever as I noticed a small tattered piece of paper sticking out from under the bed at my feet. I leant down and picked it up, it was blank on one side and had a glossy feel to it even though it looked old. I turned it over to find it was a picture of Starlight and a man.

'What have you got there, Chris?'

I stared at the picture closely for a moment, shocked at what I was looking at as I replied,

'Take a look for yourself.'

Andrew took the picture from me as he asked,

'When did you get this taken?'

'I didn't, don't you get it. It's really old and it's not even taken onboard a ship.'

Andrew handed me the picture back as he said,

'That is too wired. He is wearing your coat and looks just like you.'

I looked back at the picture and smiled as I said,

'Come on we should go.'

Andrew moved over to the door as I followed pushing the picture into my pocket. I stopped at the doorway and looked back into the room as I quietly said to myself,

'Goodbye my love, stay safe.'

Then I left the room as Andrew pattered my shoulder saying,

'Come on my friend, I think you need a good drink.'

'Yea, why the hell not.'

We both headed back towards the hanger bay as I couldn't help but think I might see Starlight again somehow.

HELLFIRE

Call To War

Volume 4

By Christopher J Sharman

CALL TO WAR

CONTENTS

Introduction	Pg 116
The call of war	Pg 120
Heading into enemy territory	Pg 129
Behind enemy lines	Pg 136
The pickup point	Pg 140
Into the unknown	Pg 144
No time to drink	Pg 151
Taking chances	Pg 155
Prison break	Pg 159
Intruder alert	Pg 167
No easy way out	Pg 172
Hidden foe	Pg 178
New beginnings	Pg 182

INTRODUCTION

A well dressed and heavily honoured older man walks into the busy command centre to Caridian Prime's military head quarters. He move boldly across to one of the room's command personal as he asks,

'Any word yet from General Darrin?'

The three staff manning the wide range of computer consoles and holographic readouts turn around quickly to salute him before one of them replies.

'Supreme Fuller, Sir; his ship has just arrived and he should be here in the next...'

'Few minutes.'

The voice came from behind Supreme Fuller as the staff member's words were cut short. Fuller turns to find his General standing behind him before he smiles and says,

'You took your time, now what's the news from our spy?'

General Darrin moves over to one of the computer consoles while he pulls a battered, portable tactical computer pad from his belt. He activates the computer and then turns back to Fuller as he replies,

'I will pull up the readout from the Storm's logs. Captain Artos got your spy in two weeks ago and we know he has worked his way into the construction crew for their new weapon.'

Supreme Fuller moves over to the holographic readout, looking over the information while he rubbed his chin with his right hand.

'Mmm, so if we got him in and he has not been found out. How long will it be before we can gain the information we need?'

Darrin moved over to one of the consoles on the other side of the room. He then moved one of the personal out of his way before he started to type something into the small tactical computer. Turning to one of the staff that had gone back to work at the another station he states,

'Let's find out, we should have had word back by now. Open me up a secure channel to the Storm. I need to speak with Artos.'

One of the men stopped what he was doing as he replied,

'Yes Sir, I will put it on the holo ring.'

He moved quickly over to a different computer console before he operated the touch pad. Suddenly two metallic rings lit up in the centre of the room. Darrin moved slowly over to the empty lit ring as the image of a middle aged man with a scar running down his face appeared in front of him, in the other ring.

'Captain Artos, good to see you. Now do you have word back from our spy yet?'

'No, we have not had anything back and we don't want to contact him just in case we jeopardise the mission.'

'When was the last time you heard from him?' Darrin asked.

'Two days ago. He reported in that he was going to copy the information to a data stick by tomorrow and then he would be back in touch.'

'Why is it taking so long?'

'He has lost his escape ship. It had been found by the Plotations before the last time we spoke. I have been trying to sort out someone crazy enough to pick him up. But it seems like all of our elite covert personal are known to the Plotations and I don't have anyone else that we could use.'

Darrin typed something into his tactical computer before he enquired,

'So why is your ship nearly three sectors away from our front line borders?'

'I received a call from one of our supply ship's reporting a large Falsec hive ship within our space. It had fired several shots at them before they managed to raise a distress call.

I know how essential resources are so figured I should take care of it, as all our other ships are tied up at our borders.'

Fuller moved over to the holo ring as he bluntly stated,

'One of our light cruiser's would be no match for a Falsec hive ship. So I want a real answer for why he is out there, and now Darrin.'

General Darrin turned back to the holographic image of Artos before he clearly said,

'I'm sure you heard Supreme Fuller and I know he is right. We have both had dealings with the Falsec and a hive ship could take on a fully armed and escorted battle cruiser. Now you had better give me one hell of an answer.'

Artos looked and sounded confident as he replied,

'I originally went to aid the transport, but found they had escaped before we arrived. The Falsec ship was reading very low power levels and it was running with its shields down. Also it was registering some areas of heavy damage. I opened up a communication to find they were fighting amongst themselves.'

'What happed to them?'

'From what I gathered before they turn on us, they had been attacked in the warp and then attempted to steal a Kalien transport for parts. I have a full report and it includes information picked up from the wreckage of their ship after I finished them off. I will send it over for you to read now.'

Darrin turned to one of the staff in the room as he ordered,

'When that report comes in, put a copy straight onto this computer.'

'Sending it now General.'

Darrin looked over the report while he stood in the ring before he passed the tactical computer pad over to Supreme Fuller saying,

'I think we have found our man, non military and unknown to the Plotations. What do you think?'

Fuller looked over the information as he stepped into the ring alongside Darrin,

'Do we know anything more about this man?'

Artos turned away as he asked one of his crew to send all the information over that his superiors required. Then he turned back and answered,

'I know what you are thinking, but he is just a kid and has no military training.'

Fuller continued to read over the information as he smiled and said,

'Looks like you two have history, now where can we find him?'

'I don't know. It looked like he stayed aboard the Kalien vessel when it left. He could be anywhere.'

Fuller looked up from the battered computer pad as he handed it back to Darrin. Then he bluntly ordered,

'Artos, you will find out where he is and by tomorrow. Now once you have located him, I want him bringing to me at command central, Fuller out.'

The holo rings powered down before both men stepped out and moved over to one of the computer stations while Darrin asked,

'Do you think he can do it?'

Fuller smiled as he replied,

'If he can take on the Falsec and survive, this should be easy for him.'

One of the staff in the room spoke up nervously saying,

'Supreme Fuller, Sir. We did have a Kalien transport drop a ship off here just yesterday. Shall I, check it out?'

'Dam right you will, and bring its crew in. I will be on my command ship.'

The call of war

'Hay Captain, the ship should be ready to leave. Are you sure you want us to stay here with Hudson?'

Richards jumped out from the shuttle's door as he confidently moved over to me putting his hand on my shoulder. I smiled at him before I replied to his question,

'It's ok. This is just a short journey and I'm sure Andrew and I can handle this one. Besides it will be nice to have some space for a change when we're travelling.'

'Ok, but you know it's going to kill us having to stay here taking in the sun, while you two are out making the money.'

We both laughed as I replied,

'Hudson still needs time for his leg to heal and you guys are the only people he knows on this planet. So you had better make sure he is ok.'

'We will, safe journey and stay out of trouble.'

Andrew popped his head around the door as he stated in a sarcastic voice,

'Trouble really. We are only dropping off some computer stuff to the nearest colony. What could possibly go wrong?'

'He's right you know, we will be gone for a few days tops. Then when we get back, you two can do the next run while we take some time off.'

I pattered Richards shoulder as I moved away from him and boarded our shuttle saying,

'Later.'

I then hit the door control sealing the ship's inner hull from the outside world before I moved over to the co pilot's seat. Sitting down next to Andrew I looked over the controls as I sighed before activating the shuttle's main landing thrusters.

'You sure you're ok mate, you have been quiet since we left the Enlightenment?'

Andrew looked across at me with a concerned look on his face as I replied,

'Yea, I guess I just need to keep busy. Now shall we make this delivery or what?'

Andrew started the take off as I felt the shuttle leave the ground, before the ship quickly picked up speed while we headed towards the planet's outer atmosphere.

'You miss her don't you?'

'Yea, it was weird how quickly we became close. Still nothing I can do about it now.'

I didn't want to let on how much I was still hurting, but then I guessed he kind of already knew. We were starting to head into the planet's lower orbit as I noticed a very large war ship close by on the scanner. So I checked the readout and found it was monitoring all the traffic in the immediate area.

'What the hell do you think all this is about?' I said as I pointed to the display. Andrew looked over before he replied,

'War stuff; nothing to do with us. I will just set our fight path and then maybe we should get a coffee.'

Andrew started to type in our flight path out of the system as the war ship started to move quickly in our direction. Our ship's communication's console kicked in with an incoming call as both Andrew and I looked at the console while it flashed and beeped before I said,

'I guess we should get that right?'

'I guess so.'

I moved my hand over to the communication's console and opened up the channel as a sharp voice said,

'Pay-Check, you will disengage your main engines and dock in our open hanger bay.'

Both Andrew and I looked at each other again before he said,

'Maybe it's just routine.... you know.'

I opened up the reply com before I said,

'Hi, we are just running some computer equipment to one of your colonies. Is there a problem?'

'No problem, just dock in the open bay, Iron Grip out.'

The communication cut as I turned to Andrew and said,

'No trouble ha, we had better do as they are asking.'

Andrew cut the main engines and started to pilot the shuttle towards the massive war ship while he continued to say,

'I'm sure the Iron Grip is the Caridians lead flag ship. It is rumoured that it is commanded by their Supreme leader.'

'What the hell do they want with us then?'

'I guess we are about to find out mate.'

I watched from my seat as we approached the massive fortress like war ship. We were now only minutes from landing in the ship's open bay as Andrew turned to me and said,

'You don't think it has anything to do with the destruction of the Nightfall, do you mate?'

'I hope not, but next time we find a drifting military ship. I say we leave it alone.'

'I agree, so what is our story if they ask?' Andrew enquired nervously.

'No stories, just tell it the way it was. I will take any blame, as I was in Command.'

Our shuttle was now passing through the atmospheric shielding of the hanger bay and it was clear we were not being checked as part of a routine shipping check. By the hundred armed troops that were waiting for us.

'Do you think they are all here for us?' Andrew asked.

'Maybe they have mistaken us for someone else mate.'

The shuttle bumped lightly onto the deck before I got up from my seat and moved over to the shuttle's door. I turned back to see Andrew getting up slowly before he moved over to my side signaling for me to leave first. I picked up my long command coat and put it on before I asked,

'Are you ready mate?'

Andrew nodded in reply so I hit the release door button. The shuttle's door hissed as it slid open and the two atmospheres mixed, while a blast of cold air hit me in the face. I stepped out onto the deck of the war ship before turning to find that the first row of troops all had their guns trained in on me. Stepping forwards I raised my hands and said out loud,

'We are unarmed.'

Andrew stepped out and moved to my side, also with his hands raised as he said to me in a low voice,

'I guess we're in trouble right.'

I watched a middle aged and well dressed uniformed man moved out from the score of troops accompanied by around ten heavily armed men.

They kept their guns trained in on us as they drew close, before the middle aged man held up a battered, portable computer pad. Then he smiled at us before he ordered,

'Check them for weapons.'

One of the troops held up a small device that he waved in front of us both before he replied,

'They are both clean Sir.'

'Troops you can lower your guns, but stay alert.'

Then he looked back at me and continued to say,

'Captain Sharman, I presume?'

'Yes, and who are you?'

'General Darrin of the Caridian military. I need you two to come with me.'

I lowered my hands while I asked,

'And do you mind if I ask what we have done to be brought here?'

'It's not what you have done, but more what you can do that brings you to my attention. Now follow me, Supreme Fuller wishers to meet with you.'

The General turned and headed towards a door on the other side of the hanger bay, while two troops followed and the others waited for us to move.

'Come on gentlemen, Supreme Fuller is not a patient man.' The General stated in a loud booming voice.

I looked at Andrew as he again made a hand gesture for me to follow him first.

'Thanks.' I replied before following the man, then the other troops followed us as I caught up with the General. The two troops in front of me now moved in front of the General. So I moved to his side while we travelled the long straight corridors of the ship. I looked across at the man's stern face before I then asked.

'So, if it's not what we have done, then why are we here?'

The man didn't waver as he replied to my question.

'Well maybe some of this is due to what you have done. But I cannot discuss this matter until we are in Supreme Fuller's office.'

'So what is it that we have done that has made you notice us?' I asked.

Again the man did not waver as he replied,

'You ask a lot of questions Kid. But saving that Kalien vessel from a Falsec hive ship, and then taking on a Falsec pirate in hand to hand combat. You are just what we need right now.'

The two troops stopped at a sealed door before the General moved over to the wall panel and began typing in a long code.

The door quickly side open and the General moved into the room before both Andrew and I followed. The room was fairly large with one wide window on the opposite side of the room. There was a desk in front of it which had an open computer panel, and there was also a large gun sitting on the other end of the desk next to a very grand looking, older man. He looked both Andrew and I up and down before he said,

'Take a seat gentlemen, I am Supreme Fuller.'

I moved over to one of the seats that were in front of the desk and sat down before I enquired,

'Ok you have us here, now what is it we can do for you?'

I spoke confidently as I sat back comfortably in the chair. The military leader signaled for the door to be locked before he lent forwards and stated,

'You don't look big enough to take out a Falsec with just a sword. But I have seen the hive ship's logged reports and communication records. Also their bridge recordings showed you to be the one who went to fight them. This is why I put together the armed escort.'

'You put an armed escort together because I faced a Falsec!'

'No, because you survived and are still walking around unharmed, now how did you do it kid?'

'Maybe I just got lucky.'

'Maybe, but that is beside the point. Look I have a job that needs doing and I will pay you well. So what do you say?'

The man sat back in his seat as he looked at both Andrew and I. I turned to Andrew briefly and could see he looked uncomfortable at the situation, while I was also feeling intimidated but curious as well.

'Depends on what the job is.' I replied.

The man smiled before he continued to say, while turning the computer panel around so I could see the screen.

'It is a simple pick up from Plattos prime. I need you to take a Plotation ship and land it at these coordinates. There you will meet a man who has been altered to look like a Plotation. Pick him up and bring him back to us. You don't need to know anymore than that.'

Andrew sat up forwards in his chair as he blurted out,

'Plattos prime is the Plotation home world. You must think we are crazy to take a mission on like that without knowing what it involves.'

Fuller looked at Andrew and then he calmly replied,

'I see your First Officer is your voice of reason.'

'He has a point, and I am not taking on any mission I don't think I know all the facts about. So this is a closed room let us know the facts.'

Fuller looked at Darrin before he spoke. I could tell the General had nodded in agreement, so Fuller replied in a low voice,

'I can give you more information, but that will mean you will have to take on the job.'

I put my hand on my chin as I asked,

'So what's the pay before I make up my mind about knowing the facts?'

Darrin moved over to my side as he passed me his battered computer pad.

'Read it kid, that is not an offer we will look to be increasing.'

I looked over the readout just as the com to the room kicked in from the bridge saying.

'We will have the last of the old fleet back in for decommissioning in two days Supreme Fuller. Do you want me to send the ships as they arrive to the salvage dock to be stripped down?'

I couldn't believe my eyes at the amount being offered. 70'000'000 credits.

'This must be one hell of a risky job. I tell you what let my first officer leave the room. Then tell me why this job is so important. I will take the risk.'

I saw Andrew as he started to protest, but I cut him short before he could speak.

'Trust me my friend, this opportunity is too good to miss out on, but we both don't need to get killed.'

'Chris, whatever this mission is we are in it together.'

'Still just wait outside and I will get all the details.'

Darrin signaled for Andrew to leave the room and once the door closed the ship's com kicked back in.

'Supreme Fuller, the Repulse just jumped back into the system, which leave the Pegasus and the Hellfire left to return.'

Fuller seemed annoyed as he replied bluntly,

'I am in the middle of something here. This can wait until I return to the bridge.'

'Yes Sir, Sorry for the interruption.'

The com cut but the message had caught my attention. Fuller turned to me handing me a new computer pad while he said,

'Now we won't get interrupted, take a look at this. It has been rumoured that the Potations are building a planet killer ship. We sent in a spy to work his way into the construction site and we now have confirmed the construction is underway. I need you to pick him up from this location and bring him back. That's all, bring him or the information back and you will get paid in full. The rest of the information you need is in that computer pad.'

Looking over the information I replied saying,

'So you want me to land just outside of the Potations highest guarded military construction yard, pick up a spy that from your report states his ship was found and bring him back into Caridian space in an enemy ship.'

'You got it in one, so when can you leave?'

'The sooner the better, but there is just one thing?'

Fuller looked at me with interest as he enquired,

'What is it kid?'

Your tannoy mentioned a ship called the Hellfire. What is it, and if it is being decommissioned can I have it as part payment?'

General Darrin quickly piped up stating,

'We said there would be no increase in the payment offer.'

Fuller held his hand up to signal for his officer to hold off then he replied,

'The Hellfire is an old Earth built battle cruiser. She is over two decades old and due to be dismantled. So what's it to you kid, and what do you have in mind?'

'Well let's just say you half the cash payout and give me the Hellfire in full working order.'

Fuller moved back to the other side of the desk before he sat down and replied,

'With the credits we are offering you, you could buy a brand new warship. So what's the score?'

'I have my reasons. It will save you some money, and get me a good sturdy ship.'

Fuller rubbed his chin before he again replied,

'Darrin see to it the best of the warships that arrive for decommissioning is sent to our orbital base for the Captain here when he returns.'

I quickly cut in saying,

'It has to be the Hellfire or the deal is off.'

Fuller looked at me with a confused looked then he replied,

'Ok kid, the Hellfire is yours when she returns and I will have the credits transferred to your account once you complete the mission. Now while my General sorts out the ship, I will get two of my troops to show you to your temporary vessel, until you get back from the mission.

Heading into enemy territory

I left Supreme Fuller's office and was met by two armed troops and my first officer all waiting in the main corridor. One of the troops bluntly stated,

'General Darrin said you would need escorting down to our main hanger bay, just this way.'

We both followed the troops back through the corridors of the ship as Andrew asked,

'Well Chris, I know you have taken the mission but what does it involve?'

'I will fill you in when we reach the ship.'

'That bad hey mate.' He replied

The two troops led us into a large hanger filled with Caridian fighters, bombers and landing ships. We walked past the new and pristinely kept ships until we reach the far side of the hanger. The troops seemed to head towards a large troop transport vessel but carried on past the shiny new looking ship. I peered around the large vessel as we walked passed it to be met by a scruffy battered yellow shuttle. It was much larger than our ship, and in typical Plotation design it was also heavily armed for its size.

'This is it gentlemen. It may not look like much, but it took a lot to get hold of it.' One of the troops said.

'Thanks, I think.' I replied as I moved around to the back of the ship where the door was situated.

I then pulled out the small computer pad Fuller had given me and accessed the code for the ship.

I typed the code into the key pad at the side of the door which caused it to bang before it hissed loudly and lowered to the floor. Moving into the ship I worked my way through to the cockpit, before I sat down in one of the ship's four cabin seats so I could start to run my eyes over the computer consoles, control leavers and sticks. Andrew sat in the seat next to me before he said,

'So this is better than I had expected.'

I could tell there was sarcasm in his voice and it was hard to ignore the smell that lingered in the air of the ship. It was like a cross between sweat and musty cloth, I also found I didn't recognise any of the symbols printed on the old style key pads so stated,

'I think we might have a problem!'

'What the smell or the fact that this bucket of blots couldn't make it out of the hanger bay let alone the system.'

'Well no, but I don't know how to read Plotation. Do you know what any of these symbols mean?'

I looked at Andrew as he looked back at me with the same blank look before he then replied,

'Hay, you accepted this mission without know all the facts.'

'That is not helping mate.'

'Well how did you know how to get the door to open?'

'With this.' I waved the small computer pad at Andrew as he asked.

'Well have you looked to see if it has any more helpful notes in there?'

'No not yet.'

Andrew looked at me as he simply and sharply replied,

'Well in your own time.'

I accessed the pad and started to look over the information until I found a briefing on the ship we would have to use.

I propped up the small computer on the console in front of me before I pressed the play symbol on the screen.

We both watched as a Caridian military scientist explained the basic access codes and start up sequences to the ship. Then he moved on to basic controls and how to activate the jump engines, before the briefing ended.

'Well I guess you know how to get this thing flying.' Andrew said again with a sarcastic tone.

'Come on and I think we will leave the door open until we get back.' I replied.

'Where are you going?'

'Too get my sword and gun. I don't think this is going to be as plan sailing as Fuller is letting on.'

I got up from the padded metal seat I was sat in and headed out of the ship while Andrew quickly followed.

'So are you going to tell me what the mission involves or not?'

'When we are on the way, I will have much more chance of pulling this thing off if you're with me mate.'

'I had a feeling you would say that.' Andrew replied as we left the shuttle. The troops had gone and we moved quickly through the main shuttle bay back towards the corridor that led us back to the shuttle bay the Pay-check was docked in.

We entered the bay to find the Pay-check was under armed guard, by around ten troops. Andrew looked at me as he said,

'Looks like they don't want us to leave in our ship now you have taken on this mission.'

'Leave it to me.' I replied before I continued to walk towards our ship.

Two of the troops spotted me and raised their guns before moving toward us both. I signaled for Andrew to stay back while I approached the two large men. One of the troops loudly and firmly ordered,

'Halt and state your intent.'

'I just need a few things from my ship, can I pass?'

The troop pushed his gun at me, then he bluntly replied,

'I have orders not to let anyone board this ship.'

I smiled at the man as I quietly said,

'Look I don't want any trouble, but Supreme Fuller has requested I take a mission on and I am not going anywhere without my equipment. Now you can call him and get clearance while I get my stuff.'

I could see the troop was not sure what to do as he pushed the gun at me again and ordered,

'Stay where you are while I call it through.'

I pushed the gun from in front of me, then I replied,

'I'm sure Fuller will not be pleased if you shoot me, and if you want to see tomorrow you will let me pass.'

With this I moved passed him and the other troops as they trained their guns in on me. I could hear the troop calling the bridge while I casually opened the door to my shuttle before I moved inside. Once aboard I moved over to the central floor panel and opened it before I took out my sword and G8 Reaper gun. I then picked out several ammo clips and pushed them into the pockets of my command coat. Finally I picked out two of the laser pistols before tucking them into my belt. Getting up with my sword in one hand and G8 in the other, resting it over my shoulder, I could hear the troop now shouting at me to leave the shuttle. I casually left the ship as again the troops trained their guns in on me while I walked passed them all and back toward my first officer. The look of bewilderment on the troop's face as I walk back passed him was a picture to be seen. So I said out loud,

'Thanks, now that wasn't so hard was it?'

Then I headed back out of the hanger bay while Andrew looked wearily behind me.

'How did you know they wouldn't shoot you?'

'Fuller would kill them if they shot the only person they have to retrieve their war info and troops will follow orders to the end.'

'That was one hell of a chance to take.'

'I know, now we have a mission to do and when this is over we can have one hell of a holiday.'

We moved back aboard the Plotation war shuttle as I hit the close door key code, before moving back through to the cockpit and taking up the pilot's seat. Andrew sat down next to me while I placed my sword and gun down at my side. I pulled out the two pistols and passed them to Andrew before I said,

Ok, these are for just in case we run into trouble. Now let's see if we can get this bucket of bolts off the deck.'

I put the small computer pad on the front of the console and pulled up the take off info while Andrew figured out the com system.

'Ok this should get the engines started, with any luck.'

Sure enough the ship started to vibrate as it lifted off the deck. I then used what looked like an old computer joy stick to turn the ship around to face the hanger bay doors.

'Have you figured out the communication systems yet?'

'I think so, let me try this.'

Andrew pressed a few keys on one of the consoles before it beeped twice and he said out loud.

'This is the Plotation ship, err. What's this ship call?' He asked me under his breath.

'I don't know, just think of something.' I replied.

'This is the ship Rebellion, requesting departure from your main hanger.'

The com cracked before the voice of General Darrin could be heard in reply,

'You have permission to depart. I have a squadron of Shadow fighter waiting on the edge of the system to escort you to our borders. Good luck out there and we will see you when you get back.'

'Thank you; we will begin departure, Rebellion out.'

Andrew cut the com and then the hanger bay doors started to open in front of our ship.

I started to move the ship forwards slowly towards the opening space doors as I asked,

'Rebellion, really, is that the best you could come up with mate?'

'You did say anything that came into my head. Now what is the score?'

I continued to pilot the ship out into space as I started to explain,

'Well it is pretty much like Fuller explained. We have to pick up a Caridian spy from behind enemy lines. The problem is this pick up is right at the heart of the Plotation Empire and just off side from their most secret military ship yard. To top it off their spy's escape ship was found by the Plotation military. That's why we have been drafted in.'

'So what are we getting paid for this suicidal mission, if we make it back?'

'Thirty five million credits and a war ship call Hellfire.'

'Wow, so what am I hear for?' Andrew asked.

I moved the ship out into the openness of space as it began to pick up speed. While I moved us out towards the edge of the system, where the ship's scanner readout registered the fighter squadron we were to meet up with before I answered him,

'I need you to keep this ship safe. Also I have a feeling that this whole thing is a Plotation trap, and that means we will have to make a quick getaway with or without the information.'

Andrew looked at me with a worried look on his face as he said,

'But if we don't get the information we won't get paid right?'

'Look I will get the info, just make sure we have a ride home. The Caridians are paying this much because they know this is not going to be easy.'

'So you think they suspect this is a trap?' Andrew replied while trying to figure out the controls to the jump engines.

'Look there was a lot they didn't really say, but to offer a huge payout like this. Well I would say trouble will come as standard.'

I started to reduce the speed of the ship as Andrew replied,

'Great, let's hope we make it back.'

'Just open up a channel to our escort so we can make it safely into Plotation space.'

'You got it Chris.'

I listened as I heard Andrew pass on who we were before the fighters pulled alongside us to provide our escort to the jump coordinates.

I couldn't help but feel nervous riding in an enemy ship in Caridian space and I could feel the tension from Andrew as he sat next to me.

Behind enemy lines

The fighters pulled back away from our ship as the lead pilot's voice came over the com,

'Rebellion, this is your jump point. Good luck with the mission and you are on your own from here. The Storm will be at these coordinates waiting for your return.'

'Thank you for the escort, Rebellion out.' Andrew replied as he activated the ship's jump engine.

The space in front of our ship was suddenly hit by several continuous energy bolts that were being emitted from the bulky and crude jump engine built into the ship. The energy bolts started to tear a hole in the fabric of the space in front of us, creating a gateway into the red pulsating realm of the warp. I held the ship's position while I powered up the shields before I turned to Andrew saying,

'Are you ready?'

'Andrew looked at me concerned as he replied,

'Well do I have a choice?'

'No not really.'

I then powered the ship's main thrusters up and move our ship into the hellish space known as the warp. Once we had passed through the gateway Andrew shut down the power to our jump engine, closing our gateway behind us.

We found we were now completely surrounded by the redness of the warp and from the windows of our ship I could see nothing but the blood red colouration all around us. It looked like we were in a pulsating sea of blood, even though the scanners were reading nothing around the ship. The only thing to break up the redness of the warp was the orange energy bolts that seemed to come from nowhere and return to the same nothingness.

'I don't like it here.' Andrew said out loud.

'I know what you mean, but it will knock about four weeks travel off of our journey. Now I can't find anything on the scanners to worry about, and the only thing showing up is a dense energy storm but that is moving slowly away from us.'

With this I set the engines to full thrust and started to pilot the ship towards our jump out coordinates.

'Shall I see if this ship has anywhere we can get a drink?' Andrew asked.

'Yes why not, we're going to be here for a few hours now and I could murder a coffee.'

Andrew got up and moved off through to the back of the ship while I stared at the hellish redness that lay ahead of us.

It had been three hours since we entered warp space and everything seemed to be going to plan. I was starting to get the hang of the controls to this Plotation ship and I was also starting to recognise some of the symbols without having to check what they were. Andrew had found his way around the ship and made something that resembled coffee, even if it didn't really taste that good. Still with the scanners still reading clear and only an hour left before we reached our jump out point we both needed to be clear on what our story would be, just in case we ran into a Plotation warship.

Andrew moved back over to the co pilots seat sitting down before he turned to me and said,

'Ok, I have fully charged the pistols and loaded your G8, but I am not sure if I can find a power adapter for your sword.'

'That's ok, I charged it before we left for our cargo run. Now what shall we use for our cover story?'

Andrew looked at me before he sort of looked around the cockpit blankly, looking for answers as he replied.

'I don't know, we could say we are on our way to visit family.'

'That won't work, neither of us looks Plotation and we would have to have someone for them to check with. What about making a delivery, there must be something aboard we could pass off as goods.'

'No, this ship is pretty empty. How about we escaped pirates but not before we lost our cargo. That would not be too far from the truth.'

I looked at my first officer before I replied,

'Yea that could work, but why are we heading this far into their space?'

'That is simple, we are here to refuel, before moving on to see an old friend, who just happens to be working in the area.'

'I suppose that doesn't seem too farfetched, and we can give the name of the worker we are supposed to be picking up if they want to check our story out.'

'That is sorted then, now why don't we have a drink. I found some Tellon whiskey in a storage unit in the engine room and one won't hurt.' Andrew replied with a laugh.

'Well it has got to be better than the coffee on this ship. But I am going to make our jump back to normal space a little earlier than the plan states.'

'Why?' Andrew asked looking a little confused.

'Just so we look a little less organised. Also we can get some readings of the sector so we can try to avoid any contact with other ships.'

'Ok, sound like a plan. Now what about that drink?' Andrew replied as he smiled at me with a warm glow and the air of a naughty child.

'Ok, but just the one.'

Andrew got up out of his seat before he disappeared into the back of the ship again. I pulled the small computer pad back across to my side of the cockpit while I looked back over the instructions to the weapon systems.

Andrew quickly returned with a dusty orange bottle and two small cups.

He opened the bottle and poured two large dinks before he passed one to me saying,

'Sorry I couldn't find any Ice.'

I sort of laughed as I took the cup before saying,

'Well let's hope this all goes to plan.'

We both took a drink before looking at each other as Andrew stated,

'Well it's not that bad.'

'Yea; but I'm not sure which is worst, this stuff or the coffee.'

I put the cup down and then I checked the scanners to find we were almost at the coordinates where I had planned to jump back into normal space. I slowed the ship's speed and said,

'Andrew, lets open up the jump gate and I will ready the ship's weapon systems.'

'Ok, activating engines now.'

The pickup point

Andrew punched in the code to reopen our gateway and I soon found I could see the same energy bolts shooting out from our ship. They began to tear a hole in the warp and I found I was happy to see the blackness of normal space and the light from the stars again.

'Well this is it.' Andrew said as we left the warp and closed our gateway behind us. We where now deep within Plotation space and I felt my unease return all too quickly.

'Ok let's see what is in the area and hope we have a clear run from here.'

I started to check over the scanner readout just as the communication's relay kicked in with a loud beeping sound. Andrew quickly checked the system before he said,

'It looks like a scrambled message from Caridian space.'

'Well let's put it on.'

Andrew played with the key pad to the communication's relay for a moment.

'I think this should be a safe channel to speak on.'

'You think!'

'Well it safe or broadcasting to the whole sector.'

I looked at my first officer shocked as I replied,

'Really?'

'No, it is safe. Well hopefully.'

He hit a couple more keys on the console before the voice of captain Artos could be heard over the speakers as they cracked into life.

'Chris, can you hear me?'

'Yes, loud and clear. What can we do for you?'

There was a pause before Artos replied with a serious tone to his voice,

'Look kid, we are here at the retrieval point and we will wait here until you return. But there is something you should know.'

'Isn't there always?'

'Seems that way kid, look we should have had word back from our spy by now. But we have had no message and we cannot get a message to him.'

'Great, so how late is his check in call?'

'About six hours, and that's not all. He should have at least sent us his twelve hour clearing check in tag.'

'What's that?' I asked as both Andrew and I looked worried at each other.

'It's a sort of signal, nothing more than a coded beep. But it tells us he is ok and in no trouble.'

'So what you are saying is he may have been found out?'

'It's beginning to look that way. So I have changed the plan of action, I will send you the location of his living quarters and all the information he had sent us on the construction yard for their new weapon. From that you should be able to gain access to his living area and retrieve the information we need.'

'So why do we need the information on the construction yard?' Andrew asked with a nervous twinge in his voice.

'I was hoping you would ask that, if the information isn't in his quarters it must still be on him. That means you will need to find him and bring him back.'

'Great so now we're going to have to fight our way into the Plotations most protected construction yard to find a spy that may already be dead, or has been taken there as part of a trap to bring back the information he stole.'

'You got it kid, but if all else fails; download as much information as you can and blow the construction yard up. That should slow the Plotations down until we can find a way to counter act this weapon they are building.'

'That easy, right.'

'I didn't say it was going to be easy. Now you will find all the information you will need in this next message, Artos out.'

The communication cut as the console again bleeped. Andrew pushed a few more buttons before he plugged the small computer pad into the system.

'Ok, I have uploaded all the information into the computer pad and now I'm going to wipe the ship's communication logs so they cannot be used against us if we get stopped.'

'Good move, I think we should head straight to this guy's apartment and see if we can't find this information.'

Andrew accessed the small computer pad before he passed me the coordinates to where we needed to be. I put the ship into full thrust as I turned our shuttle towards Plattos prime.

'Why don't you just use the jump engines to get us there in five minutes?'

I turned to Andrew as I locked the ship in on course while I replied,

'This way we won't bring any attention to ourselves, if we jump into orbit we will be picked up by every military scanner in the system. But if we just fly on in there like we aren't concerned, this ship should be too small for the military to worry about.'

I could see one of those looks on Andrew's face that said a thousand words before he bluntly replied.

'Because that worked when we were leaving Caridian Prime, right?'

'Well not really, but then they were looking for us. There must be hundreds of ships passing through this system each day.'

'Right and the Plotations aren't looking for us?'

'Well not yet, so we are just another ship landing at some dodgy space port looking to fuel up.'

I could see Andrew wasn't convinced, but I could tell he didn't have a better idea as he started to look over the information captain Artos had sent us.

'Anything I should know?'

'All of it I think, here I will fly while you figure out what the hell we will do when we get there.'

I took the small computer pad and started to look over the information while Andrew took up the pilot's seat.

Into the unknown

We had made it passed a large warship without being hailed and we were now landing in a small clearing several blocks from where this spy had been reported to be staying. I watched as Andrew continued to check the scanners while I set the ship down. The vessel bumped to the ground before we both looked at each other.

'Well we made it here, so what now?'

I powered down the ship before getting up and moving over to pick up my sword and G8 gun as I replied,

'Let's go see if anyone is home.'

I moved through to the back of the ship as Andrew followed while I placed my gun in its leg holster. Then I typed in the open door code before asking,

'Are you ready mate?'

'I guess so, now are we just going to walk up to the door and ask if anyone is in?'

'Yes why not. We know what the guy looks like from the picture in the briefing notes. So if he doesn't answer the door we can just say we got the wrong address.'

Andrew looked at me wearily as he replied,

'You are just making this whole thing up, aren't you?'

'No, it's a plan. Well sort of, now let's get moving.'

I hit the release key and our shuttle door hissed loudly as it lowered to the ground. The air outside of the ship was cold and wet as the rain poured in through the opening door while I said,

'Nice weather for ducks hay mate.'

'Yea great, just what we need.'

The shuttle's door hit the ground and we both moved out into the rain before I closed and locked our shuttle behind us.

'Come on this way.' I pulled my coat closed as I lead the way to a building just a few blocks from where we had landed. We both stopped outside of a square shaped building with a steel stairway and gantry leading up to each door on each of the upper levels. I then checked the computer pad before I said,

'It looks like we need to be on the third level. So I guess we should be up there.'

I looked around and it seemed like the streets were empty with the bad weather. So I lead the way up the stairs until we reached a dirty red door on the third floor.

'Do you think we should knock?' Andrew asked.

I sort of smiled at him as I tapped on the door. But with the first hit from my hand the door creaked open a jar. I put my hand on my G8 gun drawing it slowly as I moved into the darkened room. I then moved my hand along the wall around the doorway until I found an old style light switch. I flicked the switch causing the strip lighting in the room to flicker on. One of the lights continued to flicker while the light on the other side of the room stayed bright. It was more than clear the place had been ransacked, as there was stuff scattered around the whole area. Even the furniture and fittings had been pulled out and turned over. I moved into the room trying hard not to trip over the debris while I quickly ran my eyes over the room before moving into the space further. It was hard to tell if there had been a struggle or not, but one thing was clear it had been searched and nothing had been left untouched.

'Wow Chris, what the hell has happened here?'

'I'm not sure, but I'm guessing that we won't find the information we need and I am also guessing that we won't find our man here either.'

Suddenly there was a repeated beeping coming from the floor.

'Andrew, cover the door and make sure it's clear.'

'Yes Chris.'

I quickly looked around the floor until I found a small fixed com unit that had been pulled off the wall. I turned it over to find it was displaying an unknown incoming call. Looking at the com unit I heard Andrew asked,

'Are you going to answer that mate?'

'No, let's see if they leave a message.'

Andrew continued to watch the doorway as the com rang until the message system kicked in with a raspy voice.

'Hay you two in the flat. If you are friends of Maltos, we can see you. You made a grave mistake coming here, now pick up the com so we can speak.'

I signaled for Andrew to keep his eyes peeled but get into some cover. Then I pulled the com over to one of the walls before I pick up the receiver and pressed the answer button.

'Hi, we were just passing through and thought we would pop in on an old friend who used to live here.'

I peered out of the window at the buildings around as the rough voice replied.

'You're just about to have a really bad day.'

'Well if we are going to have a bad day, then maybe you can tell me where my friend is?'

'You don't need to worry about him. We will take care of him once you two have been disposed of.'

The com cut just as several laser shots sprayed through the window and door frame of the room. Andrew pulled back behind the door as a second spray of shots scattered across the room. I pulled myself back up to the window's edge to find the shots where coming from a window four floors up in a block just the other side of the street. The gun fire continued to fill the room with just a short few second gap in the incoming fire every twenty to thirty blasts.

The over turned furniture was being torn to pieces around us by the laser shots and as the shots paused again. I quickly returned fire with my G8 Reaper gun, firing off just two rounds.

The heavy shots exploded as they hit the building on the other side of the street. This seemed to cause a longer pause from the incoming fire as I shouted to Andrew,

'Come on, move into the back room.'

Andrew quickly moved through into the back room as I fired another round across at the window the gun fire had come from.

'Come on, before they start shooting again.'

The shots returned but with lesser ferocity this time, so I figured that this meant I had hit one of them or they were planning something. Andrew fired a few shots in return blindly out of the window and I took this opportunity to fall back into the back room of the flat while laser blasts again continued to spray the room we had just left. Once I was in the back room Andrew quickly pushed the door shut while I pulled an over tuned wall unit in front of the door to seal it shut.

'So far so good, hay mate?' Andrew replied with sarcasm.

I sort of laughed as I looked around the room to find, there was only one closed window and no other way out. I figured that we didn't have a lot of time before whoever was shooting at us would realise we were trapped and come to get us. I looked at Andrew as he said,

'So what do you say we do now, wait till they get to that door and then use your G8 to take them out?'

'No that's what they will be expecting.'

I quickly moved over to the window using my gun to smash the glass. I put my head out of the window into the rain to find it was a three story drop down to a solid concert floor.

'Jump.' I heard in a soft voice whispered into my ear.

'Starlight?'

'What did you say Chris?'

'Nothing, well at least we have more than one choice.'

Andrew moved over to the window looking out before he replied,

'Well maybe the front door is the better option.'

I looked out of the window at the back of the building opposite to the one we were in. The building wall was about six foot away from our window. Only this building had a ladder attached to it, leading from the floor to the roof. The only problem was it was offset from our window by about a foot.

'We could jump for the ladder?'

Andrew again looked in amazement before he replied,

'Do you have a death wish?'

'No, just a will to stay alive.'

'You have a funny way of showing it.'

Suddenly there was a large explosion that bust through the door to the room. Both Andrew and I shielded our self's from the blast as debris scattered across the room we were in.

'Andrew, go jump for the ladder now, and I will follow.'

Andrew quickly moved to the window while I moved to the smashed doorway peering into the other room. Several laser shots again sprayed the room from the window. So I quickly turned around to find Andrew was still standing at the window looking out before he turned to look at me while he said,

'Are you sure about this?'

'Yes you can make it, now jump before they get over here.'

Andrew climbed onto the window ledge before he jumped saying,

'Just jump right, well hear I go.'

He disappeared from view just as there was another large explosion come from the other room. At this point the laser shots stopped and the room fell into silence, I knew this meant that it was only going to be minutes before they would burst into the flat. So I moved quickly over to the window, looking out I found Andrew making his way down the ladder. I smiled briefly just before I heard the front door bang open. Turning quickly I fired off two shots through the smashed doorway into the front room.

I then pushed my G8 back into its holster before I climbed up onto the window ledge and jumped across to the ladder. I hit the ladder with a thud as I grasped one of the wet runs with my hands. I looked down quickly to find Andrew was now on the ground as he shouted up to me,

'Come on, that was the hard bit.'

Several laser shots now sprayed straight out from the window we had just jumped from, hitting the wall to the other building just above my head. I knew time was short so I just slid down the ladder to the floor, before turning to Andrew and saying,

'Well I think now would be a good time to leave.'

'Really, you don't think we should see what they have to say, mate?'

We both ran up the back street taking the first turn out of the lane that headed back to the main road. Once out of sight we both slowed to a steady walk before we moved back out into the open rain. I pushed my hands into my coat pockets as they felt like they were on fire before I looked back up the street towards the flat we were just in. There were now about ten armed troops gathered outside of the building looking around. So I walked off back towards our shuttle. Andrew followed at my side as a large hover troop carrier tank moved passed us both.

'I guess the front door was not a good idea, how did you know?'

'I didn't, I just went on my gut feeling.'

We both turned the corner to find our shuttle still sitting there in the rain. The area looked clear so we moved back to the ship. I typed in the code to open the door before we both moved back inside and out of the rain. Andrew closed and sealed the door behind us and we both moved back through to the cockpit.

'Well what do we do now?' Andrew asked.

'Move somewhere more public and park this thing up for the night.'

'Then what?'

'Well I guess we hit the construction yard, to see what we can find.'

'How about we hit some bars first. I found this and it looks like he had a few places he liked to drink.'

I looked at Andrew as I smiled,

'Well I guess I did say we should go somewhere more public.'

With this I started up the ship's engines and we headed out of the area.

No time to drink

I again landed the shuttle just a few blocks from where the first bar on the list was situated. This time we left the ship and moved out onto a much busier side street than before. It was filled with a mixture of different alien races, many to which I had never seen before. Andrew moved his hand into his jacket pocket and I knew he was keeping his gun at hand even before he said,

'I guess we won't look out of place here, let's just hope the locals are friendly.'

Somehow I got the impression that this was not somewhere you would want to take a holiday and it was clear by the random fights that broke out every so often, that this was the kind of scum hole the military wouldn't bother with. I quickly spotted the holographic bar name we were looking for above a dirty packed building.

'Come on mate, let's see what we can find.'

Andrew made a hand gesture signaling for me to go in first as he said,

'Let's hope we don't get killed in here.'

I smiled at him before I moved into the building and pushed my way through to the bar. Andrew followed closely until we found a space where we could stand. I started to scan the room looking for a quick exit just in case we needed one, while Andrew started to speak to the bar insect server while enquiring about rum. I noticed a monitor in the corner of the room which was showing the raid on the building we had just been in. so I watched with interest unable to hear what was being said over the noise in the bar's atmosphere.

Just then a green scaled creature stood at my side as it said, to me,

'You from Earth, you must be?'

I looked at the lizard man like creature as I replied,

'Yea, we are just passing through.'

'Interested in the news?'

Andrew passed me a dark brown drink before he said,

'Bacardi and coke, well almost coke but it tastes the same.'

I took the drink before I turned to our guest and said,

'Do you want to join us?'

The creature laughed as he raised a glass with thick red liquid in it before he replied,

'I'm good, warm blood is my poison. So what's with the news report? You haven't taken your eyes of it since it came on.'

'I don't know, looks like a lot fuss over nothing why?'

The creature moved in close as he said in a low voice,

'That was the flat of a Caridian spy. He was pick up by the military just a couple of days ago. They say he was planning to destroy a military ship yard.'

'Really, guess they just killed him out right. You know made sure he couldn't escape.'

The creature took a drink from his glass before he again replied,

'No they took him to some base for interrogation, it was all over the news.'

'So why are there troops at his flat now, if this all happed days ago?'

'Well it turns out that two of his people turned up to look for him and there was a big shoot out.'

'Wow, how do you know all this?'

The creature looked down at my hand as I put my drink on the bar and while he was focused on the bandage covering my burns and cuts. I drew my gun from its holster being careful not to show it from under my coat.

'What happened to your hand?'

Oh, I cut it when I was fixing a power coupling. It's fine. So where did they take the spy?'

The creature again moved in closer still until I could smell the blood it was drinking on its breath.

'You ask a lot of questions, but I know all this because there is a good price on both your heads.'

I pushed the barrel of my G8 gun into the chest of the creature slowly while I replied,

'Good, now if you don't want to find out what a G8 will do to your body at point blank range, tell me where they have the spy.'

The creature stayed very still as he watched Andrew put his drink down and draw his pistol in readiness while he remained standing at the bar. It gulped before it replied,

'If you kill me you will find out nothing, and I have friends in here. You will not leave this bar alive.'

'Look, if you tell me what I want to know I will let you go. If you don't then I will take out this entire bar before I leave.'

'You don't look like you could take more than one person on at a time.'

I discreetly draw my sword as I felt a small gun barrel being pushed into my neck. Andrew now moved in pushing his gun into the neck of the Plotation holding the gun as he said,

'Take a step back slowly.'

The man pulled the gun away slowly before he stepped back, and I smiled at the green scaled creature as I replied,

'Look this will get very messy if you don't tell me what I want to know.'

I could see a second lizard man moving in slowly from the reflection in the mirrored bar surface.

I could also see the creature I had at gun point, had also spotted his other friend as he said,

'Ok, the spy is being held in the main military brig aboard the new orbital ship yard. The military have said he will not talk.'

'Thanks.' I replied as I plunged my sword into the creature that was now only two feet behind me. The creature fell to the floor dropping his gun as he hit the deck. I kept my G8 pushed into the chest of the green lizard man while I continued to say,

'Now that wasn't so hard, was it?'

'You have made a big mistake here today.'

I pulled my gun from his chest as I stepped away saying,

'Come on mate, we're leave.'

Andrew moved away from the pair with his pistol still pointed at both of the men. I lowered my gun and turned my back to follow Andrew, just as he shouted,

'Chris, behind you!'

He fired one shot off killing the Plotation man as I swung around with my sword cutting the lizard man's head off. The bar fell into silence for just a moment before everyone carried on about their business. I kept my weapons drew while we both left the bar and as we moved back onto the street, we headed back towards our shuttle.

'Well that went well.' Andrew stated.

'Yea, and at least we now know where we need to be.'

We walk back up to the shuttle before Andrew opened the door and we both moved inside out of the rain.

Taking chances

A loud beeping could be heard throughout the small sleeping quarters of the shuttle before I heard a laser shot closely followed by a bang, then the room fell back into silence. I sat up quickly looking around to find Andrew sitting up with his pistol in hand.

'What the hell?'

'Sorry mate. I just always wanted to shoot the alarm clock when it went off. From when I was a kid, you know.'

I rubbed my eyes before I pulled on my shirt and said,

'Well that woke me up. How about a coffee before we start?'

Andrew got up from his bed while he pulled on his cloths. I also got up and continued to dress while Andrew replied,

'Yea, I think we should be awake before we start killing anyone today.'

'Come on, it's not like we set out to kill anyone yesterday. It just sort of happened.'

Andrew laughed as he replied,

'Yea we just seem to keep running into trouble. So do you have a plan on how we are going to get aboard?'

I moved through to the front of the ship as I answered,

'I think so, I just want to check something first.'

I moved over to the controls in the main cockpit before I activated the ship's main scanner systems. I briefly looked up from the controls and out of the window at the stars that were shining bright from the dark side of the Plotation moon. I smiled to myself as the thought of Starlight entered into my mind. Suddenly I felt a hand on my shoulder and turned quickly to find Andrew standing behind me.

'Where the hell are we?'

I looked back down at the controls and replied,

'We're on the dark side of Plattos's moon. I put the ship down here last night after you went to bed. Then I stayed up monitoring fleet movements to and from the main base.'

'Is it really six in the morning?'

Andrew handed me a coffee as he sat down and looked at the controls.

'Yes, and if I am right, there should be a large war ship jumping into the system within the next few minutes.'

Andrew looked at my hands as I took a drink of my coffee before he asked,

'You have taken off the bandages, how are your hands?'

'Fine, they seemed to have healed over night.'

'That's not possible, they were burnt and cut from the side down that rusty ladder on our escape. They should have taken weeks to heal.'

The console beeped drawing my attention to an opening jump gate, just on the edge of the system.

'Great, this is what I was expecting. Now if I am right the base will lower its shields to let the ship in. Then we have about an hour before it will leave.'

Andrew watched the scanners while the ship moved into the orbital base's shielded area. The scanners tracked the shields lowering and I timed how long it was before they rose again.

'Ok we have eight minutes to get into the shielded area before it reactivates. Then once we're in we need to find a place to set down.'

'Great but how do you plan on getting passed the century guns?'

He had a point and to be fair I hadn't got that part of the plan sorted yet. I again ran my eyes over the scanner readouts to find that we would have to take a huge risk to get close enough to pass through the shield opening and then we would most likely get spotted and shot down before we could get into the base perimeter.

'I was hoping we could follow a larger ship in, but it's going to be risky.'

Andrew looked back across the read out as he replied,

'More like suicide mate. It's a shame we can't just use the jump engines to jump into the main shielded complex. At least then we wouldn't have to deal with the base's defences.'

'Wait a minute; I think you have something there mate.'

I started to pull up the plans to the base running through the different areas of the complex until I came across the main oxygen factory for the base.

'There, we could use the jump engines to jump right into the middle of that section of the base.'

'That would be great mate, but haven't you forgotten about the shields. Beside even if we could make the jump you would have to be crazy to try opening a jump gate inside an enclosed dome, as it has never been done.'

I started to pull up the base plans from the information Artos had sent us as I pointed at the display and replied,

'Look the base is using a bio camber as their oxygen factory. Basically it is a forest which has a huge open space and would be a great place to hide our ship.'

Andrew looked over the readout before he laughed and said,

'That looks great and I think we could land in there. But we still need to get through the shields.'

'Well we just have to wait till that war ship leave the base. Then we will have an eight minuet window to make the jump.'

Andrew sat down next to me to look over the plans to the base before he said.

'Ok I think I can make the jump into the base, but what do we do then?'

I looked over the plans again before I replied,

'It's impossible to tell exactly where they are holding the spy. So we will have to work on that once we're in. But from the plans Artos sent us, it looks like there are several access corridors in and out of the bio dome. So at least we will have more than one way back to the ship. We will just have to keep a low profile for as long as we can.'

'That will be a first, so how long before we can make the jump?'

I checked the timer and replied,

We have about 45 minutes, so grab your pistols and let's get ready to leave. I will send a coded message to Darrin letting him know what we're going to do.'

Prison break

I walked back through to the cockpit dressed and armed with my sword and gun. I pulled on my long military coat that Starlight had made for me and sat down in the co pilot's seat. Pulling the picture of both me and Starlight out from my coat pocket. I stared at the image of us both on a grassy hill in the sun, sitting under a tree. I smiled knowing that I would see her again as I felt a hand on my back before Andrew said,

'I still think you should have taken some time to sort your head out mate.'

'I'm fine, now are you ready? We should make the jump while the warship is passing through the opening in the shields. That way the base will be focused on that and hopefully not us.'

Andrew took up his seat as he activated the ship's main systems. I pushed the picture back into my pocket as the shuttle lifted off the surface of the moon. While Andrew prepared the ship's jump engine and turned the ship around so we had a clear path to open our gateway. I followed the scanner readout as I watched the base's shields lower. I waited for the warship to start passing through the opening in the shield before I stated,

Ok mate, activate the jump engines.'

'Activating them now.'

The space in front of us was soon torn open to reveal the blood red emptiness of the warp. Andrew moved the ship into the twisted realm of space for no more than a few seconds before he reopened the gateway back into our space. Only this time the gateway opened up to reveal trees and the metal and glass of the bio domes frame work.

I quickly activated the ship's atmospheric thrusters to compensate for the gravity of the base as our ship left the warp, while Andrew quickly closed the jump gate before setting us down in amongst the trees to cover our ship's position. I got up as Andrew turned the ship's main systems off before he followed me to the air lock door. I turned to Andrew and said,

'You don't have to come with me. You can stay here and monitor things from the ship.'

'What and leave you to have all the fun, beside who is going to cover your back if I stay here?'

I smiled at my friend before I punched in the code to open the door. The air lock hissed as the two atmospheres mixed and I quickly moved out into the fresh air of the forest bio dome. I quickly scanned the area with my eyes to see if we were alone while Andrew closed and locked the ship's outer door. He pulled a small computer pad from his pocket and accessed it before he said,

'Ok, there are no life signs in this area at present and there's a corridor out of the dome about 20 minutes walk in that direction.'

He pointed off to my right so I started to walk as I said,

'Let's get moving. Most of the base should still be asleep at the moment, so we should be able to get around without being noticed.'

Andrew followed while I drew my sword and we headed through the woodland.

'Hay Chris, you know I have heard of these types of oxygen factories. But I have never seen one before. The air is so clean and fresh.'

'Yea, it kind of makes you forget you are on a space base.'

We both continued to walk until we came to the edge of the forest. The walls here were cold gray steel and I could see the open corridor arch way. I looked around as Andrew scanned the area just as I noticed a wall computer console.

'It's clear mate, but once we leave this cover we could be spotted easily.'

I pushed my sword back into its scabbard before I replied,

'Well we can't stay here forever and I think we could find out what we need from that console. So cover me.'

I moved out into the open and over to the computer wall unit. I struggled to understand the Plotation writing, but I did recognise the map symbol and that was just what I needed. I touched the screen which bought up the plan of where we were and from there I could see that the construction yard was on the other side of the base. But the brig was only a short distance from our position. I turned to Andrew signaling for him to come over to me. He moved quickly over to my side as I said,

'Come on it looks like we got lucky. The brig is not far from here.'

I moved up the empty corridor towards the brig while Andrew followed. Then I suddenly felt a hand on my arm as I was pulled back towards the wall behind a support beam.

'Chris, I am reading several life signs up ahead, moving about. The patterns of movements look like a guard unit.'

'How many are we looking at?'

'Just four; two are guarding the entrance of the main room at the end of this corridor, and two are inside.'

I peered around the support beam to find two armed guards speaking to each other just outside of a large steel door with no windows.

'Great, any ideas of what we should do now?'

Andrew looked at me for a moment before he replied,

'Well we could just walk up to them and say we are new and lost. This is a huge base and I don't think they will know everyone.'

'What about the fact we don't look Plotation?'

'Well this is a heavily armed military base, maybe they won't ask.'

I didn't have a better idea and to be fair we just needed to access the brig. But then I got an even crazier plan.

'Wait, what about we tell them we are here to see the Caridian spy. We are spies made to look Caridian to enhance our chances of making the prisoner speak.'

Andrew just laughed as he replied,

'That is even more stupid than my idea. You can do the talking and I will have my guns at hand for the shoot out.'

'Ok then follow me.'

I walked out from behind the support beam as Andrew followed at my side. We approached the two guards as they raised their guns with a look of total confusion on their faces. I walked right up to the centre of the doorway stopping just two feet away from the sealed door. I looked at both guards before I stated in a strong tone,

'Well are you both going to just stand there, or are you going to let us in. You should have received the notice that we were coming.'

The two guards looked both puzzled and confused as one of them said,

'Sorry but we have been told nothing. Who are you both and what are you doing here?'

'Typical, we have to go through surgery to look like Caridian scum, so we can get the spy to talk and then no one tell the guards that we are going to be here. And they are part of the plan. I should get onto your base commander right now and give him a piece of my mind.'

The guards both look horrified as one quickly said,

'That will not be necessary. I'm sure we can sort things out from here. Now which prisoner was it you wanted to see and what did you need us to do Sir?'

I looked at Andrew who still had a look of shock on his face. As I stated,

'Bring up the details of the spy we need to extract information from.'

Andrew quickly pulled out the small computer pad accessing it before he handed it to me in silence. I took the computer and quickly showed the display to both of the guards. Before I ordered,

'Well, you should have been told you are to put us both into the same cell as this prisoner and then close the door. We will convince him that we are on his side and gather the information that we need. Then you will reopen the door and let us leave after we have the information we need. Then you can dispose of him. Now open the door and let's get on with this.'

'Yes Sir.'

The guards lowered their guns and unlocked the door. It hissed loudly as the heavy door was pulled open. So I gestured for the two men to lead the way and followed them into the room.

The two guards walk into the open space where they were met by two more guards, who looked very unnerved by our presents.

'What's going on, and who are these two?' One of the men asked.

The guard in front of me quickly answered,

'We've not been told about this yet, I will fill you in later. Can you have cell B37 open when I signal you from his door.'

'Yea; I guess we never get told anything until it has happened around here.'

I was surprised that we had gotten this far as we followed the guards through to the cell. I watched as the first guard pressed a yellow button on the outside of the wall. This caused the door to unlock and open as I moved into the cell with the two guards. I looked at the beaten prisoner as he said in a low voice,

'So you found me some company for this small cell then.'

Before the guard could reply I pushed my G8 gun into his back as I signaled for Andrew to take hold of the other guard. Both of the men looked shocked while I said in a low voice,

'Now both of you stay calm and quiet so no one dies.'

The prisoner laughed before he said,

'General Darrin sent you two didn't he?'

'Let's just say he made us an offer we could not refuse. Now do you have the information so we can leave?'

The prisoner got up and moved over to one of the guards. He held up his hands which were cuffed and said,

'Unlock these now then put them on.'

The troop nervously replied,

'We don't have the key codes, they are kept in the main office.'

The prisoner moved around the guard before he stood at my side. He then looked me up and down before he said,

'You're a little young aren't you? So what's the plan, or are you just making it up as you go?'

Andrew smiled as he replied to me under his breath,

'I think he knows you already.'

'Thanks, now we could stand here talking all day or we can get the hell out of here. Andrew give one of your pistols to our new friend here. Then if you two cover the guards I will take care of the others.'

I put my sword to one of the guard's necks then I pointed my gun at the open doorway before I said,

'Now call for medical assistance, say the prisoner has collapsed and you need help to get him out of the cell. But don't try anything or this sword will cut your sentence short.'

I could see the guard was now sweating as he called out,

'Delvos, Delvos, come here and bring the medical kit, the prisoner has collapsed.'

I pushed my sword against his skin a little more as I said,

'Tell him you need both of them here to help get him out of the cell.'

'Bring Enrecker as well, he weighs a ton.'

I could hear the two men complaining as they approached. Their footsteps got louder as they hit the bare metal floor until the men came around the corner. There was a look of shock on both of their faces as one of the men turned to run. So I quickly fired off a single round from my G8 taking the man down. The other guard froze on his feet so I stated,

'Now move into the room slowly.'

As the man moved into the cell both Andrew and the spy moved back towards the door. I pulled my sword away from the other guard's neck while I kept my gun trained in on the other two. We now had the three remaining guards in the cell before we moved out of the small room. Once we were all in the corridor the spy turned to Andrew and said,

'Help me get this body into the cell with the others.'

I kept my gun trained in on the guards while they pulled the dead body into the cell before pulling the door closed. The lock banged, sealing the guards in as I lowered my gun.

'Come on we need to get you out of those cuffs.'

'Wait, he can use his pistol to shoot the key code. That should break the lock system.'

The spy held out his hands while Andrew took a shot at the key pad on the side of the cuffs. The lasers shot quickly brunt into the key pad causing the cuffs to click open and fall off the spy's wrists. He then held out his hand as he said,

'My name is Maltos, thanks for the rescue. But how in the world did you get aboard this station?'

'No time for that now, this is my first office Andrew and my name is Chris. Now you said you don't have all of the information. So where is it, and how do we get it?'

Maltos moved up the corridor and over to a computer console. I could see from his movement that he was in a lot of pain as he lent over the work station. We both followed him to the console as he ran through several different computer displays at speed, bringing up a detailed floor plan of the main base.

'Ok look at this, we need to get to this storage room. I hid the main plans for the new weapon in there. I was supposed to pick it up before I left for my ride home, but got caught instead.'

'But you said you have some of the information. Where is it?'

Maltos pointed to his stomach as he replied,

'I had to swallow the date stick. It is holding the fleet movement patterns for the next two months. This could change the outcome of the war.'

I looked at Andrew and then back at the plan before I said,

'Ok get a copy of the floor plan put on that computer pad. Andrew, I need you to get Maltos back to our ship. I will pick up the rest of the information and then meet you back at the ship.'

Maltos looked at me as he stood up before he said,

'It's a long way to that store room. How do you think you will get passed all the personal once they realise I have escaped?'

'Leave that to me, you need to get back to safety and Andrew will make sure you are ok.'

Alright, and I can see why Darrin sent you. Good luck.'

He downloaded the plans and handed the small computer pad back to me as he said,

'Ok lead the way.'

Andrew smiled at me as he picked up his other pistol before they left heading back towards our ship and then I headed out of another door in the direction of the storage room.

Intruder alert

I left the brig to the space station heading quickly up the corridor towards the store room I needed to find. The station was still quiet which meant that I could move around quickly and unnoticed. I kept referring to the floor plans so that I could avoid the main corridors and busy crew social spaces. Before I then made my way down a service tube through four decks to reach the station's main storage hold level. I found this area of the station was much duller than the upper levels with the walls coloured a dirty dark gray and the floor being replaced from a smooth shiny plated surface, with a bare metal grill that rattled under my feet as I stepped on them. The walls were also now filled with fitted pips and cables which ran around the whole corridor including the roof. I moved along the corridor making sure I kept out of sight when the odd station personal passed my way. Before I again checked the computer pad to find I was just several feet from the room the information was supposed to be in. So I moved quickly up to the door and over to the access panel. The room simply had an open close door switch which I pressed causing the door to slid open. Suddenly I felt a hand on my shoulder with a firm grip and as I turned around I was faced with a uniformed Plotation man standing there by himself. He released his grip as he asked,

'Who are you and why are you here?'

'Sorry I'm new. I got lost, while looking for my work group.'

I could tell the man didn't believe me as he put his hand on a pistol strapped to his belt.

'I will need your name and ID crystal, so I can get you to the right area of the station. Now hand me your ID and then follow me.'

'Yes of course.'

I moved my hand into my coat as the man noticed my G8 gun. He drew his own pistol quickly as I drew my sword. I could see he was going to pull the trigger before he asked any questions. So I slashed my sword out, hitting the power button as I swiped at his gun. The man fired the pistol just as my sword blades hit the gun knocking it off to one side. The electrical shock from my sword blades throw the man into a spin before he hit the floor with a thud, while the pistol shot clipped my upper leg tearing through my clothing and skin. The pain was sharp and continued as I felt blood pour down my leg while it soaked into my clothing. I stayed on my feet as I quickly moved over to the man, kicking his pistol out of his hand. The gun slid across the floor where it came to a stop just a few feet from his hand. We looked at each other as I pointed my sword at the man's neck.

'Don't try anything and you will be ok. Now get up slowly and move into that room.'

The man eased himself up off the floor and back to his feet. I kept my sword pointed at him as he moved slowly around me. I could see he was moving one of his hands behind his back while he said,

'You won't get off this station alive and even if you do escape, the station's defenses will shoot you down before you get to the shield.'

'Move into the room and bring that hand back where I can see it.'

The man pulled his hand out quickly slashing a knife at my chest. I stepped back to avoid the blade before the man made a run for his gun. He grabbed his pistol from the floor as I drew my G8 from its holster. The man went to shoot at me again so I pulled the trigger firing off a single shot. The shot from my G8 tore a large hole through the man's torso causing him to fall to the floor in a lifeless pile. I moved quickly into the room and over to the crate marked with a symbol Maltos had put on it when he had hidden the information. I forced the crate open to find it was full of cables, before I noticed a small package stuffed into one of the corners of the crate. I pulled the package out of the crate and checked what was inside. I pulled out a data crystal before checking there was nothing else in the package. Quickly I pushed the data crystal into my coat pocket before I moved back to the door. Then before I had a chance to leave the room, I heard voices coming from outside in the corridor.

Carefully I peered out into the corridor to find two Plotation men kneeling down at the dead body. They examined the man while I readied my G8 gun for the coming fight. Both men were armed and looked around uneasy as I heard one of them say.

'We need to report this to command, do you have your com?'

I knew I needed to keep this from happening so stepped out into the corridor as I watched one of the men pull out a small communication device. I pointed my G8 at the men as I stated in a loud voice,

'Drop the com unit and your weapons.'

The two men quickly dived for cover behind the corridor's piping and support struts while they fired blindly in my direction. I pulled myself back behind the door frame avoiding the incoming fire, while I also fired off two shots in their direction. The enemy fire continued to rain in on me from the two men and I knew I had to solve this quickly before too many people were alerted to my presents. I took the short break in the oncoming fire to return a couple of shots while I looked around the corridor for help. More shots rained in through the doorway as I spotted a gas supply pipe running across the roof of the corridor. I used the next brief break in the shooting to shoot the gas piping. This caused the pipe to explode in a gigantic ball of flames. The whole place shook and fire quickly engulfed the corridor for a short few seconds as I was blown back across the room to where I hit the floor with a heavy thud, just as the wall to the door frame buckled with the blast. Once the flames had died down I pulled myself back up from the floor dusting myself down. Before I moved back into the corridor, finding that the whole place had been scorched black with the blast. There were flames burning from the open ends of the broken piping and I could see the two men lying lifelessly and bunt on the floor. I moved quickly back towards one of the service tubes climbing back up the ladder towards the upper decks. So I could make my way back to the ship for my escape. My leg hurt like hell from the gunshot wound and I felt battered from the blast, but now was not the time to stop.

The floor shook briefly causing Andrew and Maltos to have to steady themselves on their feet. They both stopped in their tracks and looked at each other as Maltos said,

'What the hell was that?'

'I guess the Captain has run into some trouble. Now come on the ship is just over here.'

They both continued to move back into the forest area of the bio dome through the trees and undergrowth as Maltos asked,

'What the hell are we doing in here, the hanger bays are in the other direction?'

'We didn't land in a hanger bay. Now we should get back to the ship and prepare for the Captain's return as we may need to leave here fast.'

The two continued to move quickly through the undergrowth until Andrew led Maltos to where the shuttle was situated. Maltos stopped in his tracks with a look of bewilderment on his face while Andrew typed in the door code to the shuttle. This caused the door to hiss as it began to open and lower to the ground.

'Come on, we should move inside where we can track the Captain's movements better.'

Maltos followed Andrew aboard before the two moved into the cockpit. Andrew then started to activate the ship's basic systems while Maltos sat down next to him and said,

'How did you get this ship in here?'

Andrew continued to work at the ship's controls while he replied,

'We made a short jump from the moon to this dome, I was lucky I timed it just right or we might not have made it to your cell.'

'You realise we could leave now; the information I have will change the way this war will turn out. You will be a hero.'

Andrew stopped what he was doing and looked over at Maltos.

'We don't leave until the Captain returns. He has risked his life more than once for me, so I owe him that.'

'But there is not much chance he will make it back once the station finds out where he is. Besides after that explosion they will be looking for him.'

Andrew turned to the battered spy before he replied firmly,

'Your Military leaders didn't care much if you came back, just as long as we retrieved the information they wanted on the new weapon. You don't have that, so let's hope the Captain returns with it. Now sit back and relax if you don't have anything helpful to aid this mission.'

Maltos sat back and looked at the controls while Andrew tracked the ship's systems and life readouts. Then he turned back to Andrew before he said,

'Well if we are going to get out of here we will need to get past the shield, before you will be able to make a jump back into the warp. I think I can help with that.'

Andrew turned to Maltos checking his pistols were at hand before he replied,

'Good, the Captain should be back on the main decks in the next few minutes, although the station has issued a full alert now.'

No easy way out

As I climbed up through the maintenance tube I heard the station's alert sirens start to sound and I could also hear troops moving quickly around on the floor above me. I moved up to where the service tube opened up to the level above me, stopping at the opening while I listened to two of the station personnel talking to each other.

'Station command has order that we shoot to kill.'

'Good, I heard that the spy has escaped. I am looking forwards to killing the Caridian scum.'

'Yea well he is not alone, the station Commander has stated that there were two others helping him escape. And guess what, I heard that they are the two that were found at his flat.'

I watched from the opening discreetly as one of the troops loaded a large laser rifle before he continued to say,

'And you said this was a boring post to be given. I can't wait to get some target practice. Come on we should check this corridor again.'

The two troops moved off up the corridor and I took this chance to move up passed the level to the deck above. I tried to be as quiet as I could but I was all too aware of how noisy the metal ladder was as I climbed up it. I continued to move up to the next opening and quickly checked the corridor to find it was clear. Pulling myself out into the open, I checked my com pad to see where I needed to go next. It looked pretty straight forwards on the map, as I just had to travel the length of this corridor back to the bio dome.

Suddenly a laser shot skimmed passed me hitting the wall right next to where I was standing. I quickly dropped to the floor as I draw my gun while several more shots flew over my head. Looking up the corridor I found two troops standing out in the open with their guns pointed at me. I fired one shot at them, causing them both to dive for cover while I quickly got back to my feet before I fired again in their direction, keeping them both pinned down. I moved into a doorway and as it opened it revealed a power relay cupboard. I used it for cover from the incoming fire while I figured out what I was going to do next. I could hear the troops alerting other to my position and I knew I had to act quickly.

Suddenly there were more voices from the other side of the corridor as the troops shouted to each other about my location.

Trapped or so it seemed; but then I realised this power relay cupboard was my chance of escape. I noticed a small access panel under the main power couplings and relay units. So I quickly fired blindly in both directions causing a barrage of weapons fire to rain in on the small space in response. Now I knew the troops were busy, I pulled open the access panel and then took a signal shot at the mixture of cables and relays above the hatch causing the whole thing to blow out. The corridor fell into darkness and I used this cover of darkness to climb into the small service tube, pulling the panel shut behind me.

This crawl space was uncomfortable, small and I found it difficult to pull myself through the vent on my knees. I moved as quickly as I could just as I heard a sudden explosion go off behind me. I couldn't look back but move forwards even faster as I felt my heart pounding in my chest. Quickly I came to another access panel, being careful not to raise awareness to anyone that might be there, I emerged from the cramped space quietly.

Moving out from the crawl space I found I was now in a small alcove within a different corridor and luckily for me it was clear for now. Checking my map I found I now had much further to travel to get back to the corridor and bio dome where my ship was hidden. I was now in what would lead me only to the station's main engineering and reactor section.

I took the moment's pause to figure out what was next. Before I then looked around realising that I could knock out the power to the whole station from here. But that would be easier said than done. I peered around the corner to find that there was a busy crew in the area, working at several different computer consoles unaware of my presence. Suddenly I heard voices coming from the crawl space and knew I needed a distraction.

But to cut the stations main power I would have to be in the lower levels of the main power cambers for the station and not in upper engineering. I could hear the voices getting closer and had to think quickly. I draw my sword and used it to cut several power cables on the wall next to me. This again knocked the lighting out and seemed to throw the station's engineering team into confusion. I moved quickly across the room avoiding any of the crew until I reached another service tube that would lead me down to the lower decks. I quickly moved into the service tube and down the ladder five decks until I reached the main reactor room. I stepped out of the service tube and straight into one of the crew in the main reactor room. He looked panicked as he moved quickly over to a wall tannoy unit. I knew I needed to get out of here quickly so pulled my G8 from its holster before using it like a bat to knock out the engineer. Unfortunately this drew the attention of the rest of the crew in the room and before I knew it, I was again being shot at.

I returned fire with several non aimed shots which punched large holes in the wall where they hit. Within moments the lighting in the room had turned to red and there was gas pouring out from one off the holes in the wall opposite to me. There seemed to be an air of panic set across the room as I made a break for one of the main corridors out of the room. I could hear the chief engineer shouting they had a plasma leak that needed to be contained and this gave me a chance to make it back to the main corridor, out of the reactor room.

I again headed quickly up the corridor while still under fire from the troops that had now caught up with me. I returned fire back at them into the reactor room just as I heard an explosion that jolted the whole station hard. I turned back to find a wall of flames busting out from the reactor room that continued to burn while the station's crew tried to escape the blaze. I quickly made my way to a main lift shaft pushing the call button for the lift car, before I reloaded my gun. Pulling myself up close to the wall and out of sight of the lift doors I caught my breath for just a moment, before the lift doors opened at my side. Several troops moved quickly out of the lift and headed straight off down the corridor towards the burning main reactor room. I moved out from behind the lift door frame and into the lift car pushing the button for the upper deck that lead back to the bio dome. While again I made sure I was out of sight just in case any of the troops turned back to look at the lift they had just come from. The lift doors closed and I readied myself for what may still lay ahead of me in my path.

I could feel the lift car slowing to a stop before the doors opened to reveal a corridor with just two troops in it standing just outside the lift car doors.

They turned to find I was standing there with my gun and sword ready and pointed at both their heads.

'Drop your weapons and move into the lift.'

Both men dropped their guns and moved into the large lift car while I moved out into the corridor.

'Now push the button for deck twenty five and then put your hands up where I can see them until the doors close.'

Both men did as they were asked and I waited until the doors had closed before I moved quickly back up the corridor towards the bio dome. It was painful to run with my wounded leg but I needed to escape. So ran along the wide long corridor until I came to a large sealed bulkhead door. I could tell the bio dome was on the other side by the view of the trees from the small toughened glass window built into one of the two large doors. I could also see the doors were too thick to blast through with my G8 gun, so I checked around the heavy plated door frame until I found a large key pad covered in Plotation symbols. I looked over the key pad to see if I recognised anything that would help me, but found my heart sank at the confusion of symbols I didn't understand in front of me. Then I noticed the whole panel looked like it could be removed, so I used the blades from my sword to prise the panel away from the wall. Once open I looked in the hole at the mass of cables, wires and computer circuits. But before I could find the release power feed, again I came under fire. Several energy bolts hit the doors and wall around me leaving a spray of burn marks at their impact points. I quickly returned fire while dodging more of the incoming energy pulses. While the troops ducked for cover, and during the brief break in fire I decided to blast the open panel with my G8 gun.

This caused sparks to spit out from the burnt out hole and I was pleased to find the bulkhead doors began to pull apart creating a gap between them. I again shot at the troops taking one down as the blast from my gun shot throw the man across the corridor into a lifeless pile on the floor. Again the open panel flashed and banged causing the doors to come to a dead stop only partially open. I had no choice but to try and squeeze my body through the small gap. Quickly I broke from my small amount of cover during the barrage of incoming fire as I pushed myself through the small gap. I could see the forest through the gap and feel the freshness of the air as I made it into the bio dome. Only to be hit by two of the sharpest pains, one across my right shoulder and the other across my right hand side as the energy bolts tore through my clothing and flesh.

The shots burnt as they throw me to the floor, but I knew I had to keep moving. Pulling myself back to my feet through the pain, I continued to head back to our shuttle at my best speed. I could see more troops emerging out from different corridors leading into the dome and soon found the air was filled with another barrage of laser and energy shots. I found cover within the trees of the forest before I leaned myself against a large tree while I tried to gather some strength so I could carry on moving. My wounds hurt more than ever now as my clothing began to stick to my skin with my own blood. I pulled myself back up and again fired several shots back at the troops as the barrage of incoming fire increased cutting the forest surroundings to pieces.

I was pinned down but knew I needed to move just as I heard the thunderous roar of the Scorpion class shuttle's engines firing up. I held my position while the shuttle flew low over the trees before it pulled in front of my position. The shuttle lowered down to just a foot from the floor as the rear door lowered to the ground so I could get onboard. Then the shuttle fired its large cannons at one of the groups of troops causing them to scatter and find cover, while I took the brake in fire to make a run for our ship. I pulled my aching body aboard the ship and quickly hit the door close button. The door began to close again so I made my way through to the cockpit as I ordered,

'Get us out of here now.'

Andrew didn't look up from the controls as he piloted the ship upwards towards the top of the dome. With the bang from the magnetic locks as the bulkhead door sealed closed, Andrew blasted a large hole through the thick glass and steel of the outer hull wall of the bio dome into space. Our shuttle shot out into space and headed straight for one of the many shield generator projectors. Maltos took control of the ship's weapon systems as he started to fire our weapons at one of the heavily armoured generators before its own cannons fired back at us in retaliation.

'This is going to get bumpy.' Andrew said while he dodged the incoming weapons fire.

I sat myself down in one of the free chairs as we drew closer to the over sized shield generator just before Maltos asked,

'Are you ready with the jump engines?'

'Just take down that shield and we are out of here.' Andrew replied.

I noticed the ship's proximity sensors starting to bleep and checked the monitor to find we now had several fighters closing in on us fast.

'We have incoming, six fighters approaching fast.'

Suddenly there was a large explosion come from the generator in front of us just as Maltos yelled out,

'Hell yea, it's all up to you Andrew.'

Andrew activated the jump engines as our shuttle began to tear a hole in the fabric of space in front of us. Before we soon found ourselves back in the warp. Andrew quickly closed the gateway behind us while he sighed with relief and Maltos checked the scanners before he turned to us both and said,

'Well I didn't think I would ever get out of there alive. I guess I owe you both my life.'

'No problem, now I think I need a drink.' I replied breathlessly

Andrew locked the ship's course in as Maltos got up to look for something to drink.

I pulled myself up out of the chair I was sitting in and moved over to the co pilot's seat before I sat down with a moan.

'Are you ok mate?'

'I've been better; now open me a channel up to the Storm, so I can tell Artos we are heading back.'

Hidden foe

Andrew finished dressing my wounds with a concerned look on his face before he pulled the small computer pad off the main control console. He activated it and started to run a scan of my body while he asked,

'So you are sure you only got shot three times mate?'

'I think so; I guess I was just lucky.'

'Lucky, how did you work that one out?'

'Well the troops there were really lousy shots. I mean if just one of them could have shot straight, I wouldn't have made it at all.'

Andrew's face changed from a worried look to a sort of smile before he continued to say,

'It looks like you should be fine by the morning.'

'What!'

Andrew passed me the computer pad as he showed me the information being displayed while he replied,

'Looks like your injuries are healing themselves and your life stats are almost reading normal. If you look at the computer prediction you should just have some scarring by the morning and probably feel a little sore.'

'Really mate?'

'Really; I guess Starlight gave you a gift before. Well you know.'

I looked over the readout again and could see that my injuries had already reduced by around five percent. Then I noticed that Maltos had disappeared,

'Where's Maltos, didn't he go to find something to drink?'

'You're right, stay here mate and I will go and see.'

'No, let's both go and take your pistols just in case.'

Andrew looked around for his guns before he found just one of them behind my command coat.

'Funny I left both of these on the main flight console before we made the jump into warp space. Now I can only find one and it's missing its power cell. I pulled myself out of the chair I was sat in before I passed my G8 gun to Andrew and drew my sword.

'You should stay here mate, as you still need time to heal and anyone else would be bed ridden for weeks with your injuries.'

'Well I'm not and we need to check this out together, ok.'

Andrew didn't look happy but replied as he signaled for me to lead the way.

'Ok mate, you are the boss.'

We both moved slowly and quietly back through the ship checking the different areas as we went. Finally we came to the engine room; well it was more a sort of long thin corridor filled with power cables and the ship's main power core. The whole room hummed with the buzz of power as we entered the space slowly. There we found Maltos in the far corner of the room with his back to us. He was using a holo emitter communicator, so I signaled for Andrew to hold position while we listened into his conversation.

'What of the two who help you off our base?'

'Ha, they have no idea who I am and won't be a problem. Besides one of them is pretty badly shot up and I don't think he will make it back to their pick up ship.'

'And what of the information on our Obliterator ship?'

'The Captain has it in his coat. But that is of no concern. The Caridians will lose this war with the information I will give them on our fleet movements.

We will be able to end this war in just weeks.'

'Kaltar, I need you to destroy that data crystal and kill both of the spies before they reach their pickup location.'

'The plan was you would kill the captain before he escaped and now it's up to me.'

Kaltar, you have your orders. Kill them both and destroy the data before you reach the pickup location, and do it for the Empire.'

'Yes Commander, I shall kill them in their sleep. For the Empire, Kaltar out.'

He cut the holo communication link and turned slowly to leave finding my sword blades at his neck.

'Going somewhere Kaltar?'

The spy got up slowly as I kept my sword blades to his neck while I asked,

'So what happened to the real Maltos?'

The spy smiled with an evil look before he replied,

'I killed him as I ripped the data crystal from his stomach. Then I hid the information once we realised that you would be coming to save him. Let's just say you were predictable and troublesome.'

'So this whole thing was a set up just to get false information to the Caridians?'

'Yes, but I didn't count on your friend's loyalty to you, or your survival and escape from the base. Now are you going to kill me before I kill you?'

I held my nerve as I replied,

'Come on move. I'm sure the Caridian military will want to speak to you.'

The spy smiled as he held his stance,

'I'm fine right here thanks. So what are you going to do about it?'

I pushed my sword blades into the man's neck a little harder as I calmly replied,

'Just move unless you want to die.'

Just then Kalter pulled a small knife throwing it quickly at me. I used my sword to block the blade knocking it to the floor as Kalter pulled a second knife from his sleeve. He plunged it deep into my shoulder wound before pushing me to the ground as he twisted the blade. I fell back hard to the floor with a thud as I held the blade still stuck in my shoulder. Kalter quickly moved past me pulling the laser pistol from his belt, pointing it at Andrew. The two now stood face to face with just a few feet space between them, guns pointed at each other as Kalter stated,

'Now we both know you are not going to shoot me with that thing in here. I mean if you miss we will all end up dead.'

Andrew didn't waver as I tried to reach for the knife that lay just inches from my hand. But before I could pick it up Andrew bluntly replied,

'You talk too much.'

Then he fired a single shot taking Kalter out. The close quarter blast from the G8 gun tore a huge whole through the man's chest, throwing him back several feet to the floor where he lay lifeless on the deck while his blood drained from his body. Andrew walked over to him as he lay dying before he said,

'And I never miss.'

New beginnings

'Captain's personal log; we are now making good time back to our pick up location. I have checked over the information on the new Plotation weapon and have it safe for the Caridian military. Andrew has patched me up again and I am looking forwards to seeing our new ship. But after all that has happened over the last few months. I think I am most looking forwards to getting some rest, Log end.'

I felt a hand on my arm as Andrew spoke,

'Chris, we are ready to make the jump back to normal space.'

'Ok, have you contacted the Storm yet?'

'No, I figured you would want to speak to Captain Artos yourself. And Chris, ask them for some medical help. I am not happy with you just leaving it, you are not indestructible you know.'

I pulled my aching torn body up from the hard bed as I replied,

'I can't mate, if the military finds out about my body healing itself. They will have me locked up for tests and cut me to pieces to find out the secret. Now you know that will kill me and put the Kalien race at risk. So trust me when I say I will pass on that one.'

Andrew didn't look happy as I moved through to the cockpit before sitting down while he opened up a channel to the Storm.'

'Caridian ship Storm here, state your intent.'

'Captain Artos, good to hear from you. We are ready to make the jump back into normal space.'

'Chris, glad to see you both made it. Do you have the information and our man?'

'We have the information and I will fill you in on the rest of the mission once we dock.'

'Good, I will ready our hanger bay, Artos out.'

The communication cut as Andrew said,

'Opening the jump gate now.'

The twisted blood red space in front of our ship was quickly ripped open to reveal the blackness of space and the beauty of the stars. But the most pleasing sight I could see was the light gray star ship call Storm, which was our ride home. I sighed with relief while Andrew piloted our shuttle back to safety.

I was glad to be back aboard our own shuttle the Pay-check and it was good to see my crew back together again. The payment from our last mission had been completed and we were now on our way to the Caridian war fortress to pick up our new ship. Miller piloted our shuttle in close to the Caridian base just as the communication's console burst into life beeping loudly.

'Channel open Captain.' Richards stated.

'Approaching shuttle please identify yourself.'

'Independent shuttle Pay-check, requesting permission to dock.'

'Captain Sharman, of course General Darren informed us you were coming. Please enter by bay four. I will have our landing lights set up for you, just follow them to your docking point.'

'Thank you and Pay-check out.'

The com cut just as a huge set of hanger bay doors began to pull open. Miller flew our shuttle in through the gap into the fortress as I looked intently out of our forward windows at the busy interior of the base while Richards asked.

'Which ship do you think is our?'

'I don't know, but any of these would be great.' Andrew replied.

Miller followed the landing lights passed several light and medium sized war cruisers as I could feel the tension and excitement build in the air.

'Let hope it not a bucket of bolts.' Hudson said thinking out loud.

The communication's relay beep loudly again leading Richards to reopen the link.

'Pay-check, we have opened the bay doors to your ship, Hellfire. You are free to dock, Command out.'

'Thank you Command.'

Miller continued to follow the landing lights as they guided our shuttle around a large shipyard wall. I couldn't believe my eyes as we followed the landing lights towards a huge white and heavily armed Earth built battle cruiser.

'That cannot be ours.' Hudson said in disbelief as he moved closer to the shuttle's forward windows. Miller flew our shuttle along the side of the huge ship and I watched as we passed the ship's name, Hellfire.

'It's ours alright; the Hellfire. Now let's set down and take a look around.'

I smiled to myself as Miller began to land our shuttle in the open bay. He set our shuttle down gently while the doors closed behind us. Richards checked the atmosphere in the bay before he said,

'Atmosphere readings normal and I am picking up twenty two life signs moving into the hanger bay.'

Andrew moved over to the door before he signaled to me to leave the ship saying,

'Captain, you should go first as the ship is yours, by the official documents.'

I smiled at him as I pulled my aching body over to the door. Andrew pressed the release button causing the door to slid open to reveal the large and mainly empty hanger bay, except for a group of people standing there in civilian clothing. I stepped out and moved over to the group as I was followed by my small crew. One of the civilians stepped forwards to greet us. He was an older man with a rounded face and gray hair.

He smiled and held out his hand before he said,

'Captain Sharman?'

'Yes' I replied as I smiled back at him while he stood there looking a little nervous. The man paused for a moment before he spoke saying,

'Hi my name is Tannor and the people you see behind me are some of the crew that used to serve aboard this ship. We are here because all of our military service contracts ended with the decommissioning of this ship. None of us wanted to sign up again to the military to serve aboard other vessels, as this had become our home. So when we learned that the ship had been saved, we hoped the new owner would need some crew.'

This was unexpected but I knew we would need a much bigger crew to run this ship effectively.

'You're right we do need a larger crew, so who do we have here and what roles have you all done?'

The group started to introduce themselves one by one to me and my crew. I couldn't help but smile as each person showed their own love for the ship and different job role they had been doing. I could tell I now had the start to a good crew that would help get this ship running smoothly and I could also see that with this ship, my adventures had only just begun.

HELLFIRE

Planet of the Dead

Volume 5   By Christopher J Sharman

CONTENTS

Introduction	Pg 188
From out of nowhere	Pg 189
Offered help	Pg 198
All that has been before	Pg 207
The lost planet	Pg 214
Facing the dead	Pg 227
Temple of the dammed	Pg 232
Death will not stop	Pg 240
Overrun and out of time	Pg 246
Starlight	Pg 256
A world ends	Pg 266
The Darkness war	Pg 275

INTRODUCTION

'Personal log; It has been just over three months since I gained the battle cruiser Hellfire as my ship and now it feels like home to me. Over the last few months I have built up the crew from fifty to two hundred and twenty four. I could still do with another hundred personal at least, but this is something I can look into later due to the fact that we are not attached to any military body. This also means I can choose when to take work and fit it around the crews needs.

But for now we are heading back towards Earth. The whole crew could use some shore leave and it has been a long time since any of my original crew have been home to see friends and family. I am personally looking forwards to seeing my family again as I have left it far too long since my last visit. But on a more personal note; I still find myself thinking about Starlight. It was strange how quickly we became close to each other and when I found the old picture of us both... Well I'm sure it will all become clear to me one day. Even if sometimes I think I see her behind me out of the corner of my eye in the mirror or feel like see is watching me sleep. But for now I guess I just need some time with my family. Log end.'

From out of nowhere

I walked onto the large and brightly lit bridge. As I looked around I could see several of my crew working at the various computer consoles that were positioned around the military styled bridge. I moved over to my chair that was situated in the middle of the room before I sat down. Looking passed the helm and out of the giant run of forward facing reinforced windows, I could see nothing but space.

The stars were so clear and bright against the blackness of space and the only thing to break up the view was the magnificence's of a greenish blue nebular, which seemed to cross our path.

I smiled to myself at the view as I heard the bridge doors slid open, before the soft voice of Miss Carr then spoke from behind me while she said,

'Captain hi, do you have a few minutes?'

I turned my chair around to see her standing there. The ship's doctor, she was a young woman with a slim figure and mousey long blonde hair that was tied back into a pony tail. She smiled at me as I replied,

'Yes of course, what can I do for you?'

'Nothing much Captain, but I noticed that we will be passing an Earth colony. So I hoped that we could pick up some much needed medical supplies and equipment.'

'Make me a list of what you need and I will make sure we pick it up.'

'Thank you Captain.'

She smiled again while she stood there for a moment, so I asked,

'Is there anything else Doctor?'

She continued to stare out of the windows for a moment before she replied,

'No but you have a great view from up here, sometimes I spend so much time in sickbay that I forget I am in space.'

'Feel free to take it in, we have a quiet day ahead of us.'

I turned my chair back around to face the front of the bridge before I asked,

'Miller, do you know the colony Miss Carr needs?'

'Yes Captain, it is Delta Z47-A, a non military farming facility and space port.'

'Then Plot a course for Delta Z47 at our best speed Miller.'

Miller started to push several buttons on the console in front of him as he replied,

'Course plotted Captain and we should arrive there in twelve hours.'

'Thank you Miller.'

I continued to watch the stars just as lunch crossed my mind. But before I could decide what to have Miller grabbed my attention along with the beeping of the helm console.

'Captain, I am picking up what looks like some sort of opening gateway. It is about 15'000 kilometers off of our starboard side.'

I sat up straight as I ordered,

'Come to a full stop and go to yellow alert. Raise the shields and ready our weapon systems.'

The lighting in the room changed to an orangey glow as the ship stopped dead in its tracks. I could see Miller working at his station with a fixed determination so asked,

'Miller, what's out there?'

Miller sounded unsure as he answered,

'It's strange Captain, and looks like a cross between a jump gate and an energy distortion. I also seem to be reading what looks like a ship, but it keeps phasing in and out of my scanner readout.'

I quickly got up and moved over to the navigation control, looking over the screen's readout.

'Miller, turn us around to face it. I want to see this with my own eyes.'

'Yes Captain.'

The ship turned to face the anomaly and I watched the white lightning as it tore at the blackness of space. The lightning seemed to be coming from the bright white centre of the disturbance, while a darker more solid object seemed to fade in and out of view at random intervals.

'Miller, are you getting any readings from the object in that thing?'

'I think so, but it keeps phasing out. So it is hard to tell what it is.'

'Do you think we could get a hold of whatever it is with an energy beam?'

'Miller continued to work at his controls as he answered,

'I don't think so, well not without tearing the object to pieces.'

'Then are you reading any life signs?'

Again Miller checked back with his console before he responded,

I think so, but they don't appear to be human. It's hard to make out due to the energy and radiation levels, but I think they're Kalien.'

I stood up straight looking out of the bridge windows at the violent display of lightning from the anomaly, just as Miss Carr quickly moved in front of me saying,

'You have to help them!'

Her soft face had an intense look and her voice held a determined tone.'

'Ok I'm working on it. Miller, what do we know about the anomaly from the scanner readout?'

Miller looked over his controls before he replied,

'Captain, from what I can tell the energy is being created from within the anomaly. But we might be able to stabilise it if we match the energy field with a bust of power from our ship. That may just free the object without it being destroyed.'

Trying to think fast I asked,

'What about our jump gate emitters, could we use them to open up the anomaly?'

Miller continued to work at his post as he replied,

'I'm not sure, but it might be possible to work it directly from main engineering.'

I knew we needed to act fast as I quickly moved over to my chair activating the com panel on the arm rest.

'Hudson, I need you to match these energy output readings and recreate them using our jump engines.'

I heard Hudson reply with an air of confusion to his voice over the tannoy.

'What energy readings?'

'The ones Miller is sending down to you now.'

I could see Miller transferring the information while he continued to monitor the read out in front of him before he then continued to say,

'Captain, I have sent the power output reading to Hudson, but it looks like the anomaly is becoming increasingly unstable.'

'Hudson we don't have much time, can you do it?'

Hudson's reply over the tannoy sounded unsure as he answered,

'Captain, I can match the energy readings with no problems, but I cannot be sure if it will work or just pull us into the anomaly as well.'

'Ok, get it ready and wait on my order.' I replied before looking back out of the bridge windows at the violent electrical storm just ahead of our ship. I was hoping this would be the right course of action just as Richards called over from his post.

'Captain, I'm picking up a weak distress call from the trapped object.'

I could see the deepening concern on Miss Carr's face even before she pleaded with me.

'Captain, you must do something now, they need our help.'

'I know, Hudson, ready the engines.'

His reply came almost instantly over the tannoy.

'I have them ready and waiting on your command. But I'm not sure our engines will hold up, as they were not built for this type of energy usage.'

'Noted, now activate the jump gate emitters.'

With that order, suddenly several white lightning like energy bolts began streaming out from our ship, hitting the anomaly in front of us. Quickly moving over to the ship's tactical station I checked the readout on the object held inside. I noticed that our ship's engines were stabilising the anomaly, but we needed to do more. So I called over,

'Miller, can you use our emitters to open up the anomaly?'

'I will do my best Captain.'

Suddenly the anomaly broke open to reveal a scorched and battered small green and gray vessel. It was hard to make out what type or race it belonged to, but it was clear it needed help and quickly.

Then without warning the whole ship jolted sharply and as I checked the tactical readout, I found we were now right in the middle of the anomaly. The ship continued to jolt and shuddered sharply as Miller called over,

'Captain, we are now caught up in the anomaly.'

I hit the red alert button as I noticed the strange ship was beginning to lose its hull integrity.

'Miller, move us in really close to that ship. I am going to extend our shields around them.'

'Yes Captain.'

Miller moved the ship in close and once we were within range I quickly used our shields to protect the failing vessel.

I monitored the readout to find our shields were holding and once the failing ship had been cut free from the storm anomaly. I found the electrical anomaly stabilised quickly to our own engine output. This was great to see so I ordered,

'Miller, cut the power to the jump gate emitters.'

With the power cut, the anomaly quickly dispersed leaving just the black void of normal space and the beauty of the stars.

'Damage report?'

Richards moved over to the science station checking the console before he replied,

'No damage to the ship Captain, but we are getting reports of minor injuries from many different decks.'

'Ok Miller, hold position and then get a reading of the space around us. Let's make sure we are clear of any more anomalies.'

'Yes Captain, I will get straight on to it.'

The bridge doors slid open and my first officer came rushing into the room looking worried as he asked,

'What the hell just happened?'

I began to work at the tactical station while I replied,

'It's a long story, but I need you on the science station to check over the information on this ship we have just saved. I will send it over now.'

'Ok Captain, let me see what we have found.'

Richards pulled his attention back over to the communication's console but as he turned around he immediately called over,

'Captain, I am getting a call coming through from the damaged ship. I should be able to put it on the holo ring.'

'Ok then, open me up a channel and let's find out what has happened to them.'

I moved over to the two metallic rings built into the floor of the bridge before I stepped into the first one.

Both rings lit up, one around me and the other in front of me which stayed blank for a while.

'Richards, what's the problem?'

I turned to find Richards working at his station as he replied,

'Sorry Captain. It is a really old style signal and I am struggling to get it to work over the holo rings... Wait this should work.'

As he finished his sentence a 2D image of a Kalien man appeared in the front empty ring. He was clearly hurt and wearing torn clothing. His wings were down and his pale blue skin looked dirty and bruised. I could see he was holding his right arm and his voice was strained with the sound of pain as he said,

'Thank you, whatever you are. We would not have lasted much longer. Now we have many injured and we are in dire need of assistance, if we can put this upon you.

I gave a kindly smile as I replied,

'We will assist you and your crew in any way we can, medical and technical. Just let us know what you need from us.'

The battered man looked uneasy as he said,

'Thank you; you are too kind. We have lost our healing group and our only remaining healer was badly injured in the attack. Then we have the more pressing need to stabilise our core power unit and seal any outer shell breaches to our vessel. I know this is a lot to put on you and your people... and where are my manners. I haven't even asked your name.'

Again I just gave a kindly look as I replied,

'Just call me Chris. I will have our medical bay ready for your injured and I can bring my ship's doctor and an engineering team over to your ship to assist you directly.'

'We are at your mercy. I will have our shuttle bay doors open and ready for your arrival.

Andrew quickly interrupted as he said,

'Captain, I am reading more than one type of life form aboard their ship.'

I turned to my first officer before I asked,

'Can you tell me what they are?'

I watched as he played with the controls before he replied,

'There is too much interference bleeding from their ship's damaged power core. It is affecting our scanner's readout, but I can tell you that some of the life readings are not Kalien.'

I turned back to face the image of the Kalien man before I asked,

'You said that you were attacked, but by who?'

Again the Kalien man looked uneasy as he replied,

'Associates of the Darkness, the Falsec.'

I knew this made things a lot more dangerous as I asked,

'Do you know if any of their boarding vessels breached your ship's hull?'

The Kalien man looked around before he replied,

'It is impossible to tell with the ship is this condition. But I have received no word of hostiles aboard.'

'Ok make sure your people are armed. The Falsec are very dangerous and I will be aboard with my medical officer and engineering team shortly. Stay alert.'

'We will, Sole-light out.'

I stepped out of the holo ring as the image faded out and then I moved over to my chair while saying,

'Andrew, you have the bridge.'

But before I could leave Miller grabbed my attention as he spoke with a sense of urgency.

'Captain, you know how you asked me to check out the sector?'

'Yes.'

'Well our star charts don't match where we were before the anomaly appeared.'

'So where are we?'

'That's the thing Captain. Nothing matchers our computer's star charts and everything looks different.'

I moved over to Miller just as Andrew cut in saying,

'Captain, that is not all. I have been cross referencing the ship out there and it looks like it shouldn't even exist.'

Things just seemed to be getting stranger as I asked,

'What do you mean?'

'Well come and take a look at this. I had to check the Hellfire's history records to find a match. I mean this ship looks like it was built in the Earth year 400 BC.'

I looked over the information on screen and I could see an early Earth jump ship had found a drifting wreck of one of these ships many years before the Hellfire was even constructed. This all needed to be checked out, but first we needed to help the crew of the damaged vessel.

'Ok then, first things first. Let's help the injured. Andrew, pass any information onto Hudson that will assist on the repairs and tell him to meet me in bay two with a small engineering team. Then I need you to help Miller find out where we are and check for any other ships that may still be in the sector.'

'Yes Sir.'

'Miss Carr, I need you with me.'

'Yes Captain, but I need to pick up some medical equipment first from sickbay before we leave.'

'Do it and I will meet you in bay two shortly. Andrew you have the bridge.'

With this I left the bridge with Miss Carr before I headed to my quarters, knowing I needed to pick up a couple of things myself.

Offered help

I walked into the hanger bay to find Hudson and three engineers loading equipment onto our shuttle. Suddenly I felt a hand on my shoulder as a soft voice said,

'Captain, do you really think they are necessary?'

I turned to find Miss Carr and I could tell she was referring to my sword and gun.

'Have you ever faced a Falsec before?'

'Well no but...'

'Then trust me on this one, I have and these are needed.'

Miss Carr looked with interest as she said,

'But no one has ever survived a fight with a Falsec before, well that the records state.'

'I didn't say I did.'

Miss Carr looked both confused and uneasy as we both moved over to the shuttle before I pattered Hudson on the back while asking,

'Are you ready my friend?'

'Yes Captain and I can see you are not taking any chances this time, good. You know we all thought we had lost you to that pirate aboard the Enlightenment that day.'

I sort of smiled before I said,

'Yea, even I thought I was a goanna. But then you know me and I am just not that easy to get rid of.'

I signaled for him to move aboard with my hand before both I and Miss Carr followed. I could hear her mumbling to herself as I walked behind her while she said,

'Why do I get the feeling that I haven't been told something very important?'

Once aboard I sealed the door behind us just as Hudson cleared our shuttle to leave. I moved over to Miss Carr before I sat next to her while the shuttle lifted off of the hanger deck. I could see the stars out of the shuttle's windows as we left the Hellfire and I figured that this would be a good time to speak to Miss Carr,

'Bethany, do you know anything about the Kalien race?'

'Just what the ship's medical records hold and that is mainly speculation.'

'Ok then, you should know that they are a peaceful but closed race, that doesn't really intermix with other species.'

'Well everyone knows that, so have you met one before?'

'Yes and from that I can tell you that they don't use medicine like we do, so they will be very weary of our ways.'

Miss Carr looked at me as she curtly replied,

'Captain, I will be as understanding as I can be with them.'

I was going to tell her more but was cut short by Hudson who shouted over to me.

'Captain, I am bringing us into land.'

'Thanks Hudson.'

I got up and moved over to the shuttle door just as I felt a light bump as our ship touched down.

'That's it Captain, we are here and you can just pop the door open now.'

Again I thanked Hudson before I turned to Miss Carr to find she still looked uneasy.

'Look, just stay close to me and everything will be fine. Are you ready?'

'Yes I think so.' She replied before I pushed the door release button causing the shuttle's door to slide open. I stepped out onto the shiny metallic floor of the alien ship as I noticed that the hanger bay looked to be undamaged. I could see the injured Kalien man standing just a few feet in front of me. So I moved forwards over to him as he nervously said,

'I can see you have come here armed.'

I smiled at the man as I replied calmly,

'Yes, I didn't fancy running into a Falsec again unarmed, so please forgive me. Now let me introduce some of my crew. This is Miss Carr my ship's doctor and this is Hudson my chief engineer.'

The Kalien man still looked uneasy as he responded,

'So this is your Healer and Lead Tech Master. So what are you?'

'I am the Captain, or you can just call me Chris.'

The injured man seemed to relax a little as he said,

'I am what you would call Captain Bartell. Unfortunately my assistant Prime was killed during the attack on my vessel. So what do you need access to first?'

'I think we should look to helping your injured first, so if my doctor can use your healing facilities. Then Hudson and his team can head down to your engine room to help stabilise your ship's power core. Then if you are up to it, I would like to find out more about what happened here.'

Miss Carr moved forwards towards me as she asked,

'Captain, before you both leave I should check over Captain Bartell, if that is alright with you?'

Bartell still looked uneasy as he answered,

'As you wish Healer, but we should run the session from the main healing room.'

Miss Carr smiled before she replied,

'Of course Captain. So which way is it from here?'

'Just this way.'

We followed Bartell as we moved through the burnt and damaged corridors of the Kalien vessel while he lead us to his medical bay. It didn't take long and we soon found ourselves walking into a very busy corridor filled with injured Kaliens and a strange larger than life fur covered creature. Bartell moved over to a doorway and was quickly stopped by a battered looking Kalien man as he cut in saying,

'Ship's Prime, you cannot open that door.'

I could see Bartell looked frustrated by this as he replied,

'Tech third level, give me one good reason why.'

The injured man kept his arm out in front of his captain while he replied,

'The whole room has gone. That is why we have lost our healing team. They were all sucked out into the void.'

Bartell lowered his head as he put his hand on the door for a moment. Then he asked,

'But I was informed that we still had one healer. Who is it and where are they?'

The injured man moved away from the door as he limped while he replied,

'This way, she was on a different level at the time. But Callaltra is badly hurt. I had her moved here with the rest of the injured.'

We all followed the man over to a young Kalien woman who was slouched up against a wall, covered in her own blood and barely conscious. I turned to Bartell as I asked,

'Prime Leader, do I have your permission to move the injured over to my ship?'

'Yes please do Captain, I would be very grateful.'

I pulled my com link from my belt before I opened up a channel. I could see Miss Carr was already starting to run a medical scanner over the injured Kalien healer as I said,

'Hellfire, I need you to send over one of our transport ships with a pilot and two medics. Then inform sick bay that they will be receiving an influx of patients.'

Richards's voice came clearly over the com as he replied,

'Yes Captain; also Andrew is just letting me know that he is reading no Falsec life forms aboard.'

'Thank you Richards, Sharman out.'

This was a relief as I cut the communication. I could see Bartell looking increasingly uneasy at Miss Carr's actions before he turned to me and asked.

'What is she doing to Callaltra?'

Miss Carr continued as she began to explain, before I could speak.

'I am checking what injuries the lady has before I administer any kind of aid.'

I turned to Bartell before I kindly asked,

'Prime Leader, why don't you let the doctor look at your injuries first. Then you will know that it is safe.'

Bartell stepped back uneasily before he replied with worry in his voice.

'I am not sure about this Captain. I find your ways unnatural.'

Miss Carr injected a pain killer into the young Kalien woman before she moved over to Bartell.

'Now this doesn't hurt.'

I watched as she moved the medical scanner in front of Bartell before she continued to say,

'Now I can see that you have broken your arm in two places, but other than that you have little more than minor cuts and bruising.'

'You can tell all of this with that mechanism?'

'Yes now let me make you more comfortable and then if you do not like what I am doing, I will stop.'

Bartell agreed and stood still while Miss Carr worked on his arm. She spoke softly to him explaining what she was doing until she had fused the bones in his arm and dressed the open wounds. My com link suddenly beeped while she was working so I moved away and answered it.

'Sharman here, go ahead.'

Richards's voice came clearly over the com as he replied,

'Captain, I have our location.'

'Great, so where are we?'

'Approximately twelve hours travel from Delta Z47-A. We haven't moved in space, but there is something you should know. Are you alone?'

I moved away from the injured to a quieter part of the corridor before I replied with interest,

'Ok Richards, what is wrong?'

'You may not believe this but our star charts didn't match the space because we have moved in time. Andrew thinks that by using the small amount of difference between our charts and the way the stars look now. Well he thinks we are somewhere in the Earth date one hundred to six hundred years BC.'

I couldn't believe my ears as I asked,

'But how?'

'I'm not sure Captain, but Andrew thinks it had something to do with the anomaly we got caught up in.'

'Ok keep working on it for me. Also did you find any signs of the Falsec ships?'

'We are still working on that one Captain. I will let you know.'

'Thank you and good work. Just keep me informed.'

I moved back over to Bartell and Miss Carr to find he was looking much better. He now watched as Miss Carr began to work on his young healer.

'Bartell, do you have somewhere we can speak alone?'

'Yes of course Captain, just this way.'

I turned to Miss Carr as I said,

'Doctor, you can get me on my com link if you need me.'

Then I turned and followed Bartell to a small room with two cushions placed either side of a low table. Bartell sat down and signaled for me to do the same.

'Well Captain, what can I do for you?'

'It is more that we have a problem and as ship's Captain, I think you should know.'

Bartell looked concerned as he asked,

'So what is the problem we have?'

Before I could start to explain my com link began to sound again.

'Sorry.' I said as I answered it in front of Bartell.

'Sharman here, go ahead.'

The voice of my first officer replied with a sense of urgency.

'Captain, I have some news on the Falsec.'

'Go on, what are we dealing with?'

'Four ships and they are quickly moving towards the planet we know to be called Delta. It looks like they will arrive in around four hours. Also the planet is not what we know it to be. It has no human life signs and is reading over four billion alien life forms with very little technology to protect it, other than one small Kalien vessel.'

'I read you Andrew. I'm with Bartell now so...'

'That is the other thing Captain. The Kalien ship is registering the very same readings as the Sole-light.'

I turned to see Bartell looking very confused as I asked,

'So how many ships were there when you got attacked?'

'Just this one, but that battle happened around an hour ago. This is all just impossible; four Falsec ships attacked the planet. I had to evacuate some of the locals because of the threat of the Death Plague. The Falsec had said they would release it upon the planet.'

'Death plague, what do you mean?'

Bartell made himself more comfortable before he continued.

'It is a Darkness weapon. They use it on a world they wish to strip of its resources. The virus wipes out the population by infecting a host, then the host dies and the virus uses the body to spread the virus to another body and so on. No world has ever beaten it.'

I now knew what Starlight had been trying to tell me, but before I could enquire any deeper into the attack my com link sounded.

'Sharman here, go ahead.'

'Captain, I think you should both come aboard the Hellfire. We have another problem.'

There was concern in my first officer's voice before I replied,

'What is it? You can tell us this is a closed room.'

'It is the records in the Hellfire's history data banks. They read the name of the found drifting ship to be Sole-light and that is not all. The ship was found not far from this location and had no signs of any bodies aboard. Sort of like a modern day ghost ship.'

'Could it just be a coincident?'

'That's the thing Captain. The found ship's last log entries were wiped up to the Kalien date 26.07.2215.'

Captain Bartell cut in as he stated,

'But that is today's date. This is just nonsense, you are telling me that we have travelled in time and that your ship can monitor vessels from hours of travel away from us and still tell what they are.'

I could see Bartell was having a hard time with the situation and to be fair I could barely believe it myself. Still if all this was true and we had travelled in time then we could be at risk of effecting our own future with every move we made. I needed to know everything before we made our next move.

'Bartell, I think we need to check this all out from my ship. Also I would like to move your entire crew over to the Hellfire, until we have a better idea of what is going on. They will all be a lot safer that way.'

Bartell looked wearily at me but agreed, so I opened up the com channel to my ship and let my first officer know our initial plans.

All that has been before

I had called all my key officers and captain Bartell to the Hellfire's meeting room to discuss what our next move was going to be. I moved into the room and took up a chair before I activated the computer terminal sat on the table in front of me. I then began to bring up the information we had gathered so far before I started to run my eyes over the display. I could see we had plenty of time to intercept the Falsec ships before they attacked and from the information our scanners had on the enemy ships. I could also see that the Hellfire was more than a match for all four vessels at once.

But this was not my main concern, as if it was true that we had travelled back in time. Then we could be on dangerous ground and risk effecting our own future with every move we made. I found this to be very unnerving as Andrew was the first person to enter the room. He seemed to be very calm about the situation as he took up a seat and asked,

'Chris, how are you?'

'I'm ok, but have you managed to confirm a date yet, so I know what to tell everyone?'

He smiled at me as he cheerily replied,

'Yes, I matched the current date in the Kalien calendar from Bartell's ship with the Kalien date from last time we visited their home world. Then I compensated for the time in between our last visit and the time jump, before I fed it all into our computer. So I found we had travelled back to the Earth date 359 BC, January 17th ish.'

'Wow, I was just hoping for a rough year. Well done.'

Andrew looked pleased with himself as he continued,

'Well Chris, I figured that if we wanted to get back to our own time, then we would need to know.'

'Do you think it is possible?' I asked hoping we could.

'Well we got here, so why not?'

This was reassuring to know, but before we could explore the idea any further the door to the room slid open. Richards, Miller and Hudson all entered the room chatting as they took up three more of the seats. They were then followed shortly afterwards by a very flustered Miss Carr and our guest Bartell. I watched as she showed him to a seat before she asked,

'Captain, I am up to my eyes with patients in sickbay. Do you mind if I pick up the notes later?'

I could see the desperate look on her face so replied,

'Do what you need too. I will catch up with you later.'

'Thank you Captain.' And with this she left. I looked around and figured that we should get things started as I addressed the room.

'Thank you for all getting here so soon. This is ship leader Prime or Captain Bartell for those of you who haven't met him yet. He is here today because everything we decide in this room will affect his ship and crew. He may also have information that could help us. Now I asked you all here so we can work out a plan of action. The main issues we need to address are the Captain's ship, the planet and the attack that will happen, the welfare of the Sole-light's crew and finally. How we can get back to our own time. So with the information I asked my first officer to send you all, where shall we start?'

Bartell cleared his throat before he spoke first saying,

'I guess we should look to helping the injured. I know my ship is unable to help but we did have a colony on Telltorzis. The planet you call Delta. That colony holds a full healing team, most students but I am sure they will be more than enough to help out your own healers.'

'Great, can you get me the names of the healers and the coordinates of the colony? So this brings us to the planet. Can we help it without effecting our own time line?'

Andrew raised his hand as he calmly replied,

'I don't see why not. I checked out the Hellfire's archives on Delta Z47 and found out that Earth only colonised it around thirty years ago, well in our time. The planet was just recovering from a planetary burn out. The records don't say what happened to the planet, but they do show that the planet suffered a major nuclear fire that destroyed everything thousands of years before it was colonised. Earth landed its first colony once the planet started to show signs of vegetation. Now as you know it is a farming colony, well in our time.'

'So we have to look at the possibility that this planet was lost in this attack. But do we know of any survivors?'

Miller interrupted as he answered,

'Well when we last visited the Kalien home world, I read about a species of creature that matchers the creatures we moved over to our ship from the Sole-light. Other than that there has been the odd fairy tale of their existence.'

I looked around the room before I replied,

'Ok so that means we can offer assistance. So let's work out a plan of action. First we need to work out how many life's we can save and bring aboard. Then Miller, I need you to time our arrival just after the Sole-light departs the battle. Richards, I need you on our communication's channel, keep your ears open for anything that may help us from the Falsec or calls for help from the planet's surface. Andrew, I need you to work with Bartell on settling in his crew, then get to work on how we can rescue the colonists so we can ease Miss Carr's predicament. I will sort out our landing ships and troops while Hudson makes sure the Sole-light's logs match our historical records. Any questions anyone?'

Hudson spoke up as he asked,

'Captain, just how long do we have before we have to leave?'

I turned to Miller for the answer before he said.

'We will need to leave in around two hours if we travel at one quarter thrust through the warp. I will let you all know when I have an exacted time.'

'Ok then, you all have your orders and let's make sure we are ready to go in one and half hours. Now let's get to work and after this is all over we can look to finding our way back to our time.'

The room quickly cleared leaving only me, my first officer and Bartell. I watched as Bartell spoke to Andrew while handing him a small alien computer pad. Bartell then left the room while Andrew looked over the information on screen. He held a concerned look as he stared at the light blue lit screen so I asked,

'What is it my friend?'

He jumped at my voice and I could tell he had something on his mind, so I asked again.

'Well I know that look, what's wrong?'

Andrew moved around the table and handed me the small device before he replied,

'Chris, look at the names on the list.'

I took the device and looked over the display at the list of strange names before my heart jumped. Twelve lines down from the top of the list I read the name Falforar Starlight, aged 19, Student healer. I rubbed my eyes and took another look as I said out loud,

'Starlight!'

I could see the concern on his face as he said,

'Chris, you do not know that it is her. It may just be a coincident. Besides Starlight's father was called Talstead not Falforar.'

'That was his first name, Falforar is their family name.' I replied

'But Chris, this may not be her.'

Still I had to find out.

'I will lead the troops to pick up the survivors.'

'But Chris, Starlight said she was just over 400 years old. Remember we have travelled back thousands of years.'

'I know, but she also mentioned to her father that I matched the old war records and that they were sent to our time for their safety.'

I could see my first officer was not convinced but he replied like any good friend would.

'Look just be careful down there and don't be disappointed if it is not her.'

I smiled at him before I replied,

'I will and trust me, I am not going to be taking any chances.'

'Right, like I said before. Be careful.'

Andrew pattered me on the shoulder as he left and I found myself thinking I had plenty to sort out before we made the jump. I then pushed the pad into my pocket before heading out of the room and down to the hanger bay.

It was almost time to make our jump into warp space and I was making my way back up to the bridge. My troops were ready and our two transport ships and one shuttle were also prepped and ready to depart. All I now needed to do was check everything was ready before we made the jump. I had already picked up my G8 gun, sword and long command coat as I had passed my quarters and I was now making my way back along the short corridor that would take me to the bridge.

The large bulkhead doors pulled open to reveal a busy room with the thick air of anticipation about it. I moved into the room and over to my chair taking a seat while I watched my crew work.

'Miller, have you figured out our timing so we can join the battle at the right moment?'

'Yes Captain, we can leave whenever you are ready.'

'Good work, Richards, can you give me a communication's report?'

Richards turn to face me before he replied,

'All clear Captain, just a bit of chatter between the Falsec vessels but that is all. By the look of it, the planet is unaware of the oncoming attack.'

Andrew and Bartell entered the room as my first officer said,

'Captain good, you are here. I have uploaded the coordinates of the main Kalien colony into all of the landing ships computers and I can confirm that all of the Sole-light's crew are now aboard.'

'Good work, can you check if Hudson is ready?'

'Yes Sir, I will get onto it.'

I watched as Bartell moved over to the windows at the front of the bridge. He stared intensely out into space at his ship, so I moved over to his side and asked,

'Are you alright?'

Bartell didn't move as he replied in a low uninterested tone.

'Yes, I just don't think I should leave my ship drifting out there.'

I put my hand on his shoulder and replied,

'Look it is the way it needs to be; besides she will be found many years from now in the same state as you left her.'

'It still doesn't feel right.'

Andrew interrupted as he reported back to me.

'Captain, Hudson is back aboard and we are all set to leave.'

'Thank you Andrew.'

I could tell Bartell was unhappy with losing his ship, but it was time to make our move.

'Miller if we leave now, can you still make our jump out deadline?'

'Yes Captain, I will adjust our speed in the warp to compensate.'

'Good then go to yellow alert, raise the shields and arm all primary weapon systems. Miller, activate the jump engines and let's make our move.'

I watched the energy streams from our jump gate emitters grasp hold of the space ahead of us before they quickly ripped a hole through to the twisted red space known as the warp.

'Take us in and close the gateway behind us. Andrew you have the tactical post so keep your eyes open. I need to know if anything is out there.'

I heard my crew respond as our gateway closed behind us and we began our journey through the hellish looking red space. Bartell moved over to me before he asked uneasily,

'What in the creators name is this place?'

'It is known as the warp. It is a sort of condensed space or hell as many people have called it.'

'And you use this to travel?'

'It cuts days, months and years off of long space journeys. Trust me I don't like the place either, but it is required.'

The lost planet

'Captain, we are almost at the jump point.'

'Thank you Miller. Go to red alert and ready our primary weapon systems. Miller, open the jump gate on your call.'

'Yes Captain, opening the gateway in three, two, one.'

Miller activated the jump engines and the space in front of us was quickly torn open to reveal the blackness of space against the view of a stunning blue and green planet. Our ship quickly moved through the gateway and back into normal space, but before our gate was closed we were fired upon.

The ship shuddered again as my first officer said,

'Captain, two of the Falsec vessels are moving away from the planet and have their weapons locked on us.'

'Andrew, take your best shot and knock out their engines.'

'Yes Sir.'

Again the ship jolted from the incoming fire just as Andrew fired our main cannons. I watched as the powerful energy bolts shot across to the two enemy vessels. Each bolt tore through the enemy ships easily, leaving them drifting and burning in space.

'Captain, direct hit to both vessels, they are both now immobilised.

'Good work. Now Richards can you open me up a channel to the other ships?'

I got up and moved over to the holo ring, stepping into the first of the two rings built into the floor.

'Channel open Captain, but I cannot tell if they will be listening.'

I nodded in reply and then addressed the blank light projection in the other ring.

'This is the Hellfire, to all Falsec vessels. I order you to stand down and leave or you will be destroyed.'

I waited for a moment before Richards replied,

'Captain, I am getting no response from any of the Falsec ships. But I am receiving a call for help from the planet below.'

I turned to my first officer as I ordered.

'Ok Andrew, let's get their attention. Destroy one of the ships.'

Andrew confirmed my order before he again fired just one shot at one of the Falsec vessels. I watched as our main cannons fired and the energy bolts tore one of the Falsec vessels apart just as Richards stated,

'Captain, we are being hailed.'

'Put it through Richards.'

The blank light in front of me flicked as the flat image of a large menacing four legged insect like creature with many eyes and sharp pointed teeth now appeared in front of me.

'You speak the ancient language of the Light Warrior. Now who are you to dare to oppose the Darkness and their will to destroy all?'

I stood firm and replied in a strong tone.

'I am Captain Sharman of the battle cruiser Hellfire. This planet is now under my protection, you will withdraw or die.'

The creature laughed before it replied,

'This planet with suffer endless death until the Darkness strips this world of all that is useful.'

The communication cut while the image faded out, then Andrew gained my attention.

'Captain, the last vessel is firing a barrage of missiles at the planet.'

'Can you destroy them before they hit the surface?'

My first officer looked worried as he replied,

'No, there are too many and it looks like they are spreading evenly across the planet's land masses.'

Suddenly the ship jolted slightly so I ordered,

'Destroy that ship and then check the area for any incoming vessels.'

The ship jolted again before our main cannons fired finishing off the remaining ship.

'Captain the ship is destroyed and I am reading no other vessels within this sector.'

'What about the missiles?'

My first officer checked his console before he replied,

'All the missiles have hit the planet and none of them have exploded. But the scanner readout is showing that each impact zones life signs are going out.'

'Is it a chemical attack?'

Again Andrew checked with the console before he replied,

'The atmosphere is reading no hazardous chemicals, but the rate life readings are reducing by and the pattern the death toll is spreading. I would say we don't have long.'

I knew we would have to act fast and I had my suspicions to what was happening down there.

'Andrew, would you say the life rate is reducing much faster in the heavily populated areas?'

'Yes Captain, why?'

'The Falsec creature said, never ending death. Miller, take us into orbit. Andrew, you have the bridge and keep your eyes open for any incoming ships. I will take our landing crafts down to the planet and start to evacuate as many people as we can.'

I then turned and left the bridge heading straight for the hanger bay.

I entered the large hanger to find twelve troops standing ready and waiting for me to arrive. I moved over to the group as an older troop stepped forwards to greet me.

'Captain, we are ready and waiting.'

'Good, we don't have much time. Now I need to split us up into three groups, four troops for each ship. Once we land the troops for the two landing ships will cover the area and provide cover for our landing vessels while we evacuate the survivors. The troops in the shuttle will be with me and we will hunt for survivors and lead them your way. Are we all clear?'

All the troops replied clearly saying,

'Yes Sir.'

'Just one more thing, it is suspected we will be encountering a virus called the Death plague. If this is the case, shoot the infected in the head or you will be wasting ammo. Now let's move out, your pilots will give you more information on the way.'

The older troop split the group into three before they each move aboard one of the three ships. I follow a group of four into the shuttle Pay-Check and sat next to the pilot. She was a tall young girl with long blond hair that was tied back and platted, while her face held soft but strong features. I opened up the com link to the hanger control requesting clearance to depart. This was quickly confirmed before the gigantic hanger doors were pulled open to reveal the view of the planet below.

'Ok Riley, take us out of here.'

Our shuttle left the hanger deck just as the communication relay sounded. I answered the com while our ship left the Hellfire as it headed out into space.

'Pay-Check here.'

'Captain, I have completed the scan for chemical weapons and can confirm it is negative. But I am getting large amounts of slow movements from the areas of land with no or little life readings.

'Thank you Andrew, I guess we now know what we are dealing with. So I need you to get Richards to relay details of what the troops will be dealing with to the other ships. Tell him to use the report we took from the Nightfall and I will brief the troops here, Pay-Check out.'

I turned my chair around to face the troops before I addressed them.

'Ok I need you all to listen carefully. My First Officer has just confirmed what we will be facing. Now this is not to be taken lightly and may sound strange. The virus is not air born but it is very contagious and it has no cure. You will come across infected locals and they will be very dangerous. So don't let anyone infected get close, it takes only one bite or scratch to become infected and if that happens. Well then, it is all over for you. The virus kills the host and carries on living so that it can spread to another. The dead will feel no pain and can only be stopped if the brain is destroyed, any questions?'

A young tall trooper with short dark hair put up his hand, so I signaled for him to speak.

'Captain, so what will we do if we find anyone injured?'

'Mr. Renwick, if that happens we will have to assess if they are infected or not. That will mean that we will have to leave anyone found with the virus, any other questions?'

The group stayed silent so I continued.

'Ok Potts, Tyler and Renwick, you will all be with me. Stevens, I need you to stay with the ship. Riley, keep the ship's engines running just in case we need to take off quickly.'

Everyone confirmed the orders as Riley drew my attention.

'Captain we are coming in to land.'

'Thank you and good luck everyone.'

Riley flew our shuttle into a town like complex and landed the ship in an open area of the town. I got up from my seat and moved over to the door while I drew my sword.

'Ok troops, once that door opens we are to take this as a hostile and dangerous ground. So stay close and follow orders.'

I opened the door and moved out onto the alien world. I then quickly scanned my eyes around the area just as I heard the thunderous roar come from the engines of the two landing ships as they both set down to land behind our shuttle. Then the rest of the troops disembarked. I moved over to the troops before I split them into two groups, one to cover our ships and the other to spread out across the open court yard to provide cover while we picked up the survivors. As the troops moved into position I spotted a Kalien man peering out of one of the buildings windows.

'Potts, Renwick and Tyler, you are with me.'

I moved over to the building and tapped gently on the door. I could hear movement from within the building so I called out loud,

'Hello in there, I am Captain Sharman of the Hellfire. We are here to evacuate the colony.'

The door unlocked and opened just a few inches as the face of an elderly Kalien man hid behind it.

'Who sent you here and how do I know you are here to help?'

The man sounded scared in his speech so I pushed my sword back into its scabbard before I smiled kindly at him and replied,

'Sorry if we have come here heavy handed, but this world has been hit by the Death plague. I am here with ship's Prime, Bartell and we must evacuate as many people as we can before this world is lost. We are here to save life's.'

The old man stared deeply into my eyes before he opened the door and stepped out in front of me. I held out my hand and he took hold for just a moment before he then released his light grip and said,

'Sorry, I can feel your pain and your truth. I will gather my people Captain.'

'Thank you; please guide them to the landing ships. I fear we don't have a lot of time.'

'Of course now can I help you with anything more?'

I pulled the small Kalien computer pad out from my pocket and showed the list of names to the man as I pointed to just one name on the list.

'I need to find this Healer. Can you tell me where she is?'

'Yes, she is part of our colony and the female you are looking for is based in one of our outer settlements. It is four kelter from this town.'

I looked a little confused as I replied,

'I'm sorry but I am not familiar with Kalien terms of distance. Do you have a map?'

The man turned back into the building before he called for assistance. Within a moment a large fur covered creature with bear sized hands emerged with a small fragile looking device. The creature made a series of strange noises while it passed the device to the Kalien man.

'Thank you and you do not need to be afraid of these creatures, as they are here to help us.'

The large seven and half foot tall creature moved forwards into the doorway so I held out my hand. The creature looked down at me before it made a sort of low growl sound while it grabbed hold of me for a strong embrace lifting me off of the floor.

'Now remember how strong you are and put the male down.'

The creature put me down and stepped back while the old Kalien man continued to say,

'Now could you please be so good as to let the others know we need to leave.'

The creature sort of growled again before it turned and went back inside. Then the Kalien man pulled up some information on the small device before he showed it to me while he continued to say,

'Now the healing temple is here and we are in this settlement. The temple holds a mixture of Trellbeck and young Kaliens. There are also two teachers of the healing cast so you will be looking to pick up around sixteen to twenty soles from just the temple, provided the Death plague has not hit there yet.'

I could see the temple was located not far from where we had landed, but before I could reply screaming came from across the court yard.

I quickly turned to the troops before I ordered,

'Renwick, you are with me. Potts and Tyler, make sure these colonists get to one of the landing ships. Just keep the Pay-Check free and let Riley know we will be moving soon.'

With that order I turn and headed for the screaming just as gun fire could be heard. We both headed around a large stone building to find several large Trellbeck creatures attacking anything that moved. I could tell this was the start of the death plague due to the vacant but savage looks on the creatures' faces. I quickly drew my gun firing off just one shot at the closest creature. My shot blew the creature's head apart causing it to fall to the floor as I ordered,

'Renwick, aim for the head and take them down quickly.'

'Yes Captain.'

We both started to pick off the un-dead aliens one by one just as one of the Trellbeck smashed through a large wooden door. Immediately children could be heard screaming as a young Kalien girl attempted to stop it from gaining entree.

I ran toward the un-dead beast drawing my sword as it picked up the Kalien girl with ease. The large beast took a bite out of her side before it threw her like a rag doll across the street, where she lay still and lifeless. I closed in quickly taking a swing at the creature's neck with my twin bladed sword. The blades cut through its neck with a crunch causing its head to roll off to the floor still snarling while its large body crashed to the ground with a thud.

I turned to find Renwick had taken out the last of the un-dead for now as the court yard fell back into silence. I moved over to the severed head while its eyes looked around wildly and its jaw snapped at me. I quickly plunged my sword into its skull causing the thing to go still before I looked around at the devastation. I could see many injured Kaliens and Trellbeck lay scattered around the court yard moaning with pain as I realised that this settlement didn't have much time left.

'Renwick, keep your gun ready for any of the injured that may turn. I need to get these kids moved to safety.'

'You got it Captain, and please just call me Jack.'

'Ok Jack.'

I moved into the building to find a group of around eighteen children hiding behind a very scared looking Kalien woman. She was holding some sort of device that fitted over her hand, while she stood there shaking as she pointed the device at me, before shouting out,

'What in the makers name are you? And stay well back from these younglings.'

I lowered my sword as I said in a low calm voice,

'Hi, I'm here to help. Look I have a number of ships outside and we need to get everyone off of this planet.'

I could see the lady was still shaking as I moved slowly toward her, but before I could say anything more gun fire could again be heard from outside along with Jack's voice as he shouted out.

'Captain, I could really do with a hand out here.'

I turned back to the door as I replied,

'I'm on my way.'

I then looked at the scared lady before I said,

'Look lady, keep the children safe and I will be back shortly.'

I moved quickly back into the open to find most of the bitten were now starting to pull themselves up off the floor as they began to head for Jack. It was clear to see they had all turned by the rabid looks across all of their faces. Jack was picking off the un-dead one by one as they closed in on him so I moved over quickly cutting down the closest zombies with my sword. Once I reached Jack's side he said,

'I am so glad to see you.'

'I've got your back Jack, now let's not get mobbed. I will get the closest while you cover our immediate area.'

'Ok Captain.'

I could hear Jack's gun fire while I began to pick off the un-dead one by one with head shots to conserve ammo. I was now facing a group of about twelve zombies as I spotted two breaking off towards the school building. I knew we needed to act fast so I ordered,

'Jack, stay close. I'm moving back over to the school.'

'Yes Captain, I've got you covered.'

I began to move over to the school, fighting my way through the group of Trellbeck and Kalien zombies. I shot two more dead before I found I was too close to use my gun. I pulled up my sword cutting the heads from the closest un-dead as they grabbed at me.

'Captain, the back is clear.'

'Great now help take these out before we have an even bigger problem.'

Two shots passed close by me taking down another zombie as I realised we now had cover fire from more of my troops. I made a run for the school as the first of the un-dead Kaliens entered the building.

'Jack, put a call out to get one of the landing ships to put down here. Then tell the Pay-Check I need it here as well so we can make our way to the healing temple before it is too late.'

'I'm on it Captain, but what about the school?'

I was already running towards the zombies as I replied,

'Just leave that to me.'

I didn't look back while I removed one of the heads before I moved into the building. Again screaming could be heard from within the building just as I heard an energy shot fire, causing the zombie in front of me to fall to the floor still.

The Kalien woman stood shaking in front of me while the young Kalien and Trellbeck children coward behind her. I quickly moved over to her as she fell to her knees crying, so I asked,

'Are you alright?'

The woman looked up at me with tears in her eyes before she replied,

'What's happening here? She was my sister and she was trying to kill us.'

I held out my hand and pulled the woman to her feet as I replied,

'I'm sorry, but we need to leave now and get these children to safety. Now come on and I will explain all when you are safe.'

The Kalien lady was still shaking as she turned to the children and said,

'Younglings stay close and follow me.'

Her voice wobbled when she spoke and as I moved outside I could see the Pay-Check and one of the landing ships setting down close by. The thunderous roar of the engines filled the air as I turned to find the woman and children standing behind me looking completely lost and confused.

'It is ok, come with me.'

I took the lady by the hand and began to lead her over to the landing craft as the ship's main door lowered. The elderly Kalien man emerged from the ship and moved over to my side before he said,

'Captain, I will take it from here. Now please go and help the others.'

'Thank you and make sure you have all the children.'

The man smiled, then he took the woman's hand just as one of my troops came over to me. He stood in front of me in full salute before he stated.

'Captain, this town has gone to hell. We have un-dead everywhere and the infected are attacking anything that moves.'

'Ok Henderson, what is our status?'

'Good Captain, one of our landing ships has already left full of survivors, all checked and healthy. Once we have these kids this ship is also full.'

Gun fire could be heard again close by as I ordered,

'Great work, now once these children are aboard get them to safety and make sure we withdraw all our troops to a secure area while we save as many souls as we can. Then bring the landing ships back to pick up the last of the survivors.'

'Yes Captain. Do you need anything more from us?'

'No, I will take the Pay-Check and head over to the healing temple. Good luck.'

'No problem Captain. You can count on us.'

Henderson turned and headed over to the landing ship as I heard Jack shout over,

'Captain, we are ready to go.'

I made my way over to the Pay-Check before I moved aboard.

I hit the door close button and moved over to the cockpit where I sat down next to Riley before turning my chair around to face my troops.

'Great work out there Jack. Now listen up troops, things are starting to get very messy out there and I want to see you all back here alive. So we are heading over to the healing temple to pick up the Kalien healers first....'

My words were cut short as the ship's com beeped loudly before Riley answered it.

'Pay-Check here.'

'Good Riley, is the Captain with you?'

'Yes he is here.'

I turned to face the control console as I replied,

'What's the problem Andrew?'

'Captain there is something you should see, so I am sending the visual flight recording from Delta one. It picked up the creature Bartell says is a Death Dealer.'

'Ok, I will take a look.'

'No Captain, I mean Bartell has said that no one has ever survived an attack by one of these creatures.'

The console beeped so I began to watch the footage as I saw a huge creature knocking down trees with its long blade like front appendages.

'What the hell is that?'

Andrew replied over the com while he answered,

'It is a plague carrier and the Kaliens say that it is a creature from the Darkness home world, that has been infected with the virus we came across on the Nightfall. They also say that it is unstoppable.'

I continued to watch the footage as suddenly I got a clear view of the thing. It must have stood over twelve feet tall with six large pointed legs.

The creature also had two large front limbs that looked like stabbing weapons. But to make matters worse all of this was attached to a heavily armoured exoskeleton. I couldn't get a clear view of its large plated head as it tore through the woodland killing anything that got in its way. So I replied saying,

'Thanks for the tip off, we will try to avoid it.'

'That's just it Captain, each missile that hit the surface had several of these things in it and we don't know where they are. All that we do know is that one of the missiles hit near to the healing temple. So stay alert.'

'Noted, but trust me we don't plan on staying long, Pay-Check out.'

I turned to the troops and said,

I need you all to see this, then due to this new information we will now not be fully landing. So Potts, Renwick and Stevens, you are with me. Tyler, I need you to stay with the ship, cover us when we leave and again when you pick us up. Now Riley, once we are on the ground I need you to take the ship up to a safe distance until I call for a pick up.'

'Yes Captain.'

'Good so if anyone has any questions, now is the time.'

The troops stayed quiet, then Riley said,

'Captain, we are nearing a clearing, this is as close as I can get you to the temple. So are you ready?'

'Yes.'

I got up and moved over to the shuttle's door before reloading my G8 gun. I then turned to my troops, who had gathered behind me as I said,

'Ok, once we leave the ship I need you all to stay close. If it looks like we are going to get mobbed, then cover each other's backs and finally. No one breaks from the group unless I say so. Now ready your weapons and good luck out there.'

The troops readied themselves as the shuttle began to descend and I found myself concerned about our journey ahead.

Facing the dead

I opened the shuttle door as Riley called over,

'That's as low as I can take her Captain.'

I looked out to find the ground was now only about three feet below us so I ordered,

'Fall out troops.'

The three men quickly left the shuttle guns ready before I followed close behind them. My feet quickly hit the soft wet grassy earth and as I looked up, I found my troops already covering the immediate area around me. I stood up and pulled out a portable scanner checking the area for movement.

Nothing was reading close by as the Pay-Check lifted off high up into the air. The woodland became eerily still and the only thing that could be heard was the movement coming from my troops and the rustling of the trees around us while the Pay-Check's engines faded out to background noise.

'Ok troops, I'm not picking up any life signs or movement but that doesn't mean much right now. So Jack and Potts, take up the front. Steven's, cover our backs and let's move out.'

We started to move toward the temple at a good speed, as I knew we had a couple of miles to cover before we reached the complex. And I also didn't want to be this exposed for any longer than we needed to be. I kept checking the scanner as we moved deeper into the undergrowth, before suddenly the scanner beeped repeatedly.

I signaled for our team to stop while the scanner continued to beep with several movement patterns but no life readings.

'Captain what's up?' Jack asked with concern.

'Movement about twenty five meters ahead, it looks like around ten to twelve signals.'

'Survivors?' Potts asked.

'No, so ready your weapons.'

I drew my sword as groans began to emerge from the trees ahead. While the scanner continued to beep with the closing movement, the groaning became louder just as I could now see the movement was only a couple of meters away from us. Then the first of the zombielike Kaliens emerged into view.

The vacant look on the un-dead Kalien's face change to a wild look once it spotted us. Its groans became louder and its pace picked up as it began to stagger faster in our direction. Potts open fired with a single round, blowing the things head clean off. While the body continued to stagger forwards for a few steps before it then fell to the ground in a lifeless pile.

The sound of the gun shot echoed throughout the woodland but as it faded suddenly there was a rush of un-dead Kaliens and Trellbeck that emerged from the cover of the woodland, almost running in our direction.

'Take them down and quickly.' I ordered as the troops began to open fire with a barrage of energy bolts. The sound of gunfire filled the air while the un-dead were slowly cut down as they moved ever closer to my team. I took out the closest Kalien as it grabbed for Jack, removing its head with my sword. The severed head rolled off into the undergrowth still snapping its jaws just as I heard Potts cry out.

I cut down another zombie in my path before I turned to find a Trellbeck quickly overpowering Potts. He struggled to fend off the over sized fur covered, rabid corpse as I moved over with urgency, while the beast forced Potts to the ground. In desperation I plunged my sword into its skull with a crunch as it lashed out with its oversized arm knocking me several feet back into the undergrowth. I quickly grabbed for my G8, pointing it at another of the closing zombies before I fired off two shots tacking it down. Potts pulled himself to his feet before he started firing wildly at the remaining un-dead. I picked myself back up as fast as I could to find the last of the zombies had now fell to ground, causing the gun fire to stop.

The area around us fell back into a relative silence other than the movement from my team and the remains of disembodied heads that still snapped at us from the earthy ground.

I quickly checked myself for injuries and sighed with relief, but as I looked around it was more than I could say for my scanner that lay smashed on the ground. I then moved back over to the dead Trellbeck before I pulled my sword from its skull with another crunch.

'Is everyone ok?'

Stevens and Jack quickly confirmed that they were unharmed while Potts seemed distracted.

'Potts, are you alright?'

He looked back at me as he replied with an unsure tone to his words,

'Yea, yea, it just caught me off guard. I'm fine.'

'Ok good, now the gun fire seems to have drawn them into us. So I need everyone to stay alert, now let's get moving.'

I quickly realised that without the scanner I didn't know which way we needed to be heading. So as I set off in the direction we had been heading in before the attack. I pulled my com link from my belt and opened up a channel to the Pay-Check saying,

'Riley, do you read me?'

'Loud and clear Captain, what can I do for you?'

'The scanner got smashed when we had a run in with some of the infected. I need you to keep us going in the right direction.'

There was a moment's pause before Riley's voice can back over the com.

'Captain, you all seem to be heading in the right direction. But to make sure I will fly the Pay-Check over to the healing temple and hover above. Then I will send you a homing signal to your com link. It will beep faster when you are heading in the right direction. Is that ok for you?'

I smiled to myself before I replied,

'Sounds like a plan. Also can you tell if the un-dead that we ran into came from the temple? I know it is a long shot.'

'Sorry Captain, all I know is that there is a collection of buildings not far from your position but it is not reading any life signs.'

'Thanks Riley, just let me know when you are over the temple.'

'Yes Captain and I will send you the signal now, Pay-Check out.'

A slow steady beep began to sound from my com link and as we continued to walk its speed increased very gradually.

We had covered a lot of ground and only run into a few more of the un-dead Trellbeck creatures as I noticed that Potts was starting to sweat heavily as he moved ahead of me.

'Potts, what's wrong?'

He didn't answer, then he suddenly stopped and stood still just a few feet in front of us.

'Potts report, what have you seen?'

Again no reply as we all stopped in our tracks. Then he suddenly dropped his gun before he began to moan. I signaled for the rest of my team to hold back before I stepped forwards with my sword drawn ready. Again I called out but louder this time.'

'Potts, I need you to say something and now.'

My voice got his attention but as he turned around it was clear that the man I knew as Potts was gone. I could see the emptiness in his eyes before it turned to rage and he began to move towards me.

His eyes turned black before he lunged for me trying to bite. I had no choice but to cut him down as I thrust my sword at his head. The twin blades stuck deep into his skull before his body became lifeless and fell to the ground. I pulled my sword from his head before I turned to the rest of my team.

They both looked as shocked as they looked uneasy before I said,

'Ok keep this area covered while I find out what happened to him.'

The troops moved in closer while I examined his dead body. It didn't take me long to find a bite mark on his chest. So I pulled out my com link and opened up a channel,

'Riley, we have lost Potts.'

'What happened, Captain?'

'It looks like he was bitten on our last big run in with the infected. I had to put him down. Can you do me a favour and pass it on to the Hellfire, saying he died saving others.'

'Of course Captain, but I have to warn you that you are near the temple and I am reading a lot of movement with very few life readings.'

I sighed as I realised that we would have a long fight ahead of us if we ran into any more trouble, so said,

'Riley, Thanks for the tip off and can you tell me what we may be facing?'

'Well it looks like there are ten life readings coming from within the temple and one from just outside of it in the nearby forest. But as for the movement, well it looks like it is focused on the area around the main building. I cannot get exact numbers as the movement patterns keeps stopping and starting, but at a guess I would say you could be looking at around a hundred infected, maybe more.'

'Ok we will head for the group first, and keep me informed.'

'Yes Captain, and good luck down there.'

The com line cut as I turned to my two remaining troops before I said,

'Jack, take Potts's weapons and ammo. Then both of you stay close, I don't want to lose anyone else out here.'

I watched while Jack took the weapon and shared the ammo between them before we continued towards the temple at a good speed.

Temple of the dammed

The three of us continued to move through the thick woodland until we came to a small break in the trees. I could see a collection of buildings in front of us standing in the shadow of the tall stone temple that towered above them. As I looked up I could now see why we could not have landed here due to the lack of space to put a shuttle down on. The building surrounding the temple were all tightly packed together with little more than a meter space between them, while the tower seemed to have no real platforms to land on. We moved out of the woodland and stood just in front of the first two buildings. I could see that the confined space maybe a problem and without the scanner, we would have no idea of what would possibly be all around us. So I turned off the beeping to my com link before I opened up a channel to the Pay-Check.

'Riley, can you give me an idea of how to get into the temple?'

'Yes Captain, if you take one of the pathways between the buildings and continue forwards for about fifty meters, you should come to the outer wall of the temple. Then you will need to follow the wall to your right for about eighteen meters until you come to the temple's main entrance.'

'Sounds good, but what about the infected?'

'I cannot tell for sure, the movement patterns keep fading on and off of the scanners. Just be careful.'

'What about the survivors?'

'That is easy, they are all held up on one of the higher levels of the temple. So once you are in, just head up until you find them. Can I help you with anything more Captain?'

'No thanks, just stay ready.'

I cut the com line and turned to my two troops as I knew things would get more dangerous from here on in.

'Ok let's make this as easy as we can. Now we know that the sound of our guns seem to attract the infected toward us. So do either of you have a bladed weapon?'

'I do Captain.' Stevens replied as he pulled a large military style dagger from his boot. I turned to Jack to find that he was looking a little lost as he shook his head as if to say no.

'Ok then, Stevens cover our backs. Jack, keep your gun ready just in case we need some firepower and I will lead. Now let's move out and stay alert.'

Both troops confirmed my orders as we began to move into the narrow path between the buildings. All was quiet until an infected Kalien man staggered out in front of me. It limped as it staggered forwards due to it walking on the stump of its leg. I could see that its foot had been torn off. But this didn't seem to faze it, as it groaned while heading straight for me.

I moved quickly forwards towards the drooling Kalien man before I plunged my twin bladed sword into its torn head with a crunch. Then I quickly removed the blade as the now dead Kalien fell to the floor silent. We continued along the narrow pathway and were now around half way through, just as a window smashed at my side and an oversized Trellbeck grabbed at me from the broken window with its large bear like hands.

Jack staggered back a few steps before he opened fired with his gun, firing off several shots at the hairy beast. The shots blasted the thing back into the building but the sound from the gun suddenly seemed to bring the whole place to life.

Infected Kaliens and Trellbeck now seemed to pour out from every door, window and opening. It looked like we were going to get mobbed, but the narrow pathway seemed to be our saviour. The un-dead built up quickly both in front and behind us as I ordered,

'Jack, help me clear a pathway ahead. Stevens, keep them off of our backs.'

I pulled my G8 gun from its holster firing off a shot at the closest zombie. The large shell took down the first of the Terllbeck as it tore off its head while Jack started to fire.

We pushed forwards towards the temple as I could hear my com link beep repeatedly while more of the un-dead seem to gather around us. I could see the temple wall just a few feet away from us as I now shot zombies at point blank range while using my sword to take out the overwhelming numbers. Jack's gun clicked empty as Stevens shouted over to me,

'Captain, there are too many. We need to move.'

Jack reloaded as I again slashed out in front of us knocking down three more of the infected. I could see a large stain glass window in front of us and this gave me an idea.

'Jack, fire off a full clip of ammo to clear our way ahead then both of you follow me.'

Panicked Jack replied saying,

'Follow you where?'

Just fire and clear the way ahead.'

As he opened fired with a continuous barrage of energy bolts, I pointed my G8 at the stained glass window. Pulling the trigger several times I blasted the window into pieces. Brocken glass sprayed the area covering the unfazed infected as they continued to grab for us. But just then there came a blood curdling screech from behind me.

'Captain, we have another problem.'

I turned to find a Death Dealer starting to gain on us as its large front bladelike appendages began to tear through the building to get at us. I quickly cut down two more of the un-dead while I shouted out,

'Get into the temple now, come on move.'

We continued to fight through the mass of enraged infected while my com continued to beep repeatedly. I was becoming tired as we reached the wall to find the window was four foot off of the floor.

'Get into the building now.' I ordered before I turned to take out another zombie with my sword. The Death Dealer was now only about twenty meters away as I check my gun.

I had eight shots left before I needed to reload and as I turned to find both of my troops climbing through the broken window. I again turned back slashing out at another oversized Trellbeck, severing its head from its body. I needed some space so I fired off the rest of the ammo in my G8 before I returned my weapons to their holders and climbed up the stone wall to the window ledge.

Jack and Stevens both stood just inside of the building on the ledge as they fired off a round of covering fire. While I pulled myself into the building and moved out into the churchlike room as I ordered,

'Move clear of the window and back into the room.'

Both of my troops jumped down from the window as again the terrifying screech came from just outside of the building. I reloaded my G8 gun as both of my troops moved over to my side.

'What now Captain? Stevens asked.

I could see the infected, starting to pull themselves up onto the window ledge. So I ordered,

'Reload and keep them out while I find a way out of here.'

'You got it Captain.'

Both troops reloaded and began to fire. I looked around the large open empty room but before I had a chance to think, the whole building shuck and I found myself turning back to face the broken window. The Death Dealer was now looking in as its large serrated front limbs tore chunks from the stone window frame while it tore its way into the building.

'Captain, what the hell are we going to do about that?'

Both troops were firing at the creatures head, but their shots were having no effect.

'Just focus on the smaller zombies and fall back. I will take care of it.'

My troops continued to fire at the Kalien and Trellbeck zombies as I looked around. I could see that the upper floor was held up by loads of stone evenly placed pillars and this gave me another idea.

'Troops fall back to the central support column.'

Both men moved over to the centre of the room just as the Death Dealer burst fully into the building. I pointed my G8 gun at the first pillar in front of it and fired off several shots. This smashed the pillar to pieces causing some of the stone to hit the creature in the face. The creature lashed out smashing another pillar as I again shot out a third.

Suddenly the roof above caved in on top of the Death Dealer crushing it to the floor. The pile of smashed stone seemed to cover the hellish creature and blocked off the smashed window at the same time. The room then fell into silence just before Stevens shouted out,

'Hell yea, no one can kill a Death Dealer but our Captain, right!'

My com was still beeping so I pulled it from my belt before I opened the channel to hear Riley's desperate voice.

'Captain, is that you?'

'Reading you loud and clear, what's the problem?'

'I spotted a Death Dealer heading in your direction. Then all hell broke out down there before all of your life sign became very weak. Is everyone alright?'

'Yes we are all ok and that creature shouldn't bother us anymore.'

'Ok Captain, but you have another problem. It looks like the noise from the shoot out has drawn the attention of all the infected in the area and you have them heading in your direction.'

'Ok Riley, thanks for the tip off.'

'No Captain, you don't understand. You have what looks like thousands of them heading into the complex now and another Death Dealer as well.'

I knew this wasn't good as we needed to get back out so we could leave the planet.

'Riley, can you try to draw some of them away. Get Tyler to shoot at a few of them, hopefully it will draw their attention away from us.'

Just then the stain glass windows all around the temple began to grow dark as if the light from outside was being blocked by some sort of solid object. Banging started to come from all of the windows around us as Riley replied.

'I guess that is them, I will do my best for you Captain.'

The com cut just as the first of the windows smashed and as I turned to see what it was. I was horrified to see hoards of infected Trellbeck forcing their way into the room. I looked around for a way to escape just as a second window caved in under the weight of the unrelenting oversized beasts.

I looked around and found that the centre of the large hall we were standing in was filled with a sturdy stone structure that had one door.

'Jack, Stevens, head for that door and save your ammo.'

Both troops ran for the door as I followed behind them, again two more of the windows smashed as more of the un-dead poured into the building, climbing over each other while trying to get to us. We reached the door quickly and I was surprised to find that it was unlocked. Pushing it open I could see a spiral stair case heading up so I ordered,

'Both of you head up the stairs now.'

My troops ran through the doorway and disappeared out of sight just as several more windows smashed while more of the Trellbeck poured in. I didn't wait to see what was going to happen next as I ran through the door while the screech of another Death Dealer could be heard behind me. I turned around and closed the door to find that it had no lock and with nothing around to block the door with I just ran up the stairs at my best speed.

We all headed up the stairway until we emerged from the floor of another large room. This room was filled with bookcases, tables and chairs. But the stairwell had no hatch and as I looked back I could see the first of the dead Trellbeck following close behind.

'Jack, Stevens, pull some of those book cases over here to block the stairs.'

Both troops began to push the closest heavy wooden bookcase over as the first zombie emerged from the opening. I quickly pointed my G8 at the thing as it reached for Jack before I fired off one shot at the creature as it snapped at him with its jaws. The blast knocked the hairy corpse back down the stairwell and on top of another of the zombies while it climbed the stairs. Jack and Stevens quickly pushed over the large bookcase crushing another of the zombies before it could enter the room. Then I watched as the two men dragged over a heavy wooden table before they both lifted it on top of the over turned bookcase. We all sighed with relief before Jack's eyes widened as he said in an uneasy voice,

'Captain, look behind you.'

He pointed behind me and as I turned around I was faced with a young trembling pale blue skinned Kalien male. He was holding some sort of device that seemed to fit over his hand and he was pointing it at me while he trembled. The zombie Trellbeck were now banging heavily on our makeshift barrier so I said,

'It's ok, we are here to help.'

The young Kalien male's voice shook as he blurted out,

'Stay back; I know how to use this.'

Both Stevens and Jack raised their guns as I held up my hand to signal for them to hold back.

'Put the weapon down kid, we are not here to hurt you.'

I stepped forwards before I slowly put my hand out to take the device. But the Kalien male just stepped back away from me as he trembled with fear.

'Calm down, we don't want to hurt you.'

'Stay back, I don't know what you are, and if you caused this. Then....then....'

I could see Stevens working his way around behind the child while I held his attention.

'It's ok kid, trust me.' I said as again the young male shouted out,

'Stay back or I will fire this thing.'

Stevens quickly grabbed the young Kalien as I went for the device, but the moment I touched it the weapon discharged firing off a thin blue light that clipped my side, burning straight through my clothing. The pain was sharp and continued to burn as the young Kalien dropped the weapon. I pulled back placing my hand over the wound while it felt like it was still burning. Jack raised his gun so I shouted over to him,

'Let him go, he is just a kid and scared at that.'

Stevens released the kid and he ran off, before Stevens then picked up the weapon from the floor. He looked at it puzzled as he said,

'Captain, the thing has gone dead, no power at all.'

He began to move towards me just as a calm voice of another male came from behind him.

'I'm surprised it fired at all. That device has sat in a glass cabernet for the last few hundred years.'

Jack pointed his gun at the man and again I signaled for both of my troops to stand down while the Kalien man walked over to Stevens and took the weapon from him, before he continued to say,

'Still it looks to be drained now. So who and what are you?'

I stepped forwards still holding my side as I replied,

'I am the Captain of the Hellfire and these are two of my troops, Stevens and Renwick. I have a ship in orbit and we are here to take you to safety.'

The Kalien man remained un-fazed by my words as he replied,

'And what makes you think I would believe you?'

I could still hear the banging on the makeshift barrier and knew we were wasting time as I replied firmly,

'Look there are hundreds if not thousands of infected Trellbeck out there trying to get in. Now if I wanted to kill you; you would already be dead and if you want to become zombie food then fine. We will leave, but not before I have the girl called Starlight.'

The mention of her name seemed to get his attention before he said,

You had all better come with me.'

He turned and left the room, so I signaled for my troops to follow.

Death will not stop

We followed the Kalien man through many stone corridors and up many flights of stairs before we were led to a small room fill with bookshelves a table, chair and window on the back wall. A small frail looking old Kalien man sat at the desk with his eyes fix on a book. There was a scattering of books all over the room, some open but most closed. The younger man we had been following spoke up as he said,

'Great Healer, we have guests looking for the youngling called Starlight.'

The frail old man looked up from his book with a look of astonishment on his withered face. I watched as he got up from his desk slowly, before he moved around the table while his eyes remained transfixed at our presents, then he smiled and said,

'I never thought I would see you again my old friend and time seems to have been very good to you.'

I was shocked by his words but before I could reply he continued to say,

'You appear to be injured. I will find some bindings until I can get Starlight to you.'

He then turned to the other Kalien man before he stated,

'You can bring me some bindings and the youngling called Starlight to my office.'

The Kalien man now suddenly became very uneasy as he said in a low voice,

'Great Healer, she is not in the temple. She left to gather herbs from the forest for the Trellbeck before the virus broke out and we had to seal off the temple doors before she returned.'

'You mean to tell me you let a nineteen year old youngling leave the temple alone and then you sealed the temple before she had returned.'

'Well yes, but...'

'Save your words. You have greatly disappointed me Tallos, now go and bring the bindings.'

'Yes Great Healer.'

The man left quickly before I asked,

'So is there another way out of this temple, other than the main gate?'

The man looked at me with a kindly smile before he replied,

'No, not unless you can fly us all out of here. There is the landing pad on the twenty-fifth floor or the main gate. That is all.'

I turned to my troops as I ordered,

'Stevens, Renwick, head back down to the room with the book cases and check it is still secure.'

'Right away Captain.' Stevens replied before both men turned to leave the room while I added,

'And don't take any chances, if we have a breach, find a way to slow them down and get out of there.'

'You got it Captain.' Jack replied as they both quickly left the room. I found myself alone with the elderly Kalien man as he enquired,

'So Captain, how are you going to get us all out of this one?'

This didn't seem to difficult as I confidently answered,

'I have a shuttle, so if we get everyone up to the landing pad then we should be able to just leave safely from there.'

The Kalien man sighed, then he sat back down in his chair before he looked up at me and replied in an uneasy tone.

'Then we have another problem. The power to this building was cut during the plagues outbreak. Without power there is no way to lower the landing pad, so your shuttle can land. I am afraid that if the lower area of this building is overrun with the dead, then we are trapped.'

I needed a plan, but before I had a chance to think a voice came from behind me saying,

'The bindings you asked for Great Healer.'

I watched as the younger male passed the bandages to the elderly man just as gun fire could be heard throughout the building from the floors below.

'It looks like the infected have broken in. We need to move everyone to the landing pad now.' I stated as Tallos butted in saying,

'But the landing pad is completely inoperable, we will be trapped.'

'Just leave that to me.'

Tallos was just about to contest my words as the elderly man spoke up in a strong tone of voice.

'Do as he asks Tallos and quickly. We have lost too many already.'

Tallos left the room with a low level mutter to himself while I pulled my com link from my belt.

'Riley, can you locate the lone lift form, outside of the temple?'

'Yes Captain, why?'

'It's Starlight. I want you to fly over to her and tell her I sent you. Get the shuttle as low as you can and she should be able to fly up to you from there. Then get back here, I will make sure the landing pad is open for you to put down on.'

'Ok Captain, but I have to warn you that it looks like you have thousands of infected swarming into your location, including a couple more Death Dealers.'

This was something I already knew as I replied,

'Thanks for the warning, but pick Starlight up first. I need some time to figure out how we can lower the landing pad.'

'Ok Captain, I will be as fast as I can, Pay-Check out.'

The com cut just as both of my troops ran back into the room short of breath.

'Captain, we cannot hold them off, far too many of them. We blocked the hallway but it won't last long.'

'Great work, now both of you make sure we get everyone up to the landing pad and quickly.'

I watched as my men left the room again while the elderly Kalien man moved over to my side before he said,

'Captain, you need to get that injury seen to.'

'I know but we don't have time, and you seem to have me at a disadvantage.'

The man smile as he un-wrapped the bandage while he replied,

'I guess this is your first meeting with me and it makes much more sense this time around, my old friend. I am Astrail and I have known you for many years.'

I held out my hand as I replied,

'Good to meet you Astrail, now we need to move.'

Astrail smiled as he said,

'Not before I look at that wound my old stubborn friend.'

I knew he was right so I removed my coat and raised my shirt. As I looked down I could see that the gun shot had just clipped my side cauterizing the flesh. But it was deep and I could just see some of one of my ribs showing through the burnt tissue.

Astrail looked at the wound before he said,

'This must be dealt with now. I did not think the power of the shot would have done so much damage.'

'Of course power, Astrail just bind the wound for now, I have an idea.'

'But this needs to be seen too.'

'I know but later. Now that weapon, does it still hold any power or do you have any more we can use?'

Astrail began to dress the wound as he spoke,

'No, it is the only one and it is yours. It was built during the first Darkness war on our home planet. The weapon responds to you and you only.'

'So how did that kid use it to shoot at me?'

Astrail tied the bandages as he looked up at me and replied,

'You must have touched the weapon.'

I remembered the confrontation before I was shot and the moment it happened. Stevens had grabbed hold of the kid as I went for the weapon. I did touch it and this gave me an idea.

'That will hold for now, how do you feel?'

I pulled my shirt down and pulled on my coat as I replied,

'I'm ok, and thank you.'

I moved over to the weapon as Jack ran back into the room.

'Captain, you two are the last people down here and we don't have much time.'

'What's the problem Jack?'

He looked unease as he replied saying,

'Well Stevens built another barrier while I started to move people up to the landing pad, but the zombies have already started to pound on it.'

'So will it hold?'

I could see the unease grow even before he answered,

'Not for long, maybe five or ten minutes at the most.'

'I guess that means we need to leave. Get Stevens and head up to the landing pad, we will follow.'

'He has already left and said I should come get you both.'

'Ok then lead the way.' I replied making a hand gesture.

Jack headed back out of the door while I grabbed the alien weapon, before we both followed him out of the room and up more stairs.

Over run and out of time

We reached the twenty fifth floor of the temple and emerged from the staircase into a long narrow corridor with an arched roof. It seemed to run about one hundred meters across to a large open door at the other end. We crossed the space quickly even though I was finding it painful to run with the burning from the gunshot wound to my side. I could also see that Astrail was aware of my discomfort by the manner he held towards me, still he didn't say anything.

We moved into the large cargo area where all of the other Kaliens were waiting just as Stevens shouted over from the doorway,

'Captain, we have incoming.'

I turned back to find the far end of the corridor was now filled with a mixture of Kalien and Trellbeck zombies. I knew time was now running short as Jack asked,

'What are we going to do Captain? I don't think we have enough ammo left to fight them all off.'

I could see the desperate look on the young troopers face so I turned to Astrail and asked.

'You know this building right?'

'Yes, very well. Why?'

'So what is under that corridor?'

Astrail looked around before he answered,

'A large open meditation room, why?'

I held up the strange weapon in front of him before I then asked,

'Can this thing blast a large hole in the floor?'

'I do not know, why don't you put it on and find out.'

I looked at the strange device that seemed to be both metal and organic before I took hold of the handgrip. Then before I could move the device began to power up, the organic panels extended outwards from the gun as it wrapped its self around my wrist. Just as the weapon lit up and began to hum while a computer like female voice stated,

'Welcome back Captain.'

I looked around and I said out loud,

'Who said that?'

'Said what Captain?' Jack replied with confusion.

Astrail tapped me on the shoulder as he said,

'It is the weapon, it works from a telepathic link. Only you can hear it. Just point it and think of what you want it to do. It should then operate as you pull the trigger.'

I turned back to look at the corridor now filled with approaching un-dead aliens. I could see that Jack was right. There was no way we could fight off that many infected and they were to close now too try blocking the doorway. I quickly pointed the alien weapon at the massing un-dead as I thought we needed a rapid fire energy weapon. The front of the weapon changed shape to create three barrels before I pulled the trigger.

Suddenly the weapon fired a constant stream of blue energy bolts, while I continued to hold the trigger. I adjusted aim taking out the front few rows of un-dead until there was a pile of now dead corpses. I released the trigger as I heard Stevens shout out.

'Hell yea, where can I get one of those?'

But again before I could reply the infected were already starting to climb over the mass of bodies. I knew we couldn't hold them for long so I pointed the weapon at the floor as I thought that I needed a powerful energy blast to blast through the stone floor.

Again the barrel changed shape but this time it created three pointed emitter like spikes as the voice in my head said,

'Pull the trigger until you have the power build up required, then disengage the trigger to fire the shot Captain.'

I pointed the weapon at the floor of the corridor just in front of the massing zombies before I pulled the trigger. The gun vibrated as an orange energy sphere began to build between the emitters. I continued to hold the trigger while the emitters extended outwards and the ball of energy continued to grow.

'Energy output will reach maximum capacity in ten second Captain.' The voice stated in my head.

With this I let go of the trigger causing the weapon to kick back with a powerful jolt, while it fired the massed energy ball. The large sphere shot out across the corridor towards the horde of un-dead, hitting the floor with a powerful explosion. The blast throw the horde of un-dead backwards as it smashed through the floor causing the building to shake for just a moment. I turned away as the blast exploded covering my eyes and when I turned back, I could see that there was now a large hole where the floor used to be.

The horde of infected began to pull themselves back up off the floor as again they began to head in our direction. But this time as they reached the hole in the floor they stopped, reaching out towards us while the mass behind them pushed them forwards into the hole. Jack, Stevens and I moved over to the hole peering in to find the zombies starting to pile up on the floor below.

I pulled back into the room while ordering,

'Stevens, Jack, find something to barricade that door with while I work on the landing pad. I released my grip of the handle causing the gun to power down before I turned to Astrail and asked,

'Where is the access panel to the landing pad?'

Astrail replied as he moved over to the other side of the room, where a large piece of machinery stood.

'Follow me, but I must tell you that it is the power the mechanism is lacking and not a technical problem.'

'I know and I have an idea, now let's see what we have here.'

I knelt down with an involuntary moan from the gunshot wound on my side as I heard jack call over.

'Are you alright Captain?'

'Yes, just keep those things out of here for as long as you can.'

I then prised off the front panel while I heard Jack reply before I began to look through the mass of circuits and wiring, until I found the two main power cables to the landing pad motors. I ripped the cables from the main powerless feed just as I heard a quiet voice behind me say.

'Can I help you with anything?'

I didn't look up while I continued to make sure I had the right set of cables, as replied saying,

'Not unless you have a power generator I can use.'

'Ho, sorry I didn't mean to interrupt.'

I looked up to find the young Kalien male who had shot me earlier, standing there looking uneasy. I smiled kindly at him while I could see the fear on his face before I replied,

'It's ok, you can help me shortly once I have this thing rigged to work.'

I turned back to the open panel before I continued to rig the landing pad while the young Kalien said,

'I didn't mean to shoot you. I didn't think the gun worked anymore.'

'It's alright you weren't to know. Now if you can operate to landing pad from its controls, I should be able to power the landing pad with this.'

I picked up the alien weapon as the young male said,

'But isn't that going to be dangerous?'

'Probable, but it's the only way any of us are going to get out of here. Now can you activate the landing pad to lower once the power comes on?'

'Yes I think so.'

I watched the young male moved over to the control pad before Astrail showed him what he needed to do, then when he gave me a signal to say they were ready I held the handle. The gun again wrapped around my wrist before the voice returned saying,

'Welcome back Captain.'

'Hello.' I said in return while I passed the thought of what I wanted the weapon to do. Again the voice in my head replied saying,

'Captain, this is not a recommended course of action. I was not created to operate in this manner.'

I again replied in my head as I thought. I know, but it is the only way I can save all of these people. I need this to work.

There was a pause before the gun replied to me saying,

'I have disengaged my safety override.'

'Thanks' I said out load as the barrel split into two energy emitters before the gun continued to say,

'Pull the trigger, but be aware that I will only be able to hold the energy feedback from you for a short time. Good luck Captain.'

'You too and thank you.' I replied before attaching the power cables to the gun. Then I pulled and held the trigger.

The gun suddenly kicked back as the power fed into the system. This was followed by a loud bang before the wall to my left began to lower slowly. I looked up to see the sky through the opening and I smiled to myself before I ordered.

'Jack, get Riley on an open channel and tell her to be ready to land.'

I hear Jack confirm my order while the weapon I was holding began to heat up. I looked down to find that the emitter spikes were now glowing with heat from the power buildup while sparks began to spit out from the device. I again looked up to find the landing pad was now about one quarter open just as the Pay-Check came into view before hovering over the opening.

My hand was becoming uncomfortably hot just as weapons fire came from over by the door to the corridor.

'Captain, can you speed things up over there. That mass of infected are starting to climb out of the hole that is now full.'

Stevens, voice was panicked as I continued to power the platform through gritted teeth. The gun's heat was now starting to burn my hand before it said,

'Captain, I cannot hold back the power feedback for much longer.'

I replied to the gun in my mind saying,

'Just a bit longer now.'

Before I shouted over to Stevens saying,

'Just hold them back for now and get everyone as far from the doorway as you can.'

My order was confirmed and I again found myself looking up to find the platform was now about half open, then the gun stated to me.

'Captain, power buffers at maximum capacity, disengage now.'

'Just a little longer.'

I could still hear gun fire from my troops and I looked up to find Jack sending the Kaliens up to the shuttle one by one. I watched each Kalien fly up to my shuttle while it hovered close to the opening just as the gun kicked back from the system with a large and powerful bang.

I was hit with a jolt of power that throw me back across the room with force, before I came to a stop as I hit something hard.

I couldn't feel anything for a moment as I saw Astrail pull Jack back while he said,

'Let the energy dissipate first, before you touch him.'

I felt num as the barrier began to cave in under the weight of the zombies. Before Jack began to fire at the infected as they forced their way into the room. Stevens continued to fight the overwhelming odds in vain as Jack looked over at the platform before he pulled his com from his belt and opened up a channel saying,

'Riley, can you use the shuttle to force the platform down?'

The zombies were now in the room as I began to pull myself back to my feet. Astrail moved over to helped me just as there was a heavy thud followed by a grinding of metal and groans while the shuttle forced the platform down further.

Jack continued to give Stevens some covering fire while he shouted.

'Stevens, come on we have to leave.'

Astrail helped me over to the shuttle before leading me up the steep platform to the open door of my ship while he asked with concern.

'Are you alright my old friend?'

'Yes, but I feel kind of tingly all over.'

'That is to be excepted, now we must go.'

I looked back at my troops as they held back the massing horde of infected Trellbeck while hundreds of them pushed their way into the room. Gunfire suddenly came from behind us as Tyler began to lay down some covering fire to keep back the horde. I lifted the alien weapon I was still holding to find it was now still and lifeless, passing it to Astrail I said,

'Take this and get aboard the shuttle, I will provide some covering fire while my troops pull back.'

Astrail put his hand on my shoulder then he smiled before he turned and boarded the shuttle. Quickly I drew my old G8 gun firing off several shots into the mass before I shouted over,

'Stevens, Jack, fall back. We have to leave now.'

Jack pulled back while Stevens continued to fight the infected mass of aliens at point blank range now.

'Stevens, fall back that is an order.'

Stevens continued to fire at the mass as he replied,

'Sorry Captain, but no can do. I got bitten back at the last barrier while building it. Is everyone aboard?'

Both Jack and I were now standing at the doorway to our shuttle as I replied,

'Yes, everyone is safe. Is there anything I can do?'

We both continued to give him covering fire while he answered.

'Just get out of here and make sure you tell my wife I finally did something good for someone. Besides I have a little present for these monsters.'

Stevens pulled out a grenade and I could tell it was a fusion hand bomb.

'Where the hell did you get that?'

'I have always had it. My gift to whatever finally got the better of me. Now go if you want to live.'

I watched as he pulled the pin while he shouted,

'Who the hell wants to live forever anyway? Aharrr....'

Both Jack and I turned and dived aboard the shuttle as I shouted over,

'Riley, get us out of here now, fire in the hole.'

Riley started to pull the shuttle away just as there was a large exposition that jolted the ship hard. Alarms began to sound so I quickly moved over to the co pilots' seat.

'What the hell was that?' Riley asked while she struggled with the controls.

'Fusion hand bomb, don't ask. Now is the ship ok?'

Riley steadied the shuttle before she answered my question.

'Well we are still in the air, but the landing control has been damaged between the blast and me forcing the platform open. We will be ok as long as we don't have to land.'

'Good work.'

I turned back to look at the group of Kaliens looking for Starlight.

'Did you pick Starlight up?'

Riley looked uneasy as she replied,

'No Captain, she has hurt her wing and cannot fly. Should I get another ship to pick her up?'

The communication's console began to sound before I could reply while Riley opened up the channel answering it,

'Pay-Check here.'

The deep voice of my first officer could be heard as he asked,

'Do you have the Captain with you yet?'

'I'm here, well just about. What is going on up there?'

There was a serious tone to his words as he replied,

'Captain, we have a new problem.'

'What is it?'

'We have picked up five large unidentified vessels. Bartell tells me that they are Darkness death ships. Are you on your way back up to the ship yet?'

This was not good to hear so I replied,

'Not yet, I still need more time. So how long have we got?'

'It looks like they will enter the system in around one hour. But I would recommend that we leave as soon as possible due to the number of civilians we now have aboard.'

'Understood, I will be as fast as I can. Just get the ship ready to leave.'

'Yes Captain, and don't take too long, Hellfire out.'

The com cut before Riley turned to me saying,

'Captain, we are over the area Starlight is hiding and I should be able to hold the ship steady for a short time.'

'Good, just give me a moment.'

I got up and moved over to the door opening it before I looked out over the thick wooded area. I couldn't see Starlight so called out,

'Starlight, where are you?'

The tree directly below rustled as Starlight came into view from the branches. My heart jumped at the sight of her, but I could see the fear on her face and it was clear that one of her wings was badly broken.

'Starlight, I need you to trust me, can you climb up higher so I can bring you aboard?'

Starlight looked around before she then replied saying,

'I can try, but I am not sure the higher branches will hold me.'

I turned to Riley asking in desperation,

'Riley, can you take us down lower?'

'I will do my best Captain.'

The ship started to descend and I could hear the tree branches hitting the shuttle's hull as they snapped under the weight of the ship. We were now just feet away from Starlight so I knelt down and lent out of the ship's door reaching out for her hand. Starlight reached up and I found I could almost touch her hand.

'Riley, can you take the ship just a little lower?'

'I'm trying Captain, but with the damage to the landing control it is not easy.'

The ship lowered just slightly more as I reached out just a little further. I could just touch her fingers while she looked desperately back up at me.

Just then the shuttle jolted with a loud bang before it tipped sharply to its side. The jolt, throw me forwards sharply, causing me to lose my grip on the door frame. Then the shuttle pulled away quickly from the tree with another explosion as I fell forwards out of the door.

Starlight looked at me with horror as I fell quickly past her breaking branches as I went. I realised that I needed to slow my fall, so I grabbed hold of a passing branch to stop my falling. But as I grabbed hold of a branch, it snapped with the force of my fall sending me into spin. I then hit several larger branches while I quickly fell. Again I grabbed hold of a branch which stopped my fall for a moment until my grip slipped. I fell just a few feet more hitting the floor with a hard painful thud.

Starlight

I pulled myself back up off of the ground while I hurt all over. I was surprised to find I had survived while I drew my gun and looked around. The area looked clear and my com link kicked in beeping repeatedly. I pulled my com from my belt and opened the channel to hear Riley's panicked voice,

'Captain, are you alright? Your life sign suddenly became very weak.'

I sat back on the floor while I moaned with the huge amount of pain and replied,

'Yea I am still here, but remind me never to fall out of a shuttle, ever again.'

'Captain, thank god. Can you move and is Starlight with you?'

I looked around to find Starlight climbing down from the tree. I smiled at her as I pulled myself back to my feet and replied,

'Yes she is here and I can move, well just about.'

'Good, there is a clearing not far from here. If you can both make it there, I will put down to make repairs.'

'No, just head back to the Hellfire and get them to send another shuttle to pick us up.'

'Sorry Captain, but I have to land and make repairs. It shouldn't take me more than half an hour to patch up control board. Do you want me to send the troops over to you?'

'No, just keep the ship safe and send a signal to my com to tell me which way to go.'

'Sounds like a plan. Good luck Captain and I will pass on what is happening to the Hellfire, Riley out.'

The com cut before I lowered it while I winced with pain. I watched as Starlight moved out in front of me, so I pushed my G8 gun back into its holster. Starlight moved right up to me as she stared at my face before she softly said,

'By the Maker, it is you. But how and... I mean I was beginning to think you were just a dream from my childhood. But then when everything became bad around me, I remembered that you told me to hide in a hollow tree. How did you know?'

I smiled through the pain knowing she was speaking of something I hadn't done yet before I replied,

'I will explain all once we are safe, now we must get moving.'

Starlight stood still in front of me, she raised her hand and gently wiped the blood from my cheek.

'You must be in so much pain after a fall like that. I did not expect to find you alive once I had climbed down from the tree.'

'Well let's just say that this was not what I had planned.'

Starlight put her hand through the large tear in my shirt before she placed her hand against my body. I felt the sharp stabbing pain ease with the warmth of her hand as it glowed with golden light. I looked up at her pretty face to see a tear running down her cheek.'

'Why the tears?'

I moved my hand up to her face wiping the tear away as she replied,

'When I am healing someone I feel their pain. We are being taught to separate ourselves from the person we are healing, it is not easy.'

My com link began to beep so I said,

'Look we need to get moving, but thank you. I feel much better now.'

I took hold of her hand and then I held up the com link while I turned on the spot until the beeping increased.

'This way, we need to get off of this planet and soon.'

We began to walk as Starlight said,

'I wanted to thank you all those years ago for saving me when I was five, but now you are here. Well I don't know what to say.'

I turned to her and I smiled before replied,

'You do not need to say anything.'

She stopped in her tracks and pulled her hand away before she stared again at my face saying,

'You are...'

Her words were cut short as a look of horror filled her perfect face. I turned around to find an infected Trellbeck pushing its way through the undergrowth. I drew my G8 again taking just a single shot at its head. The zombie quickly fell to the ground, but before I could say anything several more of the infected appeared around us.

Starlight looked at me and quickly said,

'Wait I can help them.'

'No you can't. They are infected with the death plague, they are all dead already. It is just the virus that is controlling them and that just wants to spread.'

'But that would mean the Darkness has returned.'

'You have got it in one; now let's get out of here, as I cannot fight off a whole planet's population.'

I shot down two of the un-dead clearing a pathway ahead of us. I then gave Starlight the com before I said,

'Just follow the beeping, I will keep you safe.'

I drew my sword quickly cutting down another infected Trellbeck as it grabbed for her. Starlight moved ahead following the com's beeping while I shot down two more of the un-dead.

The gun shots were loud but the area looked clear so I followed Starlight from behind keeping my weapons ready. We continued through the thick woodland and now I was behind her I could see how badly her wing was hurt. Again I looked around and as everything seemed clear I said,

'Starlight stop, I need to take a look at your wing.'

She stopped and turned around to look at me before she replied,

'I'm ok, it hurts but like you said. We need to be safe first.'

I looked at her beautiful soft face and said,

'You should have told me how badly you had hurt it.'

I could see the pain on her face as she spoke softly,

'It didn't seem like the right time, what with your fall and those things.'

'Turn around and let me take a closer look.'

Starlight turned so I could see her broken wing. She had a large tear through her main wing membrane, but this was not where the main bleeding was coming from. I could see that one of her main wing bones had been snapped about half way down her wing, causing it to fold over on itself and this was where the main bleeding was coming from.

'Ok, I need you to hold very still while I stem the bleeding and straighten out your wing.'

I took off my coat and tore the sleeve from my shirt while Starlight replied.

'Ok, but isn't that going to hurt?'

'Yes and I am sorry, but it will feel more comfortable afterwards.'

'Just do it quickly.'

'Ok'

I drew my sword and cut a straight branch from a nearby tree before I moved back over to Starlight. Then I held up the stick with the shirt sleeve before I took gentle hold of her injured wing. Starlight flinched with the pain while I held her wing.

'Sorry, but this will all be over soon. Ready?'

'No, not really.' She said with a whimper in her voice.

I quickly straightened out her wing as she screamed out in pain. I tried hard not to move her broken bone while I tied the sleeve around the wound, closing her wing so she could not move it before I used the remainder of the material to bind the stick against the broken bone as a support.

'There that should hold, now how does it feel?'

I picked up my coat as Starlight turned around to face me. I could see tears running down her face as she said sadly.

'Thank you, it does not hurt as much now.'

I smiled back at her as I wiped a tear from her face before she throw her arms around me. I hugged her back gently for just a moment until she pulled away to look at my face.

'My Star man, I have missed you and...'

Her sentence was cut short as again a look of horror filled her face. I turned quickly to find a Death Dealer heading in our direction from the distance. It smashed its way through the trees quickly as I turned back to Starlight saying,

'Can you run?'

'From that thing, try stopping me.'

We both quickly headed away from the creature to the sound of the beeping from my com link. Starlight was starting to get ahead of me while I struggled to keep up as my whole body hurt. Starlight turned back to look at me as she said,

'Come on Star man, it is gaining on us.'

I knew I couldn't out run it, so I drew my G8 gun while I said,

'Just get to the shuttle, I will slow it down.'

I turned back to find the oversized infected monster was just over ten meters away from me and gaining fast. I pulled up my gun and fired off two shots right at its head. Both shots hit, knocking it off of its feet while I continued to run towards Starlight. She stood there looking helpless as I shouted over to her,

'Keep going and tell the shuttle to be ready to leave. Now go.'

She turned and started to run as again I looked back to find the creature was now back on its feet and looking unharmed while it again began to chase me. I ran between two large trees that were very close together just as the Death Dealer swung its oversized front cutting limbs at me.

Thud...

The creature hit the two trees hard as it seemed to be stuck between them. I saw my chance moving off to one side before I pointed my G8 at a massively oversized tree that stood over the trapped monster. I fired off several shots until the tree fell on top of the Death Dealer's back while it continued to struggle to get free.

I lowered my gun and turned back to find Starlight again standing waiting for me. I began to head for her just as a Trellbeck zombie appeared behind her.

'Get down.' I shouted out as I pulled up my gun.

I couldn't get a clear shot, but before the Trellbeck could grab her it fell to the floor with a gunshot to the head. Starlight dropped to the floor with shock while I mustered all my energy to get to her. I had my G8 ready but before I could reach her Jack appeared from out of the undergrowth. I sighed with relief and smiled at Jack as I reached the two of them breathless.

Starlight looked up in fear so I held out my hand to her. She took my hand and I helped her to her feet while she looked at Jack intensely.

'But, who... where did...'

I interrupted her as I replied,

'This is Jack, he is a friend.'

There was a hellish scream come from behind me while the sound of wood snapping could now be heard. We all turned to find the Death Dealer slowly breaking free from the overturned tree.

'I guess this means we need to get going.' Jack said out load.

'Sounds like a plan, how far is the shuttle from here?'

'Not far, it is just a couple of minutes walk from here.'

'Great.'

I looked at Starlight as I asked,

'Are you alright?'

'I think so, but how are there more of your kind here?'

Again there was another hellish scream but this time as I looked back, the creature forced its way out from the trees knocking them down before its many red eyes fixed on the three of us.

'No time to explain. Jack, lead the way and quickly.'

I took hold of Starlight's hand again and followed Jack as he ran through the thick undergrowth. Starlight held my hand with a firm grip as again wood could be heard being smashed close behind us. A large part of a tree smashed through the undergrowth just off from our sides while I could hear the heavy steps from the creature as it gained on us.

I turned back as we ran to find the creature just feet behind us as it swung its front cutting limb at another large tree. The trunk was ripped from the ground and thrown high through the air and over our heads.

'Watch out.' Jack shouted before the huge tree landed right in front of us all blocking our path.

We all came to a stop right in front of the over turned tree and without thinking I drew my gun pointing it at the oncoming oversized infected beast.

I again fired off several shots from my gun at its head knocking it to the floor. The creature struggled to get back on its feet as I ordered,

'Both of you get over the tree now.'

Jack quickly climbed up on top of the trunk while Starlight still held a firm grip of my hand.

'I need you to climb over Starlight, come on.'

She looked at me and then said,

'But I don't want you to go away again.'

'I won't, not this time. Now climb.'

Starlight let go of my hand and I helped her onto the tree.

Jack held his hand out down to her and as she reached up I turned back to find the Death Dealer back on its feet. I knew I didn't have time to climb over the five foot high overturned tree trunk, so I pulled the trigger several more times.

My G8 only shot one round off as it clicked empty and this time the creature stayed on its feet. I looked up to Jack to see that he now almost had Starlight on the top of the tree trunk.

'Jack, get Starlight to the shuttle and have Riley ready to leave. I will buy us all some time.'

'Yes Captain.'

'But what about...' Starlight's words were cut short as Jack pulled her arm while he firmly stated,

'The Captain knows what he is doing. Now come on.'

The Death Dealer was fixed on both Starlight and Jack as it began to run towards them, so I shouted out as I moved away,

'Hay, over here, come on, this way.'

I continued to shout while I moved back towards a group of trees, catching the massive creatures gaze as I went. The oversized zombie turned and began to follow me before it screamed its horrific sound at me. I quickly began to reload my gun with my last two ammo clips as again I found myself dogging the creature's large serrated cutting limbs.

I looked over to find Jack pulling Starlight out of sight as she stared at me with horror.

Click, click.

My gun was loaded and just in time. The creature snapped its jaws at me as I ran behind another tree. Again the tree was uprooted so I fired off three rounds at the creature's head knocking it back to the floor. The massive creature struggled quickly back to its feet as I moved behind it.

I knew my gun didn't have enough firepower to break through its hard thick exoskeleton, but then I had an idea. Now I was behind it I could see that its back was smashed open from the tree that had trapped it earlier. I kept out of sight until I got a clear shot of its open back wound.

Again I fired off several shots, but into the open wound this time. All my shots hit causing the creature's back legs to collapse under its own body weight. The creature pulled itself around using its front legs while it dragged itself quickly in my direction.

I ran back to the overturned tree hoping I had enough time to climb over it, but as I turned to see where the creature was I found the creature right on me. I had nowhere to run as again the relentless beast swung one of its oversized cutting limbs at me.

Its deadly sharp limb hit the tree just inches from my side where it became lodged. I saw my chance firing off another couple of shots, but this time at the creatures elbow like joint. The shots smashed through the joint severing it from the creature as it again swung at me with its other limb.

I rolled out of the way before again firing off another couple of rounds at the creatures elbow joint to its other limb. My shots ripped through the creature's limb causing it to fall to the floor. This did not stop the beast as it continued to drag itself in my direction.

I was now trapped between the tree and the infected Death Dealer as it opened its mouth wide while it snapped at me. I needed to stop this thing so I put my G8 gun on automatic, then when it opened its mouth to bite at me I pushed my gun barrel in and fired off the rest of its ammo.

The forces of the gun shots throw the creature's head back, before the whole thing collapsed on the floor in a lifeless pile next to my feet. I sighed with relief before I turned and climbed over the overturned tree.

From the top of the tree I could see my shuttle so I pulled my battered body down over the other side and headed for the clearing. I emerged from the trees to find both Jack and Tyler standing there waiting for me guns ready.

'Captain, where is the Death Dealer?'

I sort of laughed as I replied breathlessly,

'Dead, it was a piece of cake, now let's go.'

They both smiled before I moved past them and into the shuttle where I was greeted by Starlight, who throw her arms around me as she said,

'I am glad you made it.'

I smiled at her as Tyler shouted over to Riley,

'That's everyone let's get out of here.'

I looked down at Starlight to see her worried face, so I kissed her on the forehead and said,

'And I am glad I found you.'

The shuttle door closed and I took a seat which was a relief to my aching body. Starlight sat beside me and lay her head on my shoulder as I noticed Astrail staring at us both with a kindly smile, like he had seen the two of us like this before.

A world ends

Our shuttle was now leaving the planet's atmosphere and as we headed back into space the com sounded. Riley opened up the channel and Andrew's deep voice could clearly be heard.

'Riley, did you get the Captain?'

'Yes Commander, we have everyone we intended to pick up and I should have the healing team back to the Hellfire in just a few minutes.'

'Great, let the Captain know we have all of our shuttles back and that we are full of refugees from the planet.'

'I will pass that on Commander.'

I knew I should speak with him so I eased myself out of the chair as I said to Starlight,

'I will be back soon.'

Starlight smiled at me and then replied,

'Ok Star man.'

'Just call me Chris, alright.'

'Ok.'

Then I moved over to the co pilot's seat and interrupted Riley's and Andrew's conversation while I sat back down.

'Andrew, do you have any news on the approaching ships?'

'Captain, I am glad you are ok.'

'Well I wouldn't go that far, but how is it looking?'

There was a short pause before he continued to say,

'Captain, I think you should see this for yourself. I will have the information ready for you when you get back.'

'That bad right, ok just have the ship ready to leave just as soon as we can.'

'It already is, but something may have come up to complicate matters.'

'Isn't that always the case? I will head straight up to the bridge once we land, Pay-Check out.'

I closed the channel before I turned to Riley and said quietly,

'I need you to do something for me.'

'Of course Captain, what is it?'

'I need you to make sure Starlight is taken care of, just until I can get the ship to safety.'

'Ok, she can stay with me. I will keep an eye on her.'

'And Riley, I need you to tell her nothing of what you know about her. This is only the second time she has met me and last time she was just a child.'

Riley looked at me confused as she replied,

'I didn't know you met her when she was a kid.'

'I haven't yet, it is a long story.'

'Ok Captain, I will make sure she is ok.'

'Thank you.'

I could now see the Hellfire from the shuttle's windows as I thought to myself, nearly home. I turned back to find Astaril standing behind us with a look of wonder on his face as he said out loud,

'Now that is a ship I have not seen for a very long time.'

Again Riley looked at me confused so I replied,

'That is another long story. Riley, this is Astrail an old friend I have just met.'

Astrail smiled at her as he said,

'It is a pleasure to meet you again, and a little confusing to find I seem to know everyone and they do not know me this time.'

'Hi there.' Riley replied before she then turned her attention back to the controls so she could start the landing procedures while we entered the hanger bay.

The shuttle bumped gently to the hanger floor and from the windows I could see that Andrew was right. The hanger was full of Trellbeck and I knew this could make things very tricky if we got caught up in a battle.

I got up and moved over to Starlight as I said,

'Starlight, I need you to go with Riley so she can get your wing looked at. I will be on the bridge ok.'

Starlight looked at me as she got up with a concerned look on her face before she replied,

'Ok, but you need to be healed yourself.'

I smiled at her as Astrial stood by us both.

'I will, but first I need to get the ship to safety.'

I pushed the button to open the shuttle door as I said to Riley,

'Take all the Healers up to sick bay and make sure Starlight gets her wing seen too.'

'Yes Captain.'

Astrail spoke up saying,

'I may be able to help you Captain.'

'Then you are with me, now let's find out what is going on.'

We all left the shuttle and entered the busy hanger bay while Starlight stayed close by my side holding tightly onto my hand.

Then we moved passed the many creatures crowed together as we work our way out of the hanger. I found myself standing face to face with Miss Carr in the corridor. She held a medical scanner and a shocked look on her face as she asked,

'Captain, what in the world happened to you?'

Jack quickly butted in as he said,

'Well he got shot, blown up and then fell out of a shuttle which was about two hundred foot off of the floor.'

I gave Jack one of those looks before I said,

'Thanks for that Jack. Doctor, please take a look at Starlight's wing, it is badly broken. Riley has the rest of the healer and if you need me I will be on the bridge.'

'But Captain, I insisted you come to sick bay first to be checked over.'

'Not before you have everyone checked for bites or scratchers. I'm fine for now.'

I then turned to Starlight and said kindly,

'Stay with Riley, just for now. Once the ship is safe I will come and find you.'

I kissed her on the forehead before she let hold of my hand while Miss Carr was attempting to run a medical scanner over my body as I said,

'Come on Astrail.'

We both moved off up the corridor to Miss Carr's protest while Astrial said,

'You should listen to your healer my old stubborn friend.'

'I know, but the ship and its crew comes first.'

We both moved quickly through the corridors of my ship until we found ourselves standing in front of the closed bulkhead doors to the bridge. I stepped forwards just as the ship jolted sharply to one side.

The doors slid open while I steadied myself and as we both moved into the room I could hear my first officer issuing a red alert. The lighting in the room changed to a reddish colour while I asked out loud,

'Andrew, what is our situation?'

My first officer turned the captain's chair around as he got up calmly and replied,

'Captain, we have five large unknown vessels heading in fast and as you may have guessed. We are now within firing range.'

Again the ship jolted as tactical reported in.

'Captain, our shields are holding at 95% power. But I don't think they will last long once we are taking fire from all five ships.'

I needed to take control as I moved over to the captain's chair sitting down painfully hard as again the ship jolted sharply.

'Miller, move the ship behind the planet for cover to buy us some time. Richards, open up a channel asking for identification and Andrew, take up tactical while you fill me in on what I have missed.'

My orders were confirmed as Andrew began to explain,

'Captain, the five ships will not respond, but they are heading for the planet. Bartell tells me that they are Darkness vessels here to claim the planet.'

'Can we save the planet from them?'

'No Captain, it is lost to the plague and we are full to capacity. My recommendation is that we leave now with the survivors.'

I knew he was right but had to ask,

'So how many life signs are there still registering down there?'

Andrew looked uneasy as he replied,

'That is the thing, the reading are at one point two million, but that is falling rapidly as each minute passers.'

I watched Astrial moved over to the tactical station as I knew that if we were to leave now I would be condemning the rest of the planet to death.

Then Astrial moved back over to me before he put his hand on my shoulder while saying,

'Chris my old friend, Bartell is right these are Darkness battleships and they will be here to melt the planet's surface down so they can strip it of all its resources. You cannot save it, we should leave as your first officer suggested.'

This all seemed to make sense now, the Darkness killed off the population with the plague so they didn't need to fight off any resistance.

Then they melted down the planet for their own needs.

'Is there any way we can stop them?'

Andrew looked over to me as he replied,

'No Captain, the plague has the planet almost dead and if it is material the Darkness is after. Well that planet could be harvested to build an unstoppable army of ships and weapons.'

Then I remembered something, as I asked,

'Andrew, you said this planet had suffered a massive nuclear burn out, but it wasn't stripped bare was it?'

'No Captain, records show it to have been just burnt out.'

This gave me an idea as I asked,

'So would our mines be able to recreate the same burn out to match our records?'

'Yes, and it would make the planet useless to anyone for several thousand years.'

'How much time do we have before the Darkness ships reach orbit and can we save anyone else?'

Andrew looked helpless as he replied,

'We need to leave now, but maybe we can squeeze a few more minutes out to stop the Darkness from using this planet.'

I pulled myself out of my chair which seemed to take far too much effort and moved over to the tactical station before I ordered,

'Miller, start the attack run.'

I prepped the mines as I checked the planet's life readings. I could see that the falling reading were now half what they were from the last report just as Miller announced,

'Captain, once you fire the first mines I will start the run.'

I held my finger over the fire button as I said in a low voice to myself,

'Now I become death, the destroyer of worlds.'

Then I pressed the button as I ordered,

'Start the run Miller.'

The mines fired and as the first ones hit the planet's surface the explosions were clear from space. I held the button down while the ship ran its orbit, spreading the mines evenly across the planet's surface as again the ship suddenly jolted sharply. I checked the console to find we were now open to attack so I quickly fired our starboard cannons at the enemy ships while we completed the run.

The ship jolted sharply again causing me stumbled to one side. Andrew grabbed hold of me keeping me on my feet as the final mines hit the surface. The whole planet was now ablaze with a nuclear fire as I noticed that the five Darkness ships were now turning around. The tactical readout showed that they were now leaving so I powered down the cannons before I ordered,

'Bring us to a full stop Miller.'

Checking the planet's read out I could see that the whole planet was now dead and highly radioactive. I pulled myself away from the station and sat down in my command chair as I sighed with guilt.

'Miller, move us away from the planet and prep the jump engines.'

'Jump engines ready Captain.'

'Plot course for the Kalien home world and activate the jump gate.'

Miller confirmed my order while I sat and watched our gateway into hell open up. I stared out of the window while I couldn't take my mind off of what I had just done.

'We are through the gateway and I am closing it now Captain.'

'Good work Miller, ahead at our best speed.'

I sat still as my whole body hurt and I felt like I needed to sleep.

'Chris, your first officer tells me you are bleeding.'

I looked up to see Astrail standing next to me just as the bridge doors slid open to reveal Miss Carr, Starlight and Riley.

'Andrew you have the bridge.'

Miss Carr rushed over to me before she stated,

'Riley told me what happened to you on that planet, you should have reported straight to sickbay. Now let me take a look at you.'

Miss Carr waved a medical scanner in front of me as she looked concerned before she said,

'Judging by the amount of injuries you have, you should be dead, but whatever Starlight did for you on the planet seems to still be working. I don't understand it, but it works.'

Starlight moved over as she said,

'But that is impossible, once contact has been broken the healing ends. That is how it works.'

Miss Carr passed the scanner to the young Kalien as she replied,

'I took a scan of the captain before he headed for the bridge while he was speaking to you. As you can see the three broken ribs are now just fractures and all of his other wounds are reducing at an incredible rate.'

Starlight looked at the screen confused so I spoke up,

'Look I will be fine, but I need to rest. So if it is alright with you, I am going to head to my quarters!'

I pulled myself out of my chair as Miss Carr butted in abruptly,

'You will come down to sickbay so I can treat your wounds properly.'

Andrew moved over to Miss Carr before he said,

'Doctor, the captain will be fine, something happened to him before he gained command of the Hellfire. Since then his body has self healed. Let him rest, he will heal faster that way.'

Miss Carr also now looked confused as she replied,

'Well that explains why you never come to sickbay, but at least let me give you something for the pain.'

'I can help with that, if that is ok?' Starlight said softly.

'Well it looks like I am not needed here. But I should have been told about this.'

Miss Carr gave me one of those looks as I turned to leave. So I replied,

'I know, but it is not something you just drop into conversation. Now I just need to get some rest. Andrew, let me know when we reach the Kalien home world.'

'Yes Captain.'

I moved over to the bridge doors which slid open as Starlight placed her hand on my back and said,

'You don't mind if I come with you, do you?'

I put my arm around her before smiling at her, while she looked back up at me and smiled in return.

'I couldn't think of anyone I would rather be with right now.'

Then we both moved through the bridge doors and off up the corridor towards the main lift shaft.

The Darkness war

I opened my eyes to find my room was lit by only a low level light. I seemed to be alone so sat up on my bed before I looked down at my battered and bruised body. I pulled the top draw open from the unit next to my bed before I pulled out some jeans, socks and a shirt. I pulled on the jeans and socks before I stood up slowly, picking up my shirt I headed over to the bathroom. I opened the door to find Starlight standing there in a fitted black dress looking in the mirror. She spotted me in the reflection and smiled while still looking a little shocked.

'Sorry, I didn't mean to interrupt.'

'Chris, you are up. How do you feel?'

I pulled on my shirt over the dressings covering my gunshot wound and other injuries as I replied a little embarrassed to have walked in on her,

'Like I have been hit by a cargo frigate. I didn't realise you came back last night.'

Starlight continued to smile even though she still looked a little uneasy as she sweetly said,

'After your healing session I went to see Riley, she gave me some clothing, then I came back to check on you. You were fast asleep so I stayed. I guess I felt safer with you here.'

She blushed as I smiled at her before I replied,

'You will always be safe aboard this ship. Now how is your wing doing?'

'It hurts a little and your ship's healer says I should rest it for the next few weeks. Also I will need to get Riley a new dress as I had to make adjustments to it for my wings.'

'I will sort that out, don't worry about it. Now have you had anything to eat?'

But before she could answer the tannoy sounded.

'Excuse me for one moment.'

I moved over to the wall tannoy control and opened up the channel.

'Captain, we are entering the Kalien solar system.'

'Thank you Richards, I am on my way.'

I cut the com before I turned back to Starlight and said,

'If you want to stay here you can, or feel free to explore the ship.'

She moved over to me before she asked,

'Do you mind if I come with you?'

'Not at all, are you ready?'

Starlight nodded in agreement so I buttoned up my shirt covering my bruised body before I found out my shoes. She watched me intensely as I got ready and although I was overjoyed to see her again, I could see that she didn't really know me yet.

'We should get going.'

We both headed out into the corridor before we started to make our way up to the bridge, then Starlight asked while we walked,

'Do you mind if I asked what happened to you? You know, that means that your body heals its self?'

I suddenly felt very awkward at this question so stopped and looked at her.

'That is a long story, but to cut it short before I gained this ship. I had just a small shuttle, it was damaged and we needed help. A Kalien ship offered assistance and while we were aboard, the ship was attacked.

I offered to help and was nearly killed trying to save both crews. A Kalien girl who I fell in love with, saved me from the brink of death. I think it was her healing power and the amount needed to help me that changed the way my body heals. So that is kind of that. No one but my closest crew knew about it, well until now.'

Starlight looked disheartened as she replied,

'Can I meet her?'

I sighed as I looked down to the floor for a moment before I replied,

'No, she is no longer with me. It took too much of her life energy to save me.'

'I am sorry. She must have really loved you.'

'She did; that is why I try to help others. I hope she would be proud. Now we should get going.'

Starlight took hold of my hand as we continued up to the bridge before she said,

'I can see why she would have loved you. I have not stopped thinking about you for the last fourteen years.'

I smiled at her as we walked until we reached the bridge. We both entered the room as Starlight asked,

'What should I do?'

'Just take a seat in my chair and enjoy the view.'

Starlight moved over to my chair taking a seat just as Andrew turned to face me

'Captain, you are looking much better this morning. But I think Miss Carr wants to have a meeting with you.'

'I kind of figured that, now what is the situation?'

Andrew replied in a relaxed way saying,

'Well we have managed to save three hundred and twenty one Trellbeck, all unharmed and we have a total of eighty six Kaliens on board between the colonists and the crew of Bartell's ship.

Things are a little pushed, including space but we should be arriving at Kalass, in just under three hours.'

'Great work Andrew.'

Things seemed to be working out; then the proximity alarms sounded as Miller grabbed my attention,

'Captain we have a large gateway opening just one thousand kilometres off of our port side.'

'Go to yellow alert and raise the shield. Turn us to face it and bring us to a full stop.'

The space outside of the ship began to flicker and flash just as a large blue lightning filled gateway bust open in front of our ship. Andrew moved over to the tactical station checking over the readout as the gateway in front of us increased in size.

'Captain, I am picking up two large ships from within the open gateway.'

I moved forwards as I stared at the gigantic gateway while two large silver and green ships began to emerge.

'Ready our weapons Andrew, just in case.'

My first officer confirmed my orders as the two ships left the gateway before it closed quickly behind them. Both large vessels stopped in front of our ship as I noticed Starlight get up from my chair.

'Chris, they are Kalien war ships.'

I didn't have time to respond as Richards cut in saying,

'Captain, we are being hailed.'

'Andrew, power down our weapon systems. Richards, can you open up the channel over the holo ring?'

'Yes Captain, it will just take me a moment to tie in the old style signal.'

I moved forwards and stepped into the first ring before I said,

'Good work Richards, now put them through.'

The holo ring in front of me lit up as the flat image of a middle aged Kalien man dressed in a military styled uniform appeared in front of me. The man held a blank look as I asked,

'Richards, can he see me?'

'Hang on, wait he should be able to now.'

The man's face changed from a blank look to a look of shock as he said,

'By the Creator's hand, forgive us High Commander of the order of light. We did not believe the reports of your ship's return.'

I wasn't sure what to say and was taken aback by the man's words as I replied,

'Thank you for the welcome party. I have some of your people aboard and the last of the Trellbeck race, after their world was lost.'

The man looked disheartened at my words before he said,

'Yes High Commander, their world is a great loss and at least some of their race has survived. But if the Darkness has gained the resources of that world, we may have just lost this war before it has started.'

'Why would the lost of one world cause the lost of the war?'

The man looked up at me with fear in his eyes as he spoke seriously,

'High Commander, the planet Telsaker holds enough metals and minerals to give the Darkness the resources to build a fleet so big it will wipe out all who stand in their way.'

I looked at the man as I asked,

'I'm sorry but what is your name?'

The man looked confused as he replied,

'I am Ship's leader Prime Welfireat, why?'

'Well you can inform your leaders that although the Trellbeck have lost their home. The Darkness will be unable to use its resources.'

The man's voice lifted as he asked,

'But how? We had received word that the Darkness had released the Death Plague upon Telsaker. There is no way back from that.'

'I know, so with no other choice after we had saved all we could. I purged the world with a radioactive fire. The Darkness will not be able to use its resources for at least a thousand years.'

'High Commander, you may have just saved us all. Please let us escort you to the home world. Then there is much we need to discuss if we are to stop the Darkness once and for all. Now I must pass on the news of your ship's return, it will bring great hope to our people, Burning-light out.'

The communication cut as the image faded out along with the light in both rings. I stepped out of the ring and turned to my first officer saying,

'Andrew, you are with me. Miller, you have the bridge and stay close to those war ships. Richards, inform me when we reach orbit and ask Astrail to join us in my office. Starlight, if you know anything of this Darkness, I may need that information so come with me. Now let's go.'

I moved into my office followed closely by both Andrew and Starlight, before I pulled several chairs around the desk that sat in the centre of the room. I sat down and set the computer to record while Andrew sat one side of me and Starlight sat on the other. I had a lot on my mind with the conversation I had just had over the holo ring and as much as I didn't like it. I had a strong feeling we would be joining this war.

I sat back in the chair as I sighed with the aches from yesterday's events but before I could say anything Astrail arrived. Andrew pulled the chair out next to him before Astrail sat down while I pushed the record key and began to speak,

'Ok, I have asked you all here because it looks like we have stumbled into a war that some of us know nothing about. Now it looks like everyone in this time thinks we have been here before but we haven't done any of this yet. So Astrail as you seem to know me and this ship, I need you to tell me what the Darkness is and why I was just referred to as High Commander.'

Astrail looked uneasy before he spoke calmly to us all.

'Well Chris, this could be difficult. I have known you all for many years but I have not seen you for over a century.'

I looked shocked by his words but before I could ask, Astrail continued,

'I know this will all sound strange and I cannot tell you direct details of what happened in the last war. But I can give you its history.'

Andrew cut in saying,

'But how can you be sure this ship and crew are the same as the one that helped you fight the first war?'

Astrial smiled at Andrew and then replied,

'Because I remember having a conversation with all of you just like this during the first war. I didn't believe it then and you could not tell me why or how our meeting had come to pass. I just had to trust you. Now it is your turn to trust me.'

I knew what he was saying made sense but we needed to know more about the Darkness as I cut in asking,

'Astrail, so what happened during the first war and what are we up against?'

'The Darkness are an evil race, hell bent on destroying all that is different to themselves. No one knows when the Darkness started to attack worlds, just that we stumbled across them around two hundred year ago. We were monitoring younger races and had done so for many years, checking their progress from a distance, so that they could develop in their own way. One of those worlds was just looking to the stars, so with interest we sent a ship to find out how they were doing. When that ship arrived it found the world under attack from a large group of unknown ships. The world was bombarded from orbit until almost nothing was left standing. Our own fleet was sent to aid the world but they were too late. Our war council challenged the unknown fleet and we soon found ourselves at war.'

'So how do we fit into this?' Andrew asked. Again Astrail smiled as he continued,

'The Darkness at first began attacking worlds it perceived to be a threat to themselves, destroying all resistance before it stripped each planet of its materials. They quickly became feared across the stars leading to many races grouping together to fight them on all fronts. Two people saw to this alliance of worlds, one was Kalien and the other was of a race no one had ever seen before. The two worked closely with many worlds to form a massed fleet across the Galaxy. But this did not stop the Darkness, even though they were now falling into retreat. Instead they created the Death Plague in the later years of the war and this plague decimated many worlds.

The two knew the only way to stop the Darkness was to remove them from the stars. Now our ships were far from the technology they are now but this did not matter. The High Commander or Light Warrior as he was named, called upon a shining white ship which appeared from nowhere.

This powerful vessel beat back the Darkness to their own hellish world and once there it destroyed all of the Darkness's ability to leave their own planet. The war lasted for nearly one hundred years from the first attack until its end. But once over the High Commander, his Kalien adviser and his shining ship left leaving one prophecy.'

'What was that?' Andrew asked.

'Let me guess, he would return when the Darkness rose back to the stars and see to it that they could not do the same again.' I answered.

Astrail smiled as he got up from his chair taking hold of Starlight's hand. He moved it over to me placing her hand gently on top of my own as he said,

'When I met Starlight at the colony and she spoke of her Star man, I knew the time for your return was close. I had kept the weapon you were given during the first war like you had asked of me. So that I could confirm your DNA matched and that this was no coincidence. Now the two of you are together and the Hellfire has returned, we stand a chance of fighting the Darkness off once and for all.'

I knew now that we had to fight this war and that it may just be the only way of making sure Earth was safe until this evil had been stopped, or there may not be a future to go back too.

I looked at Andrew as I asked,

'How long do you think it would be before we can try to recreate the time anomaly to get back to our time?'

Andrew looked unsure as he answered,

'That is impossible to tell, maybe months or years. I know that it should be possible, but I can tell you we are not going home anytime soon.'

I guessed that would be the answer and knew that we had to fight this war. I held Starlight's hand and smiled at her before I looked back to Astrail and said,

'Well if we are going to be here, I guess we should help. I just ask one thing of your world.'

'What is that my old friend?'

'I have to give my crew the choice, for all who do not wish to fight, will you see that they are given safety on your world?'

'Yes of course.'

I smiled at Astrail before I then said,

'Well then I guess we have a lot to do. Andrew, once the ship reaches orbit we will need to see that the survivors are all transported safely to the planet. I will then take a shuttle with you and Starlight to meet with The Kalien war council. Once we get back I guess I will be able to inform the crew of what we are doing. I think this meeting is done.'

Astrail and Andrew got up to leave as I knew I was probably in well over my head. I stayed seated while Starlight just looked at me with a fear in her eyes as she asked,

'I know nothing of war, so where do I fit into all this?'

Astrail moved away from the door and over to us both as he said,

'The Captain will know how to fight the evil, but you will keep him on a course of light. I am sure it will all become clear to you both soon enough.'

With this he left the room and as I passed Andrew on the way out with Starlight he said,

'Well at least we now both know why the Hellfire was so important?'

He pattered me on the shoulder before I headed to the bridge with Starlight, while my thoughts were with the coming choices I would have to make in a war that I knew very little about.

To be continued in series two...

The Darkness Wars...

ABOUT THE AUTHOR

This book is my first full series of key adventures, it covers the opening story to the series and introduces you to the small crew of the Pay-Load. Then you follow the crew through several adventures which shows you how they end up in command of the large Earth built battle cruiser. These stories have all been published as ebooks, but they have all gone through a well deserved overhaul to bring them up to the standard they deserve for this print edition. I am currently working on the second full book to follow Darkness Falls, and I will be releasing the beginning of the second series of ebooks late 2016. So sit back and enjoy this series of epic adventures, which will take you through both time and space to fight zombies, pirates and much more. Thank you for your interest and welcome to the crew.

C J Sharman

Printed in Great Britain
by Amazon